Last Bastion

Also by James Albany in Pan Books

Warrior Caste
Mailed Fist
Deacon's Dagger
Close Combat
Marching Fire

James Albany

Last Bastion

Pan Original
Pan Books London and Sydney

First published 1984 by Pan Books Ltd,
Cavaye Place, London SW10 9PG

ISBN 0 330 28238 7

Photoset by Parker Typesetting Service, Leicester
Printed and bound in Great Britain by
Collins, Glasgow

Contents

Though the aims of anti-guerrilla warfare are clear, their realization depends on local conditions. But precedents are an invaluable guide. The anti-guerrilla commander must feel his way and obtain the best possible help: the humble man who has local knowledge, the counter-gangs who acquire it first-hand, the imaginative army intelligence officer and the even more imaginative staff officer who, knowing how others did the job before them, improve and adapt tested techniques and apply new ones. Wars are not won by rules and guerrilla wars are no exception.

Otto Heilbrunn, *Partisan Warfare*

Looking back after almost a quarter of a century on the first post-war British action in Oman, the conflict seems pennyweight compared with what came later.

David Smiley's *Arabian Assignment* and P. S. Allfree's *Warlords of Oman* contain lively accounts of the SAS squadrons' assault on the impregnable rebel stronghold of Jebel Akhdar, though neither book makes mention of Major Jeff Deacon's participation. Small wonder. Memoranda of the events which took place before and after the SAS night attack of 26 January 1959 will probably remain locked in Whitehall's vaults for ever. Passing mention in Deacon's letters, however, suggested that the Major had been 'up to something' during his short term in Arabia. I was intrigued enough to undertake a certain amount of detective work and eventually traced a surviving member of Deacon's team. As I suspected, Deacon's missions in Oman, and elsewhere, were low-key and clandestine and had purposes discreetly screened by orthodox movements of the SAS groups.

The 'surviving member' is former SAS Major Maurice Harper, who now lives in New Zealand. My letter of introduction brought a speedy and unexpected reply. Maurice was perfectly willing to talk with me about his service days. But only face to face, in his own backyard. As luck would have it, I had business in Singapore a few months later and flew from there to Hamilton, New Zealand. I admit that I rather expected to be greeted by a dour and grizzled veteran whose sole intention was to warn me off or freeze me out. Nothing could have been further from the truth. I spent a splendid week with Maurice and his family at their beach house near Coromandel, overlooking the South Pacific. During my stay, Maurice talked candidly and at length of his tours with the SAS and of his friendship with Jeff Deacon. With Maurice's permission, I tape-recorded most of his dot-about narrative.

Jeff Deacon would not have approved of Maurice's candour; the Deke remained secretive to the end. I imagine that he might have enjoyed the manner of telling, though, for Dingo Harper was, and is, a first-rate raconteur. To suggest the flavour of Maurice's style I have transcribed certain passages straight from the tape recording, editing out only the more colourful expletives and, in the interests of clarity, some of Maurice's Australian vernacular. This, I suppose, might be construed as a diabolical liberty; Maurice Harper is a lecturer in English.

The meat of the book, however, is all down to Dingo.

With my thanks.

James Albany

1 Back in harness

At sunset on 17 January 1959, Jeffrey Alexander Deacon flew into Muscat in a little RAF Heron. He was the only passenger, a lean, scarred loner in his early forties. He wore casual uniform. Only a sweat-stained beret and stable belt were regulation issue. No insignia or marks of rank were to be seen on the Major's kit or clothing. Wire-framed sunglasses protected his pale blue eyes from the harsh light that stabbed into the cabin. Behind the dark lenses, the Deke could sleep or observe as he willed.

It was Deacon's first sight of Oman. He had cat-napped for a couple of hours and had missed the spectacular part of the flight. God knows, in waning light, the descent to the airstrip at Bait al Falaj was sensational enough.

Ancient Greek navigators had dubbed Muscat 'the secret port'. Deacon could see why. Mud-roofed dwellings and drab mosques were crammed into a bowl of rock. Great steep ridges walled the town, dwarfing the stone-built Portuguese forts that flanked the narrow harbour. Once the guns of the citadels had repelled pirates and invaders but the cannons were spiked and rusty now, mere ornaments. The Sultan, Said bin Taimur, steered well clear of the oppressive old town, preferring the cool hill country of Salalah, six hundred miles away.

If what he'd heard was half-way true, Deacon couldn't blame the old boy. Out of a contingent of fifty British soldiers drafted into the region last July, forty-seven had been flattened by heatstroke. Two men had died of it. Even now, in winter, Muscat had the hue of a meringue baked too long in the oven, a beige-white brittleness which contrasted with the stark brown cliffs.

The Heron bucked on a thermal and swooped towards the saddle of a ridge, leaving Muscat behind. Far off, Deacon glimpsed the heavy blue waters of the open gulf, oil tankers ploughing down the coast from the Strait of Hormuz, from Kuwait, Bahrain, Qatar and other boom towns on the Persian

Gulf. Closer, in the anchorages of Matrah, were clustered dhows and fishing craft, their triangular sails swollen with sunlight. The Heron lurched unsteadily. Deacon's gut siphoned into his gullet. He clenched his fist and pressed it firmly into his diaphragm, relaxing the muscles, the trick of a seasoned air-traveller. Crossing a serrated crest in the rugged mountain wall, the Heron levelled out and aimed for the stretch of runway dead ahead.

'There, to the right,' the pilot shouted.

'What is it?'

'Headquarters of the Muscat garrison.'

A series of neat white barrack blocks bounded a drill square. There were trees, fences, a couple of blockhouses.

'You'll be reporting there, I expect,' said the pilot.

'Absolutely,' said Deacon.

'Rum lot,' said the pilot, at the top of his voice. 'Never make soldiers out of most of them, not in a million years.'

There were soldiers and soldiers, of course; the best man on a parade ground was not necessarily the best man in the field. Deacon, however, did not argue the point.

He said, 'How far is Bait al Falaj from Muscat?'

'Not far. There's an easy route over the pass. Bait is the gateway to the interior, though.'

'Hence the old blockhouses.'

'And the new garrison,' said the pilot. 'Hold on.'

The pilot had made the ferry run hundreds of times and he came in confidently. Tyres squealed. The stench of rubber scraped by the peppery dust that coated the runway mingled with a blow-back of hot oil from the engine. The Heron rushed along an outer strip and slowed, slowed and curved to a halt.

'Okay?' said the pilot.

'Perfect,' said Deacon. He thanked the pilot and, collecting his luggage, what there was of it, clambered from the plane.

He was used to travelling light. He carried only a scuffed leather holdall and a long, quilted valise wrapped in waterproof canvas. Inside the valise was a shotgun, a Vaughan, which Deacon toted about the world like a talisman.

The Heron taxied and turned towards the tanks of the fuel

depot. There would be no formalities to delay the pilot, or the major for that matter. This wasn't Europe where a chap on military assignment had to struggle through a welter of red tape every time he crossed a national border. Democracy and its handmaiden, bureaucracy, were unknown in Oman. The Sultan ruled like a tyrant, supported by traditions as old as the barren hills.

'Major Deacon?'

Deacon had not expected red carpet treatment. He had no illusions about his welcome. Colonel David Smiley, Officer Commanding the Sultan's forces, would be well aware that he had been summoned. But it would have been indiscreet of the colonel to meet Deacon in person.

Lieutenant-Colonel Anthony Deane-Drummond, recently appointed Commander of the 22nd SAS, would be fully occupied at Tac HQ, the Northern Frontier Regiment's camp near Nizwa, briefing and settling 'A' Squadron, who had flown in from Malaya on 9 January. Even so, Deacon had anticipated that he would be met by a British officer. At worse, by a cheerful SAS sergeant driving a Land Rover; not by a solitary Arab.

The sun had slid behind the hills. The sky was like azure velvet, studded with stars. If the Arab had chosen the robe as camouflage then he had made a wise choice. He stepped from the side of a Dodge pick-up that was parked by the runway, bowed stiffly but did not offer his hand.

'I am Masud al Hasan.'

Deacon bowed in return.

The Arab was young, but no boy. He was incredibly handsome, with a full black beard and a fishtail moustache. He wore an over-robe of midnight blue. The turban wound about his head was of scarlet silk threaded with gold, a fine Kashmiri *abba*.

'I am Major Jeffrey Deacon.'

The Arab's right hand rested lightly on the hilt of a *khanjar*, an ornamental dagger, which was almost hidden in the folds of the robe. He spoke English with a clipped accent which, Deacon reckoned, had been acquired at Harrow or possibly at Sandhurst.

Deacon was the younger son of the 9th Baronet of Rathbone

and suspected that Masud might be a fellow aristocrat. Was Masud a sheikh? A nephew of the Sultan? Prince of the blood Royal, perhaps? On the other hand, he might be nothing more than a diplomat with flair, a dandified nonentity who'd sunk his baksheesh into fine clothes rather than goats. It was fifteen years since Deacon had served in North Africa but a few facts still rattled in his memory concerning Arab races.

'Masud al Hasan,' Deacon said casually, 'is a Bedouin name, is it not?'

Masud cocked an eyebrow in surprise.

'Indeed, it is so.' He waited for Deacon to display more cleverness but when the major was not forthcoming, said, 'I am of the clan of the Al Hasan, of the tribe of Ama'ir, of the Beni Khalid. My grandfather was a chieftan in the Nejid, with many fine horses and many, many tents.'

'But now you are loyal to the Sultan of Muscat and Oman?'

'My father, too, was loyal to the Sultan.'

Deacon did not ask the question which popped at once to mind; why had the father of Masud al Hasan given up life as a proud nomad of the desert and why was his son an envoy in service in Oman? The question would, no doubt, have caused offence.

Masud turned to the Dodge and opened the passenger door. He gestured to Deacon to enter. There was no driver, no bodyguard or servant. Masud had come alone.

Deacon threw his holdall into the back of the truck and, with the valise across his knees, seated himself in the cabin. Masud climbed behind the wheel, slammed the door, fired the engine and steered the Dodge across the perimeter of the strip at a fair lick. Deacon noticed that the Arab removed his ornamental dagger and placed it on a ledge above the dashboard where it jittered restlessly throughout the journey.

The vehicle left the airfield by a gate to the north-west. The gate was patrolled by two NCOs from the Muscat garrison, tall Omanis in pillbox hats, each bearing a rifle. The guards made no move to check the truck, nor did they acknowledge Masud with a salute. After the Dodge had debouched into a dusty lane, however, the Omanis hurried to close the high metal gate. To the right of the gate were houses, spruce enough and with green gardens, and a flagged road which, Deacon guessed, must lead to the barracks. But the Dodge swung left, away from the town, heading out of Bait al Falaj towards the hinterland.

Deacon asked no questions.

Masud volunteered no information.

The truck nosed past camels driven along by boys. Mean hovels replaced the better-class dwellings. There was the pungent, acrid odour of desert villages which stirred Deacon with its novelty.

Four days ago the major had been riding a tractor over the Rathbone Park estate in Shropshire, taking advantage of dry New Year weather and a fortnight's leave from his duties as Officer in Charge of Field Training at an SAS camp in Gnome Valley in the Welsh mountains. Now he was in Arabia. Allison, his wife, believed him to be in Wales. On his return he would tell her the truth. It would not dismay her to learn that he had been in Oman. She was quite used to his 'floating off' suddenly and secretly in the service of Queen and Country. Allison was well settled in the lodge of the Deacon family mansion, with young Jeffrey Edward to look after and the farm to attend, though an estate manager, Cobbold, did most of it. The situation which military prudence created was stimulating, even for an old sweat like Jeff Deacon. He revelled in illicit freedom, like a boy playing hookey from school. For this reason he could not take the mission too seriously as yet, particularly as the arrogant Masud looked like something out of a Drury Lane Christmas pantomime.

The route was shrouded in darkness, a dusty track up a wadi, one of the broad valleys that latticed the region and knit the inland villages to the coast.

Deacon had boned up on Ordnance maps of the Peninsula, which contained an awful lot of sandy yellow space. He had scanned a 'Handbook of Arabia' put out by the Geographical Section of Naval Intelligence. One of Deacon's gifts was an ability to memorise facts with rapidity. But Arabia was difficult to grasp, its 'layers', its mix of races and religious sects.

He had concentrated on the topography. He had the notion that Masud was driving up one of the great wadis that would soon wander into the watersheds of the Al Hajar range whose south-eastern prospect rose to the ten-thousand-foot mark on the plateau of Jebel Akhdar.

Deacon had no idea what would be required of him in Oman. There was no longer a Colonal Holms to seduce him into dangerous missions. He was ordered by signal or by a telephoned command. He would be fully briefed only when he arrived at the scene of the action. Nonetheless, Deacon had tried to keep abreast of what had taken place in the remote, archaic territory around the rhino snout of Arabia. His rank entitled him to privileged information. He was aware of political 'sensitivity', why there was pressure on the British commanders to tidy up the mess before April. A full UN debate on the Middle East would take place then. The Foreign Office would have enough trouble with Russia and Egypt on the floor without having a war going on in an oil-rich country to add fuel to the enemies' fire.

In background reading, in the context of the action, Deacon found no obvious niche. Once he might have been summoned as a rock climber, the best in the regiment. But surely there were several young tigers more supple and daring than him on the ground under the slabs of Jebel Akhdar, raring to pick a route up the sheer rock walls. In fact, the SAS seemed to be in complete charge of the situation – as usual. Why, then, had he been whisked from England post-haste? Mellowed by years of army experience, Deacon rather enjoyed the mystery. It was all part and parcel of being back in harness.

From the window, pale in the light of the winter moon, Deacon saw a village, a dismal cluster of mud-walled houses, a few date palms, around which the trail looped as if to give them as wide a berth as possible. The air was cooler now. The palms amplified a faint whispering breeze.

'Dinner,' said Masud al Hasan, solemnly breaking the silence, 'in two hours. You are hungry, Major?'

'Famished,' said Deacon.

'Hunger is the best appetite, as it is said in England.'

'Absolutely,' Deacon agreed.

Once more the Arab lapsed into silence. The Dodge bored on through the drab dusty landscape. Deacon, eyes open and alert behind the sunglasses, allowed his thoughts to rove over the background to the fight which he would soon be involved in.

Tribal, territorial and religious wars had been part of life's rich pattern for the sheikhs and chieftains of Arabia since the dawn of recorded history. Nobody in the western world had paid too much attention, not, that is, until oil had oozed out of the bosom of the desert back in 1937 when the Saudi Arabians had brought their first well on stream. Since then the territories east of the Red Sea had been regarded hungrily by brokers, bankers and politicos. In the last half dozen years attention had focussed on Oman, an independent nation, in particular on its hinterland, that stretch of abysmal wilderness which formed an ill-defined border with Saudi Arabia and over which Sultans and Imams had squabbled happily for centuries. In 1952 the Saudis attacked, captured and occupied a strategic oasis at Buraimi. The Sultan was dissuaded, at first, from sending forces to retake the oasis. But an international court of arbitration in Geneva failed – thanks to corruption on the part of the Saudis – to find a diplomatic solution to the problem. The Sultan of Oman finally redeemed the place, in 1956, by a swift, bloodless *coup de main*. This, however, did not end the crisis. It only created a lull.

The Imam of Oman was, at that time, one Ghalib bin Ali, a Saudi puppet. He was supported by powerful sheikhs, including his brother, captain of Rostaq, a shrewd, intelligent warrior by the name of Talib. Backing Ghalib too was the evil ruler of the mountain kingdom of Jebel Akhdar, Suleiman bin Himyar. These gentlemen were the principal enemies of the Sultan and, by inference, threatened the British government's oil interests in the area.

Talib's first attempt to overthrow the Sultan failed. Rebel forces rallied to the mountain fastness of Jebel Akhdar which became a base for violent raids against the Sultan's units and oil company installations and transports. Even with the aid of the RAF, the Sultan's three small armies could not root out or deter the rebels, secure in their craggy stronghold. Matters reached a head with the slaughter of the Muscat and Oman Field Force, a unit composed of trained native troops led by British officers. The death toll was high, the loss of face considerable. Sultan Said bin Taimur had had enough. He appealed to HM Government for direct military aid.

First a squadron of the Life Guards had added their weight to the Trucial Oman Scouts and Northern Frontier regiments. Air strikes, by Shackleton bombers and Venom fighters from Aden, were intensified against rebel positions. Blockade tactics pressed the errant tribesmen into applying for 'peace talks' with the Sultan, really to gain breathing space. Negotiations, of course, foundered and fighting continued. At this juncture, Colonel Smiley had induced the new commander of the 22nd SAS to fly to Oman and appraise the country and the enemy, in the hope that Lieutenant-Colonel Deane-Drummond would discover a challenge worthy of his outfit's talents. Deane-Drummond did. Enter, thus, the SAS.

They came in piecemeal lots, a company followed by two squadrons from Malaya, hard men, battle-hardened toughs, fresh, not wearied by years in the jungle. They surveyed the scene, shrugged and promptly guaranteed to do what no other military force had been able to do – take and hold the heights of Jebel Akhdar.

Preparations were well advanced. Major John Watts's 'D' Squadron had been installed since November. 'A' Squadron, under Major John Cooper, and a company from 'K' Squadron, commanded by Captain Christopher Pemberton, had flown in from Malaya a bare week before Deacon.

Though 'nervous' about this turn of events, it was reported that Talib's rebels remained undaunted and had so far parried every assault upon the slopes of Green Mountain. Deacon had not been informed of the ground forces' exact plan. He had more than enough experience, however, to predict that a major thrust would be made at the end of the month, a night attack, probably at the period of the full moon. He would be in ample time for that – if his presence was required on the mountain at all. He could think of no other reason for being summoned from England, except to fight.

The track climbed up the wadi, the air colder now. The Dodge growled protestingly over rough terrain. Deacon trusted that it wouldn't pack in. God knows, he was no mechanic. He doubted if Masud al Hasan was much cop with a spanner. The prospect of a night without a hot meal and a horizontal bed, and a long walk come morning, was not appealing. Peering from the window, Deacon tried to read the line of the hills. He could not properly separate sky from mountains. It was on the tip of his tongue to ask Masud where they were when he heard an alien sound and saw faint light up ahead. No nomads' fire-flicker, it had the ghastly pale glare of neon.

Masud grunted, grinned. 'Zambat,' he said. 'Dinner.'

It wasn't neon at all, only a bright white electric bulb under a coolie-hat of chipped enamel. It projected on a stalk from the roof of a prefabricated building, like a new-town cricket pavilion which, with a couple of similar structures, formed an isolated community in the middle of the wasteland. Two stumpy derricks. Four Leyland trucks. Oil Boys, Deacon realised, lived here.

With his forefinger, Masud tamped the truck's horn. Three rude notes, like a code. Immediately a door on the verandah of the main hut was flung open. Two figures were silhouetted against the light of the room within. Out wafted the delicious aroma of cooking meat. Definitely Oil Boys. Wherever they alighted, uncased their instruments. charts and drilling bits, there was a kitchen to shame the Ritz. Their concern with cuisine outdid by a mile the attention they paid to geology.

Masud braked, prowled the Dodge up by the three broad steel-track steps that led to the verandah. The verandah was also constructed from metal sections, used like planks. The place looked as if it had been lowered, intact, from a Martian spaceship.

'Zambat,' said Masud again.

It was, after all, the name of the station, not the Bedouin word for 'dinner'. By Deacon's calculation, which was usually pretty accurate, they had travelled about a hundred miles. The

Arab had kept up a steady fifty mph, the rocky road notwithstanding. With the Dodge's engine cut, Deacon could hear the thrumming of electric generators, loud in the crystalline night.

'Zambat is our destination, Major Deacon,' said Masud al Hasan. 'We have arrived.'

Cradling the valise in his arms, Deacon got out of the pick-up. A rotund little Englishman sporting a bristling moustache scampered down the steps, hand outstretched. His attitude was one of such fervent eagerness that Deacon was tempted to back away, as if he was being accosted by the club bore.

'Deacon?' the man chirruped. 'Pleasure, pleasure. Welcome to Zambat. My name's Bressol. Major. William. Bill. Old Bill the chappies call me. Come along. You'll want a wash and brush-up. Masud will bring the baggage. Won't you, Masud?'

Sullenly the Arab nodded. An effluvium of colonial patronage surrounded the Dodge for a moment or two. Deacon would have been more polite and persuasive in inviting an Arab like Masud al Hasan to do anything, let alone perform the chores of porter. Bressol's hand upon Deacon's shoulder guided him towards the steps.

Major William Bressol? The name meant nothing to Deacon. In his forties, the little man was crisp and cool in clean, pressed khakis. Rank flashes but no regimental badges, Deacon noticed. He wore a stainless-steel Rolex Oyster on his wrist, and leaked a barbershop whiff of Bay Rum aftershave. In the doorway, watching, was another khaki-clad figure. Hands in his trouser pockets, a thin black Turkish cigarette in his mouth, he eyed Deacon calculatingly.

'Mr Gore.' Bressol halted Deacon before the tall man. 'Major Deacon.'

Gore was older, middle fifties, unhealthy-looking, with tousled mouse-brown hair. Clean-shaven, he had a puckered mouth, as if a slice of lemon was permanently stuck in his cheek. Gore did not remove the cigarette from his lips. It seemed to take him all his time to slide his right hand from his pocket. The hand-shake, like the man, was languid and unconvincing.

Mr Gore and Major Bressol; the long and the short of it. They might have been an ENSA double act, though they had no cross-talk and seemed strangly intent upon ignoring each other. Deacon, however, was not taken in by appearances. He remembered Tim Dalinart, an SAS officer in Malaya, a soft-skinned, babyish sort of fellow, yet as tough as teak. There was something of that in Bressol too. The boorish joviality never reached his eyes.

Gore stood by the threshold until Masud brought in Deacon's holdall, then, with the Arab in the room, closed the door.

The air within the building was cool, almost cold. Westinghouse air-conditioning units, sunk into plyboard panels, purred. A trestle table was set with ferns and aromatic pot-plants which gave the long low room the hint of dankness that Deacon associated with greenhouses. The furniture was functional, wicker and rattan, like a down-at-heel club for Indian officers. There was a bar of sorts littered with bottles, and a beaded cooler.

'Drink?' Bressol offered.

'Beer would be very welcome.'

Bressol handed the major a bottle of Carlsberg lager, uncapped and ice-cold. Deacon drank it in three long swallows. Masud al Hasan, Deacon noticed, had not been offered a drink but had pulled a Coke from the cooler for himself.

Bressol showed Deacon into a corridor which ran from the rear of the three-apartment hut and led to a lavatory – Elsan – and a washroom. The water flow was meagre but Deacon stripped and washed away the dust of travel, shaved, and put on fresh underwear, socks and shirt. When he returned to the lounge, he found that a table had been brought in. It was set with a white linen cloth and all the paraphernalia required to support the serving of dinner. Deacon drank another Carlsberg, from a glass this time. Bressol and Gore played with glasses of gin and tonic, tinkling with ice-cubes and split with fresh lemon twists. Masud al Hasan, having removed his midnight-blue robe, was already seated optimistically at the table.

Obviously the Arab was important; not liked – tolerated. The Sultan's man, probably. Treaty relations with Britain were strong, but Oman was still the Sultan's realm. Nothing could be done here without his knowledge and approval.

It was significant that the meeting was taking place in an oil station. Ironic too. Oil was the tide that would wash away the old ways and traditions, that would make Oman as rich as Eldorado, and as westernised as Tulsa. The price of the king's ransom was two thousand years of tradition; desert piracy on a scale never dreamed of by the bearded ruffians and scented hierarchs of the Rub' al Khali. Deacon wondered if Gore was an oil executive. Later he decided that the man was the area's political agent.

Dinner began with seafood cocktails. Delicate, fluted glasses were filled to the brim with tender shrimps and balls of crabmeat which had been fried in butter and rolled in almond paste. The sauce was smooth and light, sharpened by the juice of sweet limes. The appetiser, like the courses which followed it in generous succession, was that-day fresh. Delivered by helicopter from the coast? By private plane from Abu Dhabi? These minor matters occupied Deacon's thoughts during the early part of the meal. But he did not frame them as questions. Bressol engaged him in a dull conversation about cricket. Deacon's interest in 'the great game', as Bressol called it, was nil. But he made polite responses which was all that Bressol required of him.

The courses were carried in on wooden trays by Negro house-servants. Black, tall and graceful, silent as mutes, they wore skirts and shirts of white cotton, and round, white skullcaps. On their feet were brown plastic sandals. Consommé was followed by vegetable dishes, spiced with piquant herbs, then by a side of lean roast beef. Gore carved expertly with an implement that resembled a bayonet. Bressol stuffed slices of hot meat into his mouth like a wolverine. By contrast, Gore ate with surgical precision. The wine was of fine quality. German Riesling, French Beaujolais. No Algerian substitutes for the Oil Boys.

Masud did not touch alcohol. He sipped iced water, kept his

gaze on his plate while he ate. He had excellent manners, and used his fingers not at all. Neither Gore nor Bressol made any attempt to draw the Arab into small talk but when Gore set his fork and knife precisely upon the centre of his platter and dabbed his lips with a linen napkin, Deacon noticed that the Arab's eyes were no longer downcast but raised to the languid Englishman, as if passing a subtle command.

Gore said, 'Accommodation is limited, Major Deacon. We will take coffee at table.'

Deacon said, 'By all means, sir. Thank you for an excellent dinner.'

Gore nodded. 'Do you know where we are?'

'Zambat,' said Deacon.

'Do you have an inkling as to what this place is?'

'An oil installation?'

'A survey site, to be precise,' said Gore. 'We are guests of the Felix Oil Company.'

He paused while the Negro servants brought in dishes of dates, bowls of fruit and an ornate array of coffee cups and pots. As in most Arab countries there was a great ceremony to the serving and drinking of coffee. There was, too, a bottle of brandy, Napoleon five-star, and globes. Bressol waved his paw at the servants who withdrew down the corridor to the rear and closed the door.

Masud al Hasan's dark eyes glittered, switching from Gore to Deacon as the elder continued.

'There is no oil here,' said Gore, with a little sigh. 'Not a damned drop, as it happens. The field is further to the north. Inland, alas. At Fahud. It promises to be very large.'

'Fahud,' put in Bressol, 'has become a name to conjure with in the world of oil speculators and prospectors.'

'An exceedingly isolated spot,' said Gore. 'A circle of hills, with one passage through them.'

'And, at the back door, the Empty Quarter and the border of Saudi Arabia,' Bressol added.

Deacon said, 'I gather that the site at Fahud is vulnerable.'

'An understatement,' said Bressol.

'Is there an airstrip?' Deacon asked.

'Yes,' Gore answered.

'Who owns Fahud?'

'Sultan Said bin Taimur,' said Masud.

'Of course, of course,' said Gore, soothingly.

'The country around Fahud is inhabited by the Duru tribe of the Bedouin,' Masud explained to Deacon. 'Their chieftain did not put his signature to the infamous Treaty of Sib, and the men of the tribe are loyal.'

'Yes, old chappie,' said Bressol, 'but let's not confuse the major. Overlooking Fahud, not quite on its doorstep, is a mountain range, and that range belongs – lock, stock and barrel – to Suleiman bin Himyar.'

Deacon said, 'Lord of the Jebel Akhdar.'

'The same,' said Bressol.

'The villagers in the inner mountain regions are extremely xenophobic,' said Gore.

'The legality of the Sultan's right to tender oil concessions to the British government is in question,' Masud said. 'But it is necessary to Oman that oil be brought out of the ground. It is necessary too to the British economy to have a source of much oil.'

Bressol cleared his throat. 'I doubt if Major Deacon's interested in all that stuff. He's a soldier.'

'Go on, Masud,' said Deacon.

Gore could be miffed if he liked. The political agent would not divulge one iota of information more than he deemed necessary to let Deacon function. Deacon needed as much data as he could obtain. When it came to the crunch, to the attack, he could wrest it from Deane-Drummond without bother. But the seedy, furtive dealings of the backstage boys, that he had to discover for himself. He might never have a better opportunity. He assumed that Gore and Bressol were used to dealing with regimental soldiers and hadn't had much experience with units like the SAS.

Ignoring Bressol, Masud al Hasan said, 'Your nation, Great Britain, has lost its strongholds in the Middle East. It is of much concern that the treaty with the Sultan is not broken. The Egyptians and Saudi Arabians threaten it with intrigue. It is especially important to Great Britain that they have a share in the oil revenues from Fahud. Fahud is a place ideal, with a pipeline south to the Indian Ocean where terminals can be built, avoiding the Persian Gulf.'

Deacon said, 'I understand that in ten years, the ruler of Kuwait has become the biggest new money investor in the London exchange.'

'It is truth,' said Masud al Hasan. 'His estimated income from the petroleum revenues is one and a quarter million sterling pounds each week of each month, year following year.'

'Is that what you're after – a finger in the money pie?' said Deacon.

'For my country, such riches would be a salvation.'

Gore said, 'You may as well tell the major the rest of it.'

Masud leaned forward. He looked quite in control of himself. There was even a smile half-hidden in the beard. But there was also a hint of fanaticism. 'Sultan Said is the ruler of the lands of Oman and Muscat. He has the right of inheritance to the kingdom. It is heretical to him, and to me, to imagine the territories broken into parts by foreign patronage.'

'That,' said Deacon, 'goes without saying.'

'Oh, we all understand it, old chappie,' said Bressol. 'The problem is doing something positive about it.'

'Positive,' said Gore, 'but not too obvious.'

'Taking the heights of the Green Mountain and chasing the Imam and his rebels out of Oman is, I assume, only a part of it,' said Deacon.

'There has been a peace before,' said Masud. 'It lasted one year. It was broken, without conscience, like a dry twig.'

Deacon helped himself to coffee. He held the tiny cup in the palms of his hands and sipped slowly. Bressol poured a brandy for himself and for Gore, offered the bottle to Deacon who shook his head.

Deacon said, 'I've never heard of the Felix Oil Company.' Masud al Hasan laughed and threw himself back in his chair.

Gore put down the brandy globe. 'There's no "company", as such.'

'A front?' Deacon said.

'It is the duck upon the water,' said Masud. 'The duck which has no feathers.'

'He means,' said Bressol, 'a decoy.'

'What's the purpose of a decoy here at Zambat? Is it to lure the rebels into an attack, to take pressure off the site at Fahud, or what?'

'We've too many soldiers, of one shade or another, in the foothills of the Jebel Akhdar to allow the rebels much opportunity of attacking the rig from that direction,' said Bressol.

'In that case,' said Deacon, 'may I assume that Zambat is not concerned with oil at all?'

'A shrewd guess, Major Deacon,' said Gore. 'It does no harm to let certain people believe we have discovered another oil source. But, in reality, Zambat is a nest of agents.'

'Agents,' said Deacon, 'as in espionage?'

'Agents,' answered Gore, 'as in Military Intelligence.'

Deacon had worked hand-in-glove with undercover units many times during his career with the SAS. Colonel Holms had been a spymaster. Deacon's first encounter with an enemy – German Panzers – had been as a lieutenant on a spying mission. Interrelationships between one covert group and another were hazy at best. He felt that he should establish the chain of command. He had no desire to be severed from contact with the Special Air Service squadrons in the area. After all, this was a *bona fide* military operation, even if the damned Foreign Office was embarrassed by it.

'Are you an Intelligence officer, Major Bressol?' Deacon enquired.

'Sort of, old chappie.'

'Mr Gore – a political agent?'

'I am,' Gore said.

'And you, Masud?' said Deacon. 'What are you?'

'I am a Bedouin, Sahib,' Masud answered, with patronising innocence. 'I am here only as your guide.'

'Ballocks!' said Deacon, grinning.

Masud said, 'I am a son of the Sultan's administrator. I was sent to England, five years, to learn to be a vizier.'

'At the London School of Economics, of all places,' said Bressol.

'At other schools, also,' said Masud.

'What do you want from me?' said Deacon, deciding that it was high time he brought the meeting to the point.

From the breast pocket of his shirt Gore produced a stained, brown envelope. He opened the flap and extracted a single-page letter, with an onion-skin carbon copy attached to it by a paperclip. Gore reached over the coffee cups and placed the letter upon Deacon's plate.

The original was handwritten in Arabic, the carbon typed in English.

The letter was formally addressed to Ghalib bin Ali, the Imam of Omam, and began with flowery phrases and a scribble of titles and honours.

It was, however, the signature which caught Deacon's attention.

'Good God!' he exclaimed. 'It's from Nasser.'

'Gamal Abdul Nasser, saviour of modern Egypt. Saladin, the dragon slayer. He of the loud voice and cheesy smile,' said Bressol. 'Yes, it's from Nasser all right.'

'Read it, please,' said Gore.

Deacon scanned the translation, absorbing the contents quickly. Now he understood why it had been necessary to fund a discreet little nest of spies, out of harm's way and clear of the gossip centres of towns and cities.

Ghalib bin Ali had applied to be permitted to join the Arab League as an independent sovereign; the pretentious bastard. Nasser's letter was friendly to the point of being gushing. Egypt and Saudi Arabia would back the Imam's application to the hilt, but, Nasser warned, entry to the League might not be possible, unless the Imam proved his loyalty, and his authority, to the Arab cause.

There the letter ended. It was apparently one missive plucked from a series. Deacon glanced up expectantly at Gore.

The agent shook his head. 'Only one, alas.'

'Where did you come across it?'

'It was part of a mass of communiqués we picked up in the fort at Nizwa when we took over,' said Bressol. 'It's old hat, the letter itself. We know that the Imam did not gain entry into the Arab League.'

'He is, however, still trying,' added Gore.

'What else did you find at the fort?'

'Arms, of course,' said Bressol. 'Thousands of rounds of ammunition and things to fire them with.'

'Where did the weapons come from?' said Deacon. 'Were they Czech, by any chance?'

Gore said, 'No, they weren't part of that infamous "buy" Nasser made from the Communists. In fact, they are American.'

'Supplied, no doubt, quite "officially" to the Saudi government through the American-Arabian Oil Company?' said Deacon.

'There's more to it,' said Bressol.

'There always is,' said Deacon.

'Ghalib, Talib and Suleiman aren't stupid,' said Bressol. 'Believe me, old chappie, they are well aware that the SAS might flush them out of the heights of the Green Mountain.'

'But that won't be an end of it?' said Deacon.

'Not by a long chalk,' said Bressol. 'Talib is a fanatic. He won't rest until the traditional lands of Oman are under his control, until he has say-so over the distribution of oil concessions.'

'Egged on and financed by King Saud, of course.'

'And by others,' added Bressol.

'Others?'

'It's the others, the shadow-men, that we're most interested in.'

'Agitators?' Deacon asked.

'Agitators of a very skilful sort. Dangerous influences,' Gore confirmed. 'It's the old story. Whatever heinous acts are done in Oman over the next five or six years, Talib will take the blame. But the real blame will lie with the shadow-men.'

'What's more, we have to handle them with kid gloves,' said Bressol. 'Gingerly. *Très* hush-hush.'

'And these "shadow-men" are my targets?'

'They are,' said Gore.

Once more the agent fished in his shirt pocket. He brought out two small photographs, hardly more than snapshots. He passed one to Deacon.

'Nasir Salim Azzi, citizen of Egypt. Educated in Kiev and, most oddly, at the Massachusetts Institute of Technology.'

The features were clear enough. The man wore a double-breasted suit of lightweight material and a floral necktie. He was seated at a café table in a country where the sunlight was strong. The subject was of indeterminate age. Large, hearty, with a bald forehead and a small dark moustache. If Deacon had not been informed of his nationality he might have mistaken him for an Italian.

'Nasir is presently in Oman. In and out of Oman,' Bressol said. 'He's target number two.'

'And target number one?'

'This fellow.' Gore handed Deacon the second snapshot.

It was of poor quality, as grainy as a newspaper clipping. Head-and-shoulders, it showed a lean, lantern-jawed man of about thirty or so. He had a Marine-style crewcut and his hair was either blond or prematurely white. His expression was utterly blank, and revealed nothing of his character.

'Who is he?' Deacon asked.

'He has several aliases,' said Bressol. 'Actually we haven't a clue what his mother called him. We know him as George Seback.'

Deacon glanced up sharply.

'Nationality?'

'A Yankee-doodle,' said Bressol.

'Good God, you want me to kill an American?'

'Only if you have to,' said Mr Gore. 'We'd prefer you to take him alive.'

*

Dingo Harper

Lilli Marlene had died of old age, so the line that kept chasing round in my head, as we crouched among the rocks, came from a Canto by Ezra Pound: *Another war without glory, and another peace without quiet.* On the button, Ezra. Tell it like it is.

The sand kings of Oman, a surly bunch of cut-throats if ever there was, had had it in for the Sultans of the Coast for about ten thousand years. If it had been up to me, mate, they would have been left to get on with it, oil or no bloody oil, for another millennium. Fact is, if it hadn't been for the old black gold and the so-called strategic advantage of hanging on to a foothold on the Gulf, nobody would have cared a toss about the God-blighted place. Yet there we were, three of the Empire's finest, plus one toothless wog, creeping up a ravine in a chunk of landscape the name of which could only be pronounced by a bloke with a split palate.

We – the rag-tag of 'K' Squadron – had been yanked out of the deep Malayan jungle so fast the leeches hadn't even had time to let go of our ankles. Fortnight later we were perched seven thousand feet up in a dark and lonely canyon in the outback of Oman, where, in the hour before dawn, it was cold enough to freeze the balls off a walrus. Some time after midnight the water in our canteens had frozen solid and our mouths were dry. We daren't risk a light to heat the metal bottles for we'd heard tell how rebel marksmen could shoot out a candle at a thousand yards. 'D' Squadron had learnt that lesson the hard way by losing a corporal to a long-distance bullet during their first run at the ridge. I was taking no chances. We shivered, swallowed our spit, and forged on quietly.

We'd joked about the operation in the transport coming over, treating it like a busman's holiday. But once we got there, scanned the territory and heard what the lads of 'D' Squadron had to say, precious few of us were laughing, especially when we were sent to relieve the forward patrols out beyond Aquabat. When I learned what they had in mind for me, I couldn't even raise a sickly grin.

'Where?' I'd said.

'Here, Lieutenant Harper, in this ravine below the village.'

'Village? What village, sir?'

'Oh, there *is* a village, even if it doesn't show on the map. It's called Khahouris.'

'But it's miles into the mountain.'

'You will travel to Kamah with the rest of the unit, then move under your own steam to the ravine, lying up during the day.'

'How many of us, sir?'

'You and a couple of troopers. And a native guide.'

'What am I looking for, sir?'

'An easy way up, of course.

There was more to it than just finding a route into the hanging gardens of Khahouris. I knew it, and the boss – Korky – knew that I knew it. But nobody was giving anybody any free hints at that stage. Something furtive was in the wind, though. Considering how important it was, they might have done better by me.

The troopers were good blokes but the guide was a dead bloody loss. His name was Mohamed. He was supposed to be fluent in English. Christ, he wasn't even fluent in Arabic. When he talked, it sounded like a goat chewing a flock mattress. None of us could make out a bloody word. We had to rub along by sign language, like a bunch of dummies. Mo wasn't just sort of old. He was an antique, like the rusty Martini-Henry rifle he lugged with him. Grizzled and unwashed, he gave off a pong like camel piss after light rain. I'm surprised the rebel piquets didn't smell him as soon as we entered the ravine. Mo's odour, measured in decibels, must have boomed up that canyon like a march by the band of the Coldstream Guards. Say this for the old sod, though, at least he had the guts to come with us. By that time, it had become next to impossible to rake up Arab guides willing to venture into the ravines of the Jebel Akhdar at any price.

We'd been in the wilderness for a night and a day and most of the next night. We had no radio communication, though 'A' Squadron were supposed to be on patrol only fifteen miles away and there was a bunch down at Kamah surveying a route by which the main body could haul itself on to the summit. I had been instructed to get a first-hand squint, in daylight, at the massive limestone slab which soared up to Khahouris. The village itself was part of the cliff face, eight or nine hundred feet of tumbling terraces and sheer rock walls, notched with steps. But the slab which guarded it was twelve hundred feet from base to apex. My brief was to select a route which could be climbed by three men in full pack, in the dark. What's more, I was supposed to make this recce on the qt, without being spotted by any of the rebels who were perched on the canyon walls like bloody vultures, ready to draw a bead on your heart through the scopes of their .303s.

Dear Ma, Coming Home. Love, Maurice.

There was one other little snag – donkey-men. They were needed round Tac HQ to look after 'the transport'. They were about as trustworthy as scorpions. Crafty old Deane-Drummond was already plotting to use the donkey-men to spread false information about SAS attack plans. But nobody had fudged *our* trail, not that I knew of. It was disturbing to think that the donkey-men might have put the big X on our little party and that, when dawn came, we might find the bottom of the canyon plugged with rebel soldiers.

Captain Christopher Pemberton – Korky – had shown me an album of reconnaissance photographs snapped by our brave Boys in Blue as they streaked over the Jebel in their Venom fighters. And, to be fair about it, by seat-of-the-pants blokes in droning low-level flights. In foreshortened aerial shots, the slabs looked to be angled. Fact is, they were close to being sheer. The bed of the ravine was strewn with rock, like big scree. In the dark I hadn't much of a clue where we were, how high up the fault we'd struggled or where we would hide when the sun stuck its nose over the rim. There were caves in plenty but many were occupied by gangs of rebel piquets and I couldn't be sure of finding a vacant hole.

Twenty minutes before sun-up, I decided to halt. We were snug under the wall, under the slab, a thousand feet below the village. We got out of our packs and sat down. I could hear Mo's gums chattering in the cold. The sound of Trooper

Macgregor taking a piddle. Lance-Corporal Walrond wheezing a bit with the aftermath of a chest cold he brought with him from Port Kernan, our 'home' in Malaya. I'd worked many a jungle patrol with Rob Roy and Wally, which was why I'd picked them from 'K' Squadron volunteers to accompany me on this picnic. Neither of them could have been older than twenty-three. Yet they were seasoned veterans and wouldn't do anything stupid under pressure.

It was so ruddy murky in the bottom of the ravine I could hardly see a thing. Rob Roy, though, had eyes like a tomcat. I flinched when he touched my hand. He pressed a tin mug into my fingers. I brought it to my mouth, sniffed and tasted. Peaches in brandy. Macgregor's Ma owned a classy grocery store in Edinburgh and parcels of expensive nourishment followed her wee laddie round the globe. Two fat slippery slices of fruit slid down my throat and made me feel better at once. I could hear Mohamed smacking his chops and Wally Walrond's wheeze had ceased. Rob Roy managed to feed us all from his stash of goodies. All I wanted now was a smoke. But that wasn't on, until somebody invented a flameless cigarette.

Christ, but it was cold! It wasn't snow cold, wet cold, like you get on British mountains, not clear, skin-crimping Alpine cold either. It was tomb-like cold, dusty. There would be no mist with the sunrise. Visibility would be perfect about ten minutes after dawn. Blokes on light artillery told me they were getting thirty per cent extra range on shells in the thin air and visibility was forty miles or more. The sharp tang of brandy in my mouth, I sat still, shivering, wondering what daylight would bring.

The idea was to find a hide, lie up, make the recce of the slabs when I thought the coast was clear, lie up again until dark and pick our way down to the wadi and start along the route to Kamah. Even the wadi was 'occupied territory', and mined here and there along the track. Even so, we could make good time there and would be within sighting distance of transport by tomorrow's dawn. It was today's dawn that cramped my bowels, though, squatting under the rifles of those dead-eye dicks on the high ground.

Mumble, mumble, mumble: too faint to draw a reprimand, Mo was getting his morning prayer in early. Say one for me, mate.

It began to get light.

I put my hands round my mouth.

'Cover,' I hissed.

I only had to say it once. Macgregor and Walrond were gone like shadows. Mo went on with his prayers, his antique rifle laid lengthwise across his knees as if he was praying to it and not to Allah.

Then there was a noise, high up where the steps in the rock were. A small stone chuckled into the ravine.The sky was a thread of light overhead, so slender it looked like a crack in the ceiling. I'd been in a crevasse once, up on the Tasman glacier, in NZ, and the sky had looked like that. Unattainable. Maybe I should have joined Mohamed in prayer right there and then. I fished out my field-glasses, blew the dust off the lenses and pressed myself back against the rock. I had a pad in my thigh pocket and four coloured crayons. Korky had offered to dig me up a camera but I preferred to make sketches since I couldn't trust my hands not to shake. Anyway, photographs can lie when you get down to interpretation.

Funny, there was no breath of wind that morning. It had cut across the plateau and sliced through the jagged peaks for four solid days. The whistle of it, the sting of granules on your face got so maddening it made you want to scream. But that morning, no wind at all. Every tiny noise would echo about the canyon and ascend to the rebels' ears.

Macgregor came back.

'There's a cave, boss. Not awful deep, though.'

'Does it have a lip, an eave?'

'It would take the four of us, huddled. No lip, though.'

It was growing rapidly lighter. I could make out Rob Roy Macgregor's features, a chunky face with sandy eyebrows and pouting lips. Always seemed to be disapproving, did Macgregor, though he was no grouser. He wore a scarf around his neck, a red tartan teacloth, in fact, in which his Ma had wrapped a fruit cake. He had freckles and looked about sixteen.

'Okay,' I said. 'We'll keep it in mind.'

'Want me to keep lookin', boss?'

'Draw your breath, Roy.'

The submachine gun was no longer just luggage. Macgregor held it across his lap as he crouched beside me. He squinted up at the rocks opposite. The light starred above them gave them brittle edges.

'See anythin', boss?'

I put down my field-glasses, shook my head. We had been conversing in whispers so faint that we sounded like grasshoppers. There was nothing above us except pits of shadow, planes of limestone and the candlewax dripping of rocks pared by aeons of harsh weather.

Wally slithered around a knob of rock. He had a long, concave sort of face, as swarthy as Roy was fair. He had a twist in the bridge of his snitch, which had been broken during a para exercise.

'Got it, boss,' he murmured, gesturing with his thumb. 'Good 'un.'

We moved at once, crabbing up the ravine, hard against the base of the slab, 'our' slab. The cave was only yards away, a neat, wedge-shaped crack , like the door of a pup-tent. It had a hewn look to it, as if it had been carved as a shelter from the sun. I craned my neck. The Khahouris slab hung above us, a grey curtain. I rubbed my eyes with my fingers, dizzy with the angle, seeing the ruddy slab falling outwards. There was enough light for definition, though.

'Inside,' I said. 'Roy, Wally, keep me covered.'

'Where are you goin', boss?'

'Over there.' I indicated the far side of the ravine. It wasn't more than fifty yards wide. Below, wandering down, the canyon walls were like cork-matting in the sunlight. The ravine looked much steeper than it had seemed in the darkness. Any idea of a fast dive down it was discarded there and then. 'I'm taking a position so I can see as much of the slab as possible.'

'What if—'

'If I'm spotted,' I whispered, 'I'll only have to travel one way.'

'Tight,' said Walrond. 'Very tight.'

I took the water bottle, an M1, field-glasses and a couple of pouches of ammo on my belt, plus three grenades, and went without further ado.

I had already picked out a jumble of rocks, humped like a couple of Trafalgar Square lions. I darted across the ravine and got myself down between their paws. I could see most of the slab winging upward, even the knuckle of a stone wall left of the summit, presumably where the good folk of Khahouris dumped their trash. Also a hank of smoke purling against the sky.

I gave Wally the thumbs up.

I could see the two troopers, like rats nosing out of a hole, Mo behind them.

Once I got myself into position, I didn't wait. I took the pad out and soon had the pencils flying so fast it must have looked like the Gene Krupa drum solo from *Skin Deep*. What I was looking for, and recording, was a fault series, plus stances. The line had to be complete. What I mean is, I didn't want to lead three blokes on to the middle of that flamin' slab and get them stuck there. Starting meant finishing. Use of pitons had to be avoided. The *chack-chack-chack* of a toffee hammer on a metal spike would rise to the ears of the sentries like the cry of a gooney bird with its bum on fire. I wanted to mark natural belays, if I could spot them. Ideally I should have been scanning the wall from the cliff opposite. But the cliff was posted with rebel piquets and could be seen in all its glory from the village. I still wasn't quite sure why Korky and his bosses wanted us to enter Khahouris by the back door. A chopper could have roped a nice little team on to the rooftops in ten fast and furious minutes.

Ours not to reason why, Maurice.

I squinted through the field-glasses.

The sun had lifted now and the cold had diminished. Long slanting shadows dived down the ravine. Up top, the peak of the slab caught the sun's rays. Details began to emerge from the surface of the wall like a photographic plate swished in a tray of chemicals. But it would be three or four hours, I reckoned, before the whole drape of the slab was lighted. By that time, even in winter and even at eight thousand feet, it would be warmish. Not searing hot, right enough, but warmish. I put my canteen on the slabby rocks by my side to thaw out and lifted the glasses again.

And some bastard shot a hole through my water bottle.

Jesus! I jumped ten feet in the air.

Another shot sang off the boulder behind my neck.

Wally was yelling at me. He and Roy had flung themselves on their bellies at the cave mouth. But they hadn't let off any shots. No targets. I squirmed and curled up, stuffing the pad and glasses into my shirt. A hail of bullets whirred and chirruped about my noddle. I still couldn't see the snipers. They couldn't be directly above me. They'd never have got an angle from the breast of the cliff. They had to be on the flank or up by the vee, where the big slab and the roots of the village met. Ducked into the lion's paws, I lifted the field-glasses and probed the heights.

Too right: there they were, three or four guns in the nick of rock, lowest point of Khahouris. If I'd stayed in the cave with the others, I wouldn't have been spotted. Now I was pinned down.

Fifty yards of unprotected gutter separated me from proper cover – and that wouldn't last long. Even as I got the snipers in focus another movement caught my eye. I panned the lenses and saw the rebels. Scarecrows. Flying rags. Tall, agile bastards. Up there to my right on the saw-toothed ridge. Five, six, seven of them. Long rifles held akimbo. All of them moving fast, bounding into flanking positions. So much for my orders to keep the sortie quiet. We'd been rumbled only minutes after daylight, before I had a chance to do any decent recce work at all.

The bastards were proper sharp, I'll grant you. Talib bin Ali, or whoever was in charge on top of the mountain, had his blokes on tiptoe. A nest of rebels had already been caught napping at Jassahd, when a Marine commando force got above them during the night and flushed them out at dawn on to the barren plateau where the Venoms, summoned in for a strike, chopped them up badly. Talib had learned his lesson. I wondered what he did with men who snoozed at their posts. Slit their nostrils, cut out their tongues? Probably nothing so drastic. This was Oman, not the Yemen. Such out-and-out barbarity wasn't common. What the hell did it matter? The rebels had the drop on us and the situation was fast turning into a right cow.

'Now what do we do, boss?' Wally yelled.

There was no need to keep mum any longer.

The ravine looked miles bloody long. I had to decide. Sit tight in the cave and hold off the rebels through the long, dry, dusty day, or make a dive for it, a fighting retreat?

The snipers had the choice of both sides of the canyon. Even when we got out of the ravine, they would still own the high ground. With those modern high-powered rifles, they would be able to pick us off at leisure.

Even so, flight was better than tucking ourselves into a rat-trap cave where a mortar shell or a couple of grenades would blast us all into the kingdom.

One thing – the only ruddy thing – in our favour was the narrowness of the ravine. It meant we could hug the inner wall. It would give us a bit of a start. Not much, but something to hang on to. I decided to play leap-frog. One bloke with a gun to cover the other three – make a hundred yards – cover the rearguard – drop another man – scuttle on. It was like paying out rope, slower but safer. All of this was good thinking, Maurice. But I was still pinned in the lion's paws on the 'wrong' side of the ravine. There wasn't much Wally or Rob Roy could do to assist me since they couldn't switch their guns to that angle over the hanging slabs. And I couldn't return fire lying on my belly.

I took out a grenade, held it up like a pear for Wally to see.

'Got the picture, mate?'

'Got it, boss.'

I lobbed the grenade to my left over the back of one of the lion-like boulders. And ran like flamin' hell.

The blast was shattering. Rocks whizzed about my head as I plunged on across the bed of the ravine. Wally and Roy set up a powerful, pointless, crossfire from out of the cave; a diversion, nothing more. But it bought me a couple of minutes, as the rebels pumped slugs into the cloud of debris the grenade had put up.

I pressed down on my legs to stop them shooting me right into the cave and battered hard against the base of the slab. A bloody great rock dropped straight from above and burst like a bomb only ten yards away, stone chips rattling everywhere. Cheap ammo.

'Jesus!' I yelled. 'Let's get out of here.'

'Back marker?' Wally cried.

'You, Wally. Okay?'

'Okay.'

Mo came out last. He didn't look scared now. He held the long carbine like a flintlock pistol, balanced in one hand. He had red eyes. Honest. Eyes as red as rubies. He swung and strutted, the rifle barrel on his left palm and fired upward at a target I couldn't even see through the pall of dust.

The butt of the Martini was at crotch level, right elbow jammed against right hip joint. One neat technique for sky-shooting if you had the strength in hands, wrists and forearms to stand the recoil. Old Mo let out a maniacal laugh every time he fired. Four shots, fast as shit flying off a shovel. I couldn't believe it. One rebel scarecrow jack-knifed off the top of the notched stone steps, miles above us to our right. His death scream filled the ravine with shrill echoes.

I slapped old Mo on the back.

'Fair dinkum, Dad.'

He hadn't a clue what I'd said but he grinned, showing rotted teeth.

'Now go. Git. Scarper.'

I pushed him towards the exit of the ravine. His grin changed to a scowl.

Maybe he thought we were going to shoot it out like a bloody contest with prizes at the end of it. Maybe he'd been raised on Arabic translations of Kipling and wanted to be a hero before he died. Gunga flamin' Din.

'RUN,' I bellowed.

Mohamed got the message.

Flailing like a waterlogged swan he went off down the ravine bed at the double, Roy and me after him. Wally remained against the rock, carefully firing single shots up into the convergence of the walls.

What gave me hope, originally, was that the rebels didn't seem to have piquets on the south cliff after all. If I'd known that, of course, I'd never have set foot in the ruddy ravine. I'd have taken my observations from the facing ridge. Informationally somebody had sold me a pup. But at least we weren't under fire from both sides. If we kept ourselves slotted under the Khahouris slabs, we might even escape with our necks.

The ravine kinked about a quarter of a mile down then made a zig-zag round a limestone buttress, before widening and flattening out into the canyon-mouth which wandered over a series of scrub-spiked undulations into the Wadi Yafayn. We'd come up in darkness so I didn't have a true picture of what it was like. I didn't know how much cover we would find once we broke out of the canyon.

I glanced behind me. I could see Wally in classic sniper's stance, aiming at the rock steps and firing with caution. I couldn't make out hide nor hair of the rebels, though. They seemed to have vanished. There was a rough horseshoe of crumbled rocks around the head of the ravine. I guessed they were up there, loping across the summit to better positions, to nail us down. I had a nervous twitch about the bastards dropping grenades over the edge. Nothing, though, came from above. I couldn't see the rim for bulges in the limestone. Old Mo had gone horsing on but Roy had stopped and taken up firing position. I yelled to Wally, who let off two more shots then joined us at a fast, crouching run, trailing his rifle. Roy covered him all the way. But there was no returning fire.

It was quiet, suddenly. Too bloody quiet.

Wally was wheezing when he reached us.

'Where'd they all go?' Roy demanded.

'Up top.'

'Both sides?'

'Yer.'

'Get going, Wal.'

I moved him on after Mohamed and left Roy to it. We were nicely strung out now. Safer for it. Mo was a hundred yards to the van, with Wally next, me on the move and Roy pegging the rear. I ran out the string for three hundred yards, then whistled Roy in. Mo had vanished round the kink. I told the boys to be careful, settled myself, and looked back up the ravine. The sky had turned from shimmering blue to that lacquered viridian shade which said it was going to be a cooker by noon. Only relatively. It never got that hot in the mountains in winter. Anyhow, though I had been born and bred in Sydney, I had trekked the Northern Territories with my Dad when I was a kid, visiting the cattle stations in which he had a financial stake. And I had worked out one long simmering summer at the uranium diggings at Mount Painter. Heat didn't daunt me. But bullets did. A bullet was a bullet, no matter what its temperature. Wet or dry, hot or cold, it sank into your flesh with lethal impact. But nobody was shooting.

Anxiously I scanned the rims of the ravine. If they didn't attack now they would attack later. I mean, Jesus! they hadn't all gone home for breakfast. Omani tribesmen were shrewd fighters. They might cock things up when it came to organisation but they had a tradition of guerrilla warfare that went back to flint axes. If they appeared to have let us slip the noose now, it was only because they were sure they could reel us in further down the chute.

The bastard of it was, I was right.

We bunched up at the zig-zags, picked our way over broken rocks and rubble, then strung out again at fifty-yard intervals, going on down the slope towards the Wadi Yafayn. Mo was out front. He must have had eyes like a falcon to pick them out. I couldn't see them at all, not even with field-glasses.

I hunkered at the Arab's side, while he pointed with the Martini and jabbered away in what he thought was English. The sides of the ravine had peeled away. There was vegetation on the slopes, enough to patch them like an old quilt. Rock clusters projected from smoother ground. The measurable distance across the canyon had increased to about eight hundred yards. But where we were, in the basin, there was no cover at all, only limestone plates and sandy grit. The track wended nakedly down to join the camel route along Wadi Yafayn, with the green date groves of a hamlet away to the west.

I left Wally and Roy at the last piece of decent cover, tall stands of limestone, almost like anthills. That proved to be a lucky move on my part. If we'd all come dancing out together, the machine-gun crew would have opened up and we would have been mown down by crossfire.

The rebels had one manned gun sunk in a scoop, in a commanding position which gave an arc of 240 degrees across the track. I had the feeling that there was a bristle of rifles to my right as well, where the hill folded into the summit cone.

Mo's charcoal-black fingers tapped my wrist. I found focus. The muzzle of the rebel machine-gun leapt up, a nasty cylinder of metal against the barren earth. The crew wore sand-coloured head-dresses. I could discern them only when they moved. There was no way we could ever take them out. The wide open spaces of the basin of the wadi suddenly seemed as far away as King's Cross or Elizabeth Bay.

'G'un,' mumbled Mohamed.

He meant 'Go on'. I shook my head and gestured backwards. He sighed, disappointed at my infidel's lack of courage and trust in the hand of Allah. I preferred tactics. I also preferred to get real close to the deck and snake-crawl back to the shelter of the limestone anthills.

'Machine-gun on the hill, left,' I told Wally and Roy.

'Aye, and a bunch of snipers up there,' Roy told me, pointing.

'I don't think I like this, like,' said Trooper Walrond.

'If half a dozen wogs come down the ravine . . .' Roy shrugged.

'Or up from the wadi,' said Wally.

'Right now,' I said, 'I wouldn't spit on a flight of RAF fighters if it winged over the horizon.'

'They'd prob'ly bomb us,' said Wally, chuckling drily.

He handed me his water canteen and a hand-rolled cigarette, a fat one. I lit it from a match and the four of us sat there, passing the handmade around, and the water bottle. We could afford to be liberal with the liquid. It wouldn't have to last us more than a couple of hours, unless the rebels decided to sweat us out, which I doubted. They had several dozen blokes in arms on that part of Jebel Akhdar, and could travel freely about the summit; could summon several hundreds more from the main villages if they felt it was necessary. But it wasn't their style to take a sledge-hammer to swat four flies. They could do it with twenty men. Easy.

A half-hour dragged past. We ate a jar of asparagus tips that Rob Roy Macgregor produced from his satchel. I was surprised he had any room left for ammo, considering the weight of delicacies he'd hauled along. But the soft green stuff was welcome. We drank more water, smoked another thick cigarette, didn't say much. I don't even know what we were waiting for, come to think of it. A flamin' miracle? We were all veterans of the jungle campaigns and knew that God didn't bother too much with patrols, whether you were a Christian, Muslim or an Aussie jackeroo. Sooner or later, the Imam's boys would tug on the noose – and then we'd swing.

There was heat in the air but the wind had latched up again. Spirals of dust whirled across the wadi and whipped out from the ridges like spindrift. It was pleasant sitting there by the stand of limestone. I felt I'd abrogated responsibility by waiting for the Omanis to make the first move. Another quarter of an hour went by. We could hear the singing of the wind. No other sound, not even the bleat of a goat or a sheep flock. I tried to kid myself that the Boys in Blue were scrambling into their Venoms to come to our assistance. But in my heart I knew it wasn't true. Air strikes would not be directed against the Khahouris ravine. The boss wouldn't want to damage my climbing route.

It would be tomorrow morning before anybody began to worry about us and reconnaissance planes were sent out. I got fretful, mad, at the waste. Fact is, the patrol had been ill-advised. Anybody with any real experience could have figured out what would happen to us when we showed our arses in daylight.

None of us saw the little caravan come up the canyon from the direction of the village of Bab el Allam, which lay along the floor of the wadi, about seven miles away. First we knew of it was when the rider came around the rump of the hills, bobbing slow and black in the dust haze. When we spotted the figure we all got the jitters, wondering if this was the vanguard of another gang of rebels lugging a mortar to blast us out. If I'd been in charge of the rebels, it's what I'd have ordered. They would have us on all sides then. We were on our feet, sheltered from the flanks by the head-tall rocks, but nervous.

'I imagine they've got a mob in the ravine, too,' said Wally.

'We're no' goin' back in there,' Roy stated.

I sympathised with his feelings. If we were going to have to fight, and probably die, then I didn't want to do it in a limestone trench. In the open we at least had a chance.

Wally put his fists on his knees and bent over. I rested my forearms on his back and steadied the field-glasses.

'Rebels?' Roy asked.

'Yep,' I told him. 'One rebel. Solo. On a horse. A donkey.'

'Flag?' said Roy.

A schoolboy system of identification flags operated in the Jebel Akhdar region. Nobody in the rank and file had quite got on top of it. I didn't need to see the bright red rag fluttering, pennant-like, on a wand to guess that the rider must be a rebel scout. We were too far from Nizwa for it to be an allied donkey-man.

The bloke was wrapped in dark robes and pink-check head-dress. He carried a weapon on a sling around his shoulders. The beast was one of the small black Somalis which had been imported from East Africa but had proved useless as draught animals in the high country. Numbers of the Somalis had been lost, stolen or had strayed. It was not unusual to find one being used by a rebel scout on low ground. Focusing again, I found that the Arab had binoculars too, and was giving me the eyeball in turn.

'Ain't he got a flag, boss?' said Wally, clutching at straws.

'It's red.'

'Then he's a fuckin' rebel.'

'Too right,' I said.

I panned the glasses, expecting to see a field force hauling a mortar or another machine-gun towards us under the rider's direction. But there was no sign of movement on the valley floor. The rider was approaching at a leisurely pace, the donkey rolling between his robes, the red rebel ensign dipping and snapping.

'Up there,' said Roy.

Scarecrows again, up on the saw-toothed ridge to our right: I glanced up the ravine. Empty. I swung the glasses to the ridge, on to the rebel piquets. They were exposed for a moment or two. We could have risked a shot at their outlines but it would only have drawn retaliatory fire and I needed mobility for our final charge. Because that's what it would come to, sure as death. The bandits were waving their rifles at the donkey rider. I swivelled the lenses. The rider ignored the rebels, rode on slowly, then, even as I watched, reined the animal to a halt and simply sat there, watching.

'Boss,' Wally grunted.

Up the bed of the ravine were six or eight tribesmen. We were within range even as it was but obviously they wanted to take no chances. I'd kind of expected a back-door thrust. It worried me less than the cow of a machine-gun on the flank, and that sinister and mysterious bloke on the black Somali. If only the rider would do something, make a gesture, so we could see what the bastards were up to. It was possible, even likely, that the rebel lieutenants had got their wires fouled. Like I said, organisation wasn't their strong suit. They held all the ruddy aces, though. All four of them. One on each corner.

Urging the donkey with his heels, the rider trotted towards us. I could see him now without the aid of the glasses. When he stopped again and pivoted round in the saddle, I guessed he was summoning reinforcements. He raised his arm, the wand in his fist, and signalled with the red flag to somebody or something over the shoulder of the hill.

Dust clouds preceded the vehicle. No track, nothing except rocks; yet the lorry beat along fast, dust streaming behind it and the thin whine of its engine coming to us on the wind. It was four hundred yards from the mounted man. He was five hundred yards from our position by the limestone stalks. I glanced up at the machine-gun nest on my left. Its crew would have full sight of the vehicle. If it was an army truck they would open fire any second now. They didn't. The rebels on the Khahouris ridge were equally passive. The bunch in the ravine were the only ones in motion.

Roy said, 'D'you think they've come up from Kamah for us?'

I said, 'If they have, they must think we're dead.'

'Uh?'

'It's a Red Cross ambulance,' I told him.

Wally said, 'But there's no Red Cross . . .'

'I wonder how long it'll take Talib's boys to figure that out.'

'Aye, well, yon mob in the ravine'll have their bayonets up our kilts any minute,' said Roy. 'Unless we make a run for it.'

The transport was a Dodge pick-up, one of the 2-ton jobs. It had been rigged with a black canvas tarpaulin painted with the sign of mercy, the Rosy Cross, red on a white ground. The sign itself gave the rebels pause. Undoubtedly they recognised it and were as puzzled as we were as to what the hell it meant. There were no casualties this far north. There hadn't been any fighting so far. The Dodge bounced about like a beach-ball, then, short of the Arab on the Somali, halted. The rider drove the beast forward, and waved the red flag encouragingly. Some kind of signal? He was shouting too, but I couldn't make it out. Mo cocked his head and cupped one hand about his ear, tapping it as if to shake out wax.

'Offer,' Mo informed me. 'Anglesh offer.'

It wasn't that I doubted Mohamed's word. Possibly it was an English officer. But I'd no intention of charging rashly out of cover, not with a machine-gun overlooking the ground between us and the ambulance. Rifle fire from the depths of the ravine changed my mind.

'Run like fun,' I said.

Roy and Wally went off like greyhounds across the hardpan. I lingered long enough to pump a few rounds from the M1 at the Arabs in the ravine. It was all or nothing now. Wally and Roy knew it. They had jettisoned their packs. Against the rules of the game, but sensible under the circumstances. What did it matter? If this was a clever ruse, if Talib bin bloody Ali had set it up then we were well and truly cooked. I slapped old Mo on the rump with the barrel of my rifle. He went into the open ground too, waving the Martini-Henry over his head as if he was attacking a fox-hole instead of running for dear life. Four minutes of frantic action followed. The whole ruddy mountain turned into a hornets' nest of gun-fire. It wasn't my lot who were doing the shooting. By rights we should have been mown flat by the machine-gun. Only thing was, the machine-gun was manned by somebody on our side.

I couldn't quite work out what was happening. I was too busy keeping my nose to the ground, sprinting like buggery for that big Red Cross sign. Sure thing, the rebels were trying to give us a strafing. But they daren't show their heads long enough to draw aim. That sweet machine-gun – a US Browning .30 calibre, as it happened – was belting out bursts across the canyon. Ricochets sang from the rocks to my right, hummed among the limestone towers. The bloody weapon must be jumping on its tripod. Not only the Browning was busy. The stranger had dropped down from the back of the Somali donkey and was also giving us covering fire. He had swept the burnoose from his head. I could see white-blond hair flickering in the wind, dark-tinted sunglasses catching the sunlight like tiny mirrors. He was cool, so bloody cool.

The Somali kicked its hoofs and pranced off, so scared by the racket that it scattered dollops of dung in its wake. The blond bloke didn't worry about the donkey. He had no more need of it. The Dodge with the Red Cross camouflage was carving round to aim its snout into the Wadi Yafayn. No troopers had spilled from its flap. So far as I could make out, there was only the officer, whoever had taken out the machine-gun nest, and a driver. Some flamin' rescue.

We didn't get off scot-free, though. Roy caught one in the calf of his leg. I saw him dive, sprawl, features contorted with pain. He dropped his rifle, scrambled to reach it, while shots from the hill puffed and pocked the ground around him. Then the Browning barked and the rebel fire stopped. I slung the M1 into my left hand and caught Roy under the armpits with my crooked right arm. He was chunky, solid. It was like hefting up a meal-sack. But he yielded, got his right leg under him and, using me as a crutch, hobbled on, yelling.

Quick to spot what had happened to Roy, Wally and Mo flung themselves down and fired too, fanning shots right and left of us into the mouth of the ravine. I saw now why the Dodge had stopped short; the driver couldn't come closer to ease our retreat. Shelves of rock broke into the undulations, forming a shallow little wadi twenty or thirty yards wide. The fault was coated with crisp lichens, sheltered a couple of fleabane bushes and a lone dragon's-blood tree.

Wally said, 'I'll take him from here, boss.'

I lowered Roy to the ground.

He groaned, tried to smother it with a laugh. 'Don't leave me wi' yon lout, boss.'

Wally said, 'Shut your complainin' mouth, Macgregor. Leg up.'

I took Wally's rifle and slung it over my shoulder.

From across the wadi a familiar voice called, 'Is your chap all right?'

'I'm fine. I'm fine,' Roy answered for himself, though his assurances sharpened into a cry of pain when Wally humped him up into a piggy-back.

Now I knew for certain who the 'Anglesh offer' was. The rescue was a typical caper, natural to the man. Suddenly I felt relieved and secure.

Wally crossed the basin and climbed the rock shelves with Roy, all thirteen stones of him, clinging to his shoulders like a monkey. Funny how these things stick in the memory, odd visual fragments, like Walrond with his mate on his back going up the fault like a bloody ibex, sure-footed and graceful and quick. He climbed out of the wadi and ran for the pick-up truck.

Major Jeffrey Alexander Deacon continued to fire with a sort of arrogant casualness, though there seemed to be no retaliation from anywhere now. Mohamed and I plunged into the dell and across the bottom and up the short steep slope to the other side. I pointed to the ambulance. Mo gave me no arguments. He had guts, our old Arab, but he wasn't crazy. He knew we had a limited amount of time to get out. There would be a fresh hail of bullets coming at us from the ridge just as soon as the Khahouris rebels regrouped. I stopped by Deacon's side.

He did not appear to notice me. The jaw was set, the tinted glasses impenetrable. His hair, white as thistledown, fluttered in the wind.

I said, 'I thought you were in Wales.'

'I am,' Deacon answered, and pushed me firmly towards the transport.

It was not in Deacon's nature to form close and abiding friendships. Since Sergeant Buz Campbell had bought it in the Tennga Valley and Corporal P. B. McNair had returned to Civvy Street, Deacon kept most of the men with whom he worked at arm's length. Even so, in his capacity as a Special Force officer/instructor, he had rubbed shoulders with many decent chaps and several fine jungle fighters, and remembered them with a degree of affection, Maurice Harper included.

It had been fifteen months since Deacon had last encountered the eager young Aussie. At the Port Kernan camp in Malaya he had put Dingo through his paces. No tidy assault course, no pen-and-paper examination for Deacon's pupils. It was up-country and into the danger zone, a six-man team, the Deke as part of it. On-the-job instruction. He had been impressed by Lieutenant Harper's behaviour under fire, by the young man's willingness and stamina. There was little enough to Dingo physically. He was by no means a giant, did not emanate the bull-like strength of many of his contemporaries.

Indeed, he was almost as skinny as the Deke, with muscles like rawhide, a tobacco-leaf tan, curly brown hair bleached by the sun, and wicked brown eyes.

Dingo had been branded 'a dreamer' by certain staff assessors, stiff military types who could not understand energetic introverts and were suspicious of junior officers who carried volumes of poetry in their kit. Deacon did not share such prejudices. What he most admired in Dingo was an ability to control fear. The Australian did not ignore or disguise it. He kept it, like a large and boisterous dog, on a flexible leash. He had an instinct for survival, a 'sixth sense' which Deacon fully understood and which was a considerable gift for a Special Forces' leader to possess. If Dingo had a fault it was that he liked to talk. Given suitable opportunity, he would discuss with enthusiasm any number of subjects, from the plays of Arthur Miller, through stockbreeding in primitive communities, to the philosophy of Oswald Spengler.

Deacon was pleased with his first foray into the hinterland of Arabia. As Captain 'Korky' Pemberton had warned, it *did* seem like an episode of light relief after the hardships of guerrilla fighting against Communists in the sickly jungles of Malaya. But the bullets were real enough, and death was a serious matter whether it cloaked itself in khaki ducks or dusty *abbas*.

What galled Deacon was the fact that Harper and his team had been sent into the Khahouris ravine in the first place.

'It wasn't my idea, Jeff,' Korky had told him.

'Whose idea was it?'

'Orders.'

'From Deane-Drummond?'

'I doubt it. The message didn't come from Tac HQ.'

'Why was Harper picked?'

'Best officer for the job.'

'Didn't you realise they might be trapped?'

'It did occur to me – but it's happened before, you know. It's part of this operation. In fact, "A" and "D" Squadrons are having similar problems with reconnaissance work. Route-finding for the night assaults. They're using three separate teams, against three separate targets.'

'And "K" Squadron?'

'Diversion. We're not going for the top, unfortunately.'

'Show me the maps again.'

Deacon could not understand Bressol's impetuosity. It seemed quite ridiculous to send in a reconnaissance before he, Deacon, arrived. Time was against them, of course. Even so, wriggling a team into that part of the mountain was a serious over-estimate of what could be accomplished and, set against the risk of discovery, bordered on stupidity. It was too late to do much about it, particularly as Bressol seemed unconcerned. Typical of the attitude of Intelligence officers in recent years, expecting the SAS to perform absolute miracles.

Towards the end of the briefing session at Zambat, however, Deacon had made it clear that he didn't intend to do his job with anyone breathing down his neck. He had been told what was required and would fulfil the conditions of the mission to the best of his ability – but in his own way.

Kit 'Korky' Pemberton was an old acquaintance. It was Deacon's first stroke of luck. He would have had more flak from one of the other squadron commanders, those who did not know him well. With Korky, however, he could be sure of co-operation. He had left Zambat at dawn next morning, driving the Dodge. Masud al Hasan had accompanied him as navigator and they had reached 'K' Squadron's base camp amid the stunted date groves of the village of Munnier shortly after eleven.

In daylight, the soaring summits of the Jebel Akhdar became a dominating presence. Deacon made excellent use of the travelling time to quiz Masud, to learn all that he could of the odd, unfettered tribal war into which he had been pitched. Now that they were out of Zambat and clear of the influence of Gore and Bressol, Masud revealed himself as a quick-witted and perceptive companion.

Captain Pemberton was equally helpful.

'Oh, yes, indeed, I had a trembling in the bowels about this sortie. Dingo volunteered, you know. I mean, yes, he was ideal for the job, and all that, but I wouldn't have insisted.'

'Am I correct in thinking that Harper and the team are on a very sticky wicket?'

'You are. If I had the personnel I'd have organised a back-up unit. But I'm short-handed. All my chaps are spoken for. I hope you don't think—'

'Of course not,' Deacon had said. 'Can you spare me one man, a driver?'

'What do you intend to do?'

'Go out and field for Harper.'

'Really, Deacon, it *is* rather an unprotected route.'

'When is Harper due home?'

'Tomorrow night.'

'All right,' Deacon had said. 'I'll travel tonight.'

'A driver,' Pemberton had said. 'Sergeant Edwards, will he do?'

'Admirably.'

'Anything else you require, old man?'

'Paint and canvas,' Deacon had said. 'Oh, yes, and a horse.'

'A horse?'

'Four legs and a tail.'

'What in God's name do you need a horse for?'

'Camouflage, of course,' Deacon had said, and at his shoulder Masud had laughed softly.

Dingo Harper

For all the attention Sergeant Red Edwards gave to the speed limit, he might have been bombing down the motorway in a tooled-up Sprite. He shot the Dodge out of that canyon in seconds flat, while I hung on to my hat in the cabin.

It was some lousy camouflage job when you got close; a tarp slapped with red and white distemper. If it had rained, the vehicle would have looked like a strawberry sundae on wheels. In the back, under the covering, were straw bales, ropes and the stench of donkey piss. The Deke had brought the animal up in state, riding noisily behind. With the donkey gone, though, there was ample room for Mohamed, Wally and our wounded hero, Macgregor. Wally had put a tourniquet around Roy's thigh and would be dressing the calf wound as we travelled. I guessed there must be at least three other blokes to pick up en route, since the machine-gun nest on the southern hillside had been nobbled. Fact is, I was wrong. There was only one bloke, a wog at that. The nattiest bloody assassin I ever clapped eyes on. Right out of *The Desert Song*. He came sprinting down the hill towards us. Red Edwards cut a diagonal to meet him, braked just enough to allow him to fling himself under the tarpaulin, then revved the powerful Dodge engine and projected us at breakneck pace towards the camel road that wound along the bottom of the Wadi Yafayn.

'Who the hell is that?'

I was referring to the Arab; a loose suit of beige-tinted linen, ankle-length kid-skin boots, a single scarf wound about his brow. He had a jet-black beard and saturnine features. Dagger in his left hand, the blade stained with red stuff. I reckoned he hadn't been shaving with it. I wondered how many rebels he had gutted up there, how fast he had been to take them by surprise.

'His name is Masud,' Deacon told me.

I said, 'How did you know we'd be in trouble?'

'Guesswork.'

'Don't give me that, boss.'

'Masud knows the area. He wasn't awfully cheerful about your prospects.'

'Bloody death-trap.'

'Couldn't agree more,' said Deacon.

We were shouting the conversation above the roar of the engine.

I yelled, 'When did you arrive?'

'Couple of days ago.'

'Are you here for the assault?'

'After a fashion.'

I yelled, 'I might have known you wouldn't miss out on a show.'

Deacon said nothing for a while. We both hung on as the

sergeant mauled the big steering wheel and we bucked wildly over rocks.

'Just like the old days,' Red Edwards shouted gleefully.

He was one of the very few left of Deacon's vintage. He had been attached to the 8th Army in North Africa, one of the original Long Range Desert Group. Buccaneers like this pair were in the regimental genes, were what we had to live up to. I had seen their like in action in the jungle, had witnessed Deacon 'at work'. When all the ruddy bumf was cut away, this was what soldiering was really about. And it seemed like the modern world was ready to throw up wars to accommodate us, to make blokes like Edwards and the Deke feel at home.

The Dodge hit the dirt track, weaved and straightened. The sergeant tamped the horn to shake a goat herd and a straddle of ragged kids out of our path. The Wadi Yafayn was bleak but there were a few water-holes and palm trees here and there. And where there was water and shade there were tribesmen. And where there were tribesmen, in this quarter, there were rebel sympathisers, those who paid lip-service to the Sultan but gave their hearts to the Imam and to Suleiman, their overlord.

Deacon patted my arm.

'Did you find it, Dingo?'

'What?' I'd been dreaming again.

'A route up the slabs into Khahouris?'

'I didn't have enough time to complete the recce.'

'You did, I assume, manage a looksee?'

'Yep.' I gave him my sketch-pad. He held it flat against the dash and peered at it. 'What's your interest?'

'It's me you'll be leading,' Deacon said.

'You mean we're going back up there?'

'Indeed we are.'

'Jesus! How many?'

'Three of us.'

'Including yours truly?'

'No show without Punch.'

'Don't give me that, boss,' I said again.

'Can you find a climbable route up the slabs to the village?'

I looked at him. We were nose to nose, vibrating. He still wore the mock Arab robe, the head-dress around his shoulders like a shawl. It was warm now that we had slumped down a couple of thousand feet, getting hotter all the time. Red Edwards was sweating heavily but Deacon's skin was dry.

I took the pad from him and glanced at the incomplete sketch I'd made of the face, stitched lines in red, blue circles for possible belay stances. I'd broken new routes before now, on ice and rock; the Khahouris slab was a challenge. In daylight I'd have danced it. But in darkness and without pegs? Major Deacon, legend had it, had been the best spider in the SAS up to that time. But he was past his prime, maybe, had lost his sap for all I knew. I might admire and respect him, fair dinkum; but I didn't know how far he'd slipped.

It would be a long, gruelling haul.

I squinted to my left, at the mountain range doing the conga alongside the Dodge.

'When?'

'We would climb on the night of the twenty-sixth, to coincide with the squadron's main assault.'

'That's less than a week.'

'I imagine you're concerned about my fitness.'

'Fact is, Major, yes.'

'I'm fit enough.'

'In that case,' I said, 'I'll find us a route.'

'Good,' said Deacon.

I had only just got out of that bloody ravine yet there I was volunteering to go back, not just to skulk about in the canyon but to climb that sheer, exposed mass of limestone with only a glimmer of moonlight to give definition. Nonetheless I was flattered that the Deke, the famous Major Deacon, had selected me to be his guide. If I'd known who the third man was going to be I'd have thought twice about it, though, twice and three times. I might even have declined.

The third man was Masud, the natty assassin. And he'd never been higher off the bloody ground than a camel's bum.

2 Assault on Green Mountain

Once he had taken the first step towards becoming a spy in the service of the Sultan of Muscat and Oman, there was no turning back for Masud al Hasan.

The trouble was that Masud was not at all sure that *he* had taken the first step, that his peculiar time-out-of-joint career had not been ordained by a God in whom he no longer believed. Why had Habis al Hasan, Masud's grandfather, abandoned the nomadic existence which had sustained his little band of Bedouins for thousands of years? There would have been no access to education, no meeting with Mr Gore, no doorway to the wide, wide world for Masud if old Habis had not come in from the desert, if the flocks and herds had not been sold and the family, what was left of it, brought to the village of Jartak in the Dhofar to become, in the course of a single generation, thoroughly sedentarised civil servants to a foreign ruler.

Why a Bedouin chieftain should have decided to journey from the heart of the Nejid into backwater Oman was a mystery to which Masud had no solution. Masud's father solemnly assured him that it had been the Will of Allah that had steered Habis across the Great Emptiness in search of his future. But Masud, a cynic, suspected that the old fellow had fled from bullying sheikhs and deteriorating ranges and had alighted in Jartak simply because he had become lost during the drift. It had all happened long ago, since Hasan al Hasan was the youngest of the many sons of Habis and Masud was the youngest of the nine sons of Hasan.

The ways of Destiny were unfathomable and, so Masud strove to convince himself, inconsequential. But he had often pondered the matter, while he lay alone in bed at night in lodgings in Shoreditch or in his attic room atop the mansion house at Barthorpe; even when he resided in his father's house in the hills of Salalah, wrapped in the perfume of the frankincense trees which flourished in the walled garden. Especially there; there more than anywhere Masud al Hasan felt himslef to be a stranger. He was neither nomad nor trader, neither courtier, like his brothers, nor commoner like his innominate cousins; not even a down-to-earth engineer like his brother Salem, another of Mr Gore's protégés. Masud al Hasan was as lonely as only a man born ahead of his time can be. Mr Gore, long resident in Oman, had mongrelised him. Destiny, perhaps, was not a moving finger but a conniving Englishman.

In London, Masud had learned the language of economics and the politics of stability; yet he could not share the simple, lyrical visions of his brethren. Salem, for example, dreamed only of paved highways criss-crossing the Rub al Khali and, girding the coast, a railway on which fleets of stainless steel, air-conditioned Budd cars would cruise. Salem's vision could not be tarnished by reality. To Masud, trained in duplicity at Barthorpe, Oman was naught but a chicken in a nest of vipers. He had seen what the Americans, Egyptians and Russians – and the British too – got up to when it came to acquiring power. The West's cynical ruses made Omani tribal deals seem petty. Oman was also a dumpy little powder keg and there were times when Masud felt that he, not Sultan Said bin Taimur, might inadvertently touch flame to the fuse and reduce the dreams of his brothers to ashes.

Though Mr Gore and the pig-like Bressol had given Major Deacon the impression that they had unearthed the American plot, this was not so. He, Masud al Hasan, had unravelled the threads from a lead picked up in Cairo. It was he who had purchased the photographs of Nasir and the American, who had discovered that letters existed, who had gone disguised into Nizwa and other recaptured forts in search of them, who had finally unearthed and interpreted them. Mr Gore and Bressol had not been slow to appreciate the importance of his 'find'. But he was aggrieved at them for robbing him of credit. He might have lost his native faith but he had lost not one iota of his native pride.

Masud al Hasan had been depressed by it all. He felt cut off, left out, particularly when the SAS units arrived, bristling with arrogance and rash promises. He disliked obstreperous soldiers, swaggering officers, found them childish and often vulgar. He had great respect for their professional efficiency, however. He did not doubt that they would storm and capture the heights of Jebel Akhdar, that the numerous tribesmen who eked out a livelihood on the summit pastures would turn their coats in an instant, protected from the Sultan's wrath and retribution by their clever rustic innocence. The truth was that Masud envied both tribesmen and soldiers. He coveted their stability. It was not until the SAS major arrived that Masud's depression lifted, like mist from the mountain top.

Deacon was not what the Arab had expected. In Deacon there was a sense of danger, like an electrical cable hanging limp in the air, charged within by fierce power. This major was like no other British officer Masud had ever encountered. He was not merely complex and devious – the training officers at Barthorpe had been that – but seemed richly complicated. Experience in many theatres of war made Deacon assured. He possessed, too, an odd sense of humour, neither caustic nor patronising. The business with the ambulance proved it.

It was not until that morning in mid-January that Masud al Hasan 'found himself'. It was Major Jeffrey Alexander Deacon who showed him the way. Masud would never forget it – the Dodge camouflaged with canvas, the bed of the pick-up padded with straw, the Somali tethered within, a sergeant at the wheel. It was the first time that Masud had been on this sort of mission. It had been dawn before they had stopped, the great stooped shoulder of the Khahouris spur to the right. Deacon and he got out of the Dodge. Deacon had pointed and said, 'If you were a rebel leader where would you situate a machine-gun?'

Masud, awake at last, had pointed his knife. 'There.'

Deacon had told him, 'Take it out, please.'

And Masud al Hasan had done that which he had never done before, he had killed three tribesmen – not Bedouins – in cold blood. Never before had he clinched a blade into flesh, in the manner in which he had been taught in the mansion house deep in Oxfordshire. He suffered no guilt about the assassinations. These tribesmen would have slit his throat without a qualm. Something in the act made him feel clean, washed free of squalid deceptions. He had stalked them like a jackal stalking hares. He had pounced and struck with the swiftness of a lizard taking beetles from a crevice. One, two and three – dead before they could utter a sound. He had become a soldier, not a dealer in lies. He had felt the excitement singing in him, a sharp triumphant note that increased when he squatted behind the machine-gun and triggered it.

It was Major Deacon who had gifted him the morning which had transformed him into a warrior akin to the magnificent Bedouin sheikhs of old of whom his father had spoken. Thereafter, Masud al Hasan would do anything for the SAS officer.

Nothing would daunt him.

Nothing, that is, except a weakness of which he had no knowledge, a fear which lay coiled and dormant in a corner of his brain.

Vertigo.

Using a bayonet, which he kept as an all-purpose tool in a sheath attached to his belt, Dingo Harper prised open the lid of the plyboard crate which had come up from Tac HQ by jeep and had been duly signed for at the door of the Arab-style tent. Stooping, the Australian peered into the box and, with a whimper of pleasure, extracted a coil of cabled nylon climbing rope. He glanced round at Deacon who, with a clipboard on his knee, was seated on the end of a camp bed under a dangling fly-paper coated with insects. Deacon, like Harper, wore shorts, a grubby Aertex singlet and a pair of the black-soled hockey boots which had been found most suitable for the abrasive terrain over which SAS patrols were despatched.

'Single rope?' said Dingo. 'You prefer single to double?'

'I'm old-fashioned.'

'We could be on long run-outs, you know.'

'I expect we will be.'

'What's the drill?' Dingo weighed the coil in his hand. 'Through leads, or what?'

'It depends on the third man. He hasn't any experience of rock climbing.'

Dingo raised his brows. 'None?'

'I'm afraid not. It's Masud, you see.'

'Christ on a speedboat!' said Dingo Harper. 'We're taking a wog up a thousand foot of virgin limestone in the dark?'

'There's no alternative.'

'In that case,' said Dingo, 'I'll lead all the way. We can string matey between us. We'll need a double rope.'

'If you dig a little deeper, Dingo . . .'

Harper rummaged among the canvas bags and folded climbing sacks which lined the upper layer of the stores' container. He found two hefty coils of 1¼-inch rope, also of cabled nylon. One of the coils had already been dyed bright red. Dingo checked a hand-printed packing label.

'Two hundred feet. Nice of them to mark it.'

'Is it inked off in thirties?' Deacon asked.

Expertly, Dingo Harper paid out the waxy coil. He found a black ink daub. 'Yep, it's marked.'

Deacon ticked off the item on his sheet.

Though the tent was within the precincts of 'D' Squadron base camp, it was isolated, as if the men within it were in quarantine. Deacon was acquainted with many of the soldiers who had been flown in from Malaya. He made no attempt to contact them, however, and those who remembered the major steered clear of his billet.

Walrond had gone with Macgregor to a field hospital at Nizwa, Rob Roy's wound was serious, though no bones had been broken by the rebel's bullet. Masud had gone too; Deacon did not know where. The major was more concerned with getting himself organised for the night climb, making absolutely certain that the equipment he had requisitioned had arrived in perfect order.

Dingo extracted a pair of lightweight climbing boots.

'Kletts?'

Deacon said, 'I asked for Masters.'

Dingo studied the hand-written label strung to the lace-hole of the *Kletterschuhe*. He said, 'It's this model or standard Noddies. They can do us a nailed boot, though. Do you fancy nails, boss?'

'Not on dry limestone.'

'Nor me. I've never climbed in nails.'

'But you have climbed on limestone?'

'Sure thing,' said Dingo. 'In the Dollies. Me and a Frog I met up with in Chamonix went down there. Fair old climber this Frog was. Fact is, he could beat me by a lick. I learned a lot from Charles Cuvinot. About rhythm. God, he was smooth as smoke on those big walls. We got on famously, though I didn't speak his lingo, nor he mine.'

'What did you climb in the Dolomites?'

'Bloody-near everything. It was the bum-end of the season but the weather was perfect. We were five weeks down there, so broke we couldn't even use the huts. We lived on peanuts and oatmeal. I lost twenty pounds. I looked like an alpenstock with hair when I got home. My Ma thought I was sick.'

'Hm! But what routes . . .?'

Dingo gave the major a broad grin and winked. 'Take my word for it, boss. I'm hot stuff. You want me to brag? Anyhow, the Frog did most of the leading. We tuned up on the Sella Towers, then shifted to the Civetta. Grade Fours all the way.'

'You did some route-finding, I suppose?'

'Sure.' Dingo shrugged and returned to the treasure chest. 'I wasn't just a passenger.'

'What age were you?'

'Seventeen.'

'A tiger,' said Deacon.

Harper growled, plucked a rope of Karabiners from the box and jangled it.

'Top-notch gear. Did the lads bring it with them or was it flown in specially?'

'It came out from England by air. Deane-Drummond ordered it. Not specifically for our little toddle. After all, three units will be slogging up to the summits.'

Obviously Dingo had been embarrassed by the major's direct questions about his mountain experience, an unusual display of modesty for a climber, an SAS soldier and, most of all, an Australian. Tactfully, Deacon brought the conversation back to the matter in hand and held it there.

It was hot outside the tent but the heavy material rebuffed much of the sun and it was not desperately uncomfortable within. Two camp cots, a card table and a couple of wooden foot lockers made up the furnishings. Deacon's baggage had been stowed under the cot, together with the shotgun valise. Dingo's kit had been brought down from the barracks a mile away. The barracks were canvas too, Black's best, set around two low crumbling buildings with palm-thatch roofs.

It was hectic in the foothills as patrols returned to eat and rest up. Briefings were held for the platoon leaders and weapons' checks conducted by diligent sergeants. Towards evening, Dingo made tea on a petrol stove, safe in a metal-sided box outside the tent. The water was sweet, drawn from a well, the tea refreshing. The Australian had scrounged a tin of Penquin biscuits and the officers spent a quiet half-hour munching sticky chocolate titbits. Then came a wind to remind them that it was winter. The flaps of the tent stropped against the ropes, poles creaked and the fertile smell of grazings a dozen miles away drifted across the plain, together with the reek of a burning tar-barrel from behind the latrines.

Lieutenant Harper licked his fingers and wiped them on the seat of his shorts. He lit a Gold Flake. He did not meet the major's eye, though Deacon, within the tent, had removed his glasses.

'I suppose,' said Deacon, gently, 'you'd like to know what it's all about?'

'Up to you,' Dingo Harper answered.

'It isn't routine.'

'I'd gathered that.'

'It's Intelligence work – of a sort.'

'We aren't supposed to be there?'

'In Khahouris? No,' said Deacon. 'Khahouris is just another village. The point about Khahouris is that we – you, Masud and I – have to get there before the gentlemen we hope to find take fright and vanish into the mirk.'

'Gentlemen? You mean the Imam and his mates?'

'The Imam, Suleiman and Talib bin Ali are not our targets. Oh, I don't mean we would let them walk past us. No.'

'What are we after?'

'Other fish,' said Deacon. 'An Arab named Nasir. And an American.'

Dingo's eyes narrowed. 'A Yankee? On the plateau? Jesus! That's pretty volatile.'

'If our American friend isn't on the plateau, he won't be far away. Our job is to pick up his trail from information elicited in Khahouris or from papers we may find there – before they can be destroyed or whisked out of reach – and to track him before he can scuttle away into Saudi Arabia.'

'A plane, a helicopter, could—'

'According to local sources – all right, to Masud – there's a retaliatory coup planned, and an arsenal laid in for it.'

'Where?'

'That's the rub,' said Deacon. 'Masud doesn't know.'

'In this country, so I've heard, you can buy anything.'

'Well, perhaps,' said Deacon. 'But this piece of information is not for sale. Whoever it was that masterminded the plan was skilful enough to keep a blanket of silence wrapped over it.'

'Could Masud be having a wet dream?'

'I trust him.'

'That's good enough for me,' said Harper.

'Apart from pin-pointing the arsenal and making sure that Venoms wipe it out before it can be used—'

'What's the rebels' target?' Dingo interrupted. 'Is it the oil installation at Fahud?'

'That would seem to be favourite,' said Deacon. 'You see, even while the combined forces of the Sultan and the British are engaged upon capturing Suleiman's mountain, a reserve rebel force will be triggered to make a direct attack.'

'But the installation at Fahud isn't all British, is it?'

'No,' Deacon said. 'There's another possible target. Smaller, but with as much potential as a "symbol", if you follow me.'

'The place where the Felix Company are?'

'You've heard of it?' Deacon seemed surprised.

'A whisper. Oil blokes are everywhere, like ruddy sand fleas. Tell me what else we've got to do, apart from smothering this alleged counter-attack.'

'Bring in Nasir, if we can.'

'And the American?'

'Especially the American.'

'Is he done up, disguised?'

'It's possible. Masud thinks not. Though, of course, if we bay at his heels there's no saying what he'll do.'

'Have you been *ordered* to bring him in, boss?'

'Swift strike. Pick up trail. Nail.'

'After which he – the Yank – will be grilled and info gleaned neatly typed and clipped into a Top Secret file. And a copy of that file will happen to find its way into the hands of diplomats before the UN debate on the Middle East Question, next – when is it?'

'April.'

Dingo chuckled. He said, 'Ever read Pound?'

'Pardon?'

'Ezra Pound, the poet?'

'I'm afraid not.'

'I'm hooked on old Ezra. Lovely line in Canto One Hundred. It says, *Their technique is two lies at once, so there be no profit in conflict.*'

'I don't understand,' Deacon said.

'The Americans will never admit they have a man in Oman stirring up the soup. So we catchee man who isn't there. Put him in a bottle like a djinn, send the label to the Americans.'

'Go on.'

'We ask them, "Have you an agent in Oman?" and they say, "What, us? No sir. Not us, sir." And we say, "In that case, we can't have anything in this bottle and you won't mind if we bring it along to the UN with us." No profit in conflict, right?'

'I'd rather we talked about limestone slabs,' said Deacon.

'Only Masud can mug the blokes,' Dingo went on. 'That's why he's got to come with us, and can't be dropped in later?'

'Absolutely.'

'It's Masud that worries me.'

'Masud worries me too,' said Deacon. 'But we do need him.'

'On slabs, boss,' said Dingo, 'we need him like a dose of clap.'

Dingo Harper

Before I put my fingers on the rock and lifted a Klett to find a hold, I had no feeling for the climb at all. I was choked by a look-over-the-shoulder sort of nervousness. Which wasn't surprising. Last time I'd been in this ruddy ravine, less than a week ago, I'd reckoned the rubble was going to be my tombstone. But it was different on the night of the 26th. Maybe because of the darkness. Maybe because of the stir in the camps along the foothills of the Jebel before we lit out in a jeep for the far north-west spur. The Imam's riflemen were going to have more to occupy them, come sun-up, than sentry duty at Khahouris.

I'd seldom led a stiff rock route in darkness, only a half-hour or so on some of the long Alpine routes where the start had been before daybreak. Bracing up to a serious test with eight hours of night ahead was a new experience. Otherwise, it was more like a hike than a secret operation. We came in by hoof from a drop-point four miles to the south-west of a twenty-hut village named Alhdamar, tucked off the main drag on the wadi floor. If choppers had been in common use in Oman, it would have lopped hours off the approach. But no choppers were available. We were transported in a jeep driven by a corporal who resented being told what to do by a wog.

The wog, of course, was Masud al Hasan, done up like the

Red Shadow in a new linen outfit that must have been hand-cut for him. He had refused the use of SAS trim, even of weapons. He arrived at the meet on foot, bearing his own choice of arms – a Colt .45 Government Model. The heavy semi-automatic handgun was snug in a shoulder holster of soft kidskin leather, fastened tight against his breastbone with a thong. He had a knife too, a thing like a miniature scimitar, worn in a sheathed pocket down the leg of the linen suit. He took the big high-pack we had made up for him and didn't even check it or enquire what was in it, assuming we'd see him okay as far as food and water went. The Deke had given Masud some elementary instruction in the use of the ropes. He was dexterous enough, could tie the knots and work the spring-clip of the krabs. But he didn't betray much interest in our hardware. Getting up the slab wasn't his business.

It was all go at 'K' Squadron base. The lads were being fed real meat for a treat, then kitted and assembled. It had the usual confused look to it, like an Orphan School picnic. We left our tent quietly, sliding away before the real action started. Fact is, the real action was miles away, on the buttresses above the Wadi Kamah where 'A' and 'D' Squadrons were mustering for the main attack. The SAS were stoutly backed by units from the Life Guards and Oman Scouts. They had been in the blocks for two or three days, waiting for clear weather. Apparently there had been hail showers and even a flutter of snow up there and, after sundown, it was colder than a virgin's nipple. But tonight there would be a full moon and pale skies, for us as well as the troopers. Thank God. Some illumination would be needed to negotiate men and equipment up the buttress and across the ridge which connected it with the plateau. All being well, the lads would emerge on a pinnacle overlooking the rebel village of Habib. Venoms and Valettas were on standby alert for a dawn raid and to drop supplies on to the plateau. The only helicopters in the zone were on the ground at Nizwa, ready to act as hospital transports. My lot, 'K' Squadron, were attached to a platoon of the Muscat Regiment. Maybe it was vice versa. This group would lead a diversionary attack on the broad track from Awabi. If the Deke hadn't kidnapped me for his 'secret' mission, I would have been moving out with them, fuming at our secondary rôle.

To give some idea of how divorced the three of us were from the shooting war, think of Khahouris as the tiller of a flat-boat, on a spur to the north-west of the Jebel proper. It was easy to see why this particular village had become the hideaway for the leaders. It would be toffee for them to make a fast exit down the gnarled, indistinct track and vanish into the foothills that overlooked the wastes of the Zambat plain. This piece of nothingness had more names than Queen Victoria. But we called it Zambat after the newly-installed oil camp on its nether edge.

I hadn't been in Oman long enough to have the topography straight in my head. I never did sort it out correctly. Some villages seemed but a hop and a spit away, others were parted by hundreds of kilometres from their neighbours. Masud had it all pat. If the mysterious 'gentlemen' were as well organised as Masud believed, then they would have a fall-back line, and a bolt-hole no more than forty miles away on a line towards the sweeping dunes which protected the ill-defined border of Saudi Arabia. All this data was somewhere at the back of my mind as we tramped resolutely across the baked hillside in the early evening.

The moon was already standing cold above the Jebel. Masud led at a terrific lick, the high-pack towering over his head. He might be a spy, used to swanning it in the foyers of Cairo hotels, but he was a sturdy young buck in open country. He showed no sign of flagging as the evening wore on and the route steepened over the rump of the hills, cutting across the path around the ravine. The shapes of the houses of Khahouris, pricked by fires, appeared. The limestone slabs fell like dirty muslin shrouds into the pitch-black chasm. We covered fifteen miles across hill country in close to four hours, which was three times faster than a trek up the wadi. By nine-thirty we were ready to descend into the upper portion of the ravine. It was an abseil of about two rope lengths. The SAS assault on the Jebel would have started by now. But we could hear nary a thing from 'over the hill'. The wide bright sky was calm and unflashed.

We approached the rim on our bellies, pressed down by our packs. Against the skyline we would be extremely visible. I took a long anxious squint at the mountainscape but couldn't pick out the sites where sentries might be hidden. It was natural to assume that Talib bin Ali, who had the reputation of being smart, would have jigged up his piquet lines. On the other hand, maybe he had been deluded into thinking that the previous week's abortive little raid on this God-forsaken outcrop of the plateau had been a blind. Perhaps he had fallen for Deane-Drummond's 'false rumours'.

The three of us lay motionless, listening intently, hearing practically nothing. It was no ruddy use trying to guess where the sentries were hidden. All we could do – loony as it seems – was forget about them and get on with our job.

We didn't have to communicate. The Deke had told me the drill. I went over the edge, *sans* pack, down about ten feet. I hunted for a flake belay. Found one. Big, solid knob, like a beer-pump handle. I roped to it with a nylon sling, fixed myself into an abseil position. I had an old pair of leather-palmed mittens, didn't use fancy technique like seats. I just ran the rope through a krab at my waist. Deacon handed me the end of the double rope which I knotted to my waist loop too. I went out into space.

The Kletterschuhe found purchase on the dry surfaces. I had fine tension on the rope and didn't rush. I had no safety rope as such. The double of dyed nylon wouldn't protect me. It wasn't intended to. But I dabbed on down, safe enough. All I had to watch out for was the knot which bonded the two single ropes together. I checked it after every series so that it didn't foul the krab. After I was on to the second rope, and on vertical air, it was as easy as falling out of bed. I got to the bottom and gave Deacon a signal on the rope. He tied on the packs and I brought them down by the pulley. We hadn't rehearsed it.

Hadn't had a chance. But it was smooth and efficient. Not a single pebble clattered into the ravine. Maybe there was frost. It was cold enough to hold down dust and bind any moisture in the rock. But there was no haze, no ring round the moon.

Packs down, it was Masud next.

And I had my first hint, a preview of what was to come when we got to the main event.

Masud shot down like a bloody counterweight in an elevator shaft. He had been instructed how to pay out the rope through the krab. Deacon had him on a cradle sling, which was just as bloody well. I knew he was coming. But I didn't expect him to be dead-weight. I grabbed the rope and was almost yanked off my feet. He was dropping like a ruddy boulder, that wog. I bit off my shout of alarm, twisted against the rope and braked for him. Deacon was doing likewise up top. You could tell by the swing that Masud was dangling free. I had this batty notion he might have been shot dead. That's what it felt like, like hauling down a cadaver. You could hear the rope slapping and humming while Deacon and I tried to find some kind of harmony. In a series of jerky movements, we lowered the Arab to the ground.

Jesus! He looked like a brown spider. A dead spider. Legs bunched up to his belly, shoulders hunched, wrists tangled in the guide rope. He was doing nothing to help himself, just hanging there. He didn't even unclench when he got near the deck. He let Deacon and me lower him right to terra firma. Landing on his knees. Even then that son-of-a-cow didn't let go. His eyes were closed.I rapped him on the head. He let out a kind of shuddering sob. His hands sprang open and his legs started to work. He scrambled away from the rock like a clockwork Toby. He'd have tick-tocked on down the bloody wadi if I hadn't grabbed him by the shoulders and pulled him on to his back. I wanted to shout at him. But couldn't. I uncoupled him from the rope while he lay there, panting. I tried to pretend I didn't know what possessed him. I didn't want to believe it.

I snapped a signal up the double rope. The Deke came

down, silent as mercury in a thermometer. He was by my side in about three minutes. He ran a rolling loop up the line, got the sling loose first time. We heard the whispering skitter of the rope coming down the wall. Deacon caught it, coiling it while it was still falling. Once he had it, we both stood still, Masud at our feet.

The Deke didn't have to ask the question. I wouldn't have told him the truth anyhow. Bringing it out into the open wasn't going to serve any purpose. I put my hands under Masud's arms and hoisted him to his feet. He was shaking. Deacon slammed the pack at him and Masud struggled into it without a word. He was still breathing like a hog in heat. We sandwiched him between us and pushed on across the narrow, boulder-littered ravine. We hove left, away from the cut-stone steps, to the corner of the Khahouris slab.

From this corner I reckoned to begin the ascent. My hasty sketches had suggested a viable line. The opening section of three hundred feet would probably be comfortable enough. But I doubted if the fault would run clean to the top. I anticipated having to make a traverse left into a prominent crack that split the upper part of the slab. From photographs you could see that the angle was less steep on the section immediately below the mud-brick wall in the vee at the root of the village. Once we got on to that, we'd be home. My estimate was five pitches. My big worry was in finding natural belays, since I didn't dare batter in pegs. My notion that we should do it with just a handgun apiece and, maybe, a bayonet, hadn't met with the major's approval. He had told me that we might have to fight when we reached Khahouris and he had no liking for heavy odds. He had a pretty fair old point. Anyhow, pack-hauling wasn't new to either of us. Dragging a paralysed Arab bodily up the face was. I took a long suck at the water bottle, wrapped in a towel to keep it from freezing. It wasn't all that cold, though. The limestone held the day's heat. The temperature was no sharper than an autumn night in Llanberis, and a ruddy sight drier.

'All right, Masud?' Deacon breathed.

'Okay, okay, okay,' the Arab croaked.

'Dingo?'

'Ready when you are, boss.'

'Okay, okay.'

'Shut it, Masud, please,' said Deacon.

'Sorry, sorry. I am so sorry.'

Christ! I thought. I put my fingers to the rock, lifted my right leg like a dog about to pee, found a nice edge for my Klett and hoisted myself up. My nervousness fell away. I hadn't time to fret about piquets or bullets or what we would do if our darlin' Masud froze. I had the Khahouris slab to concentrate my mind. Fact is, I suddenly felt ballsy. Twenty-six, you're immortal anyhow. I knew I was good at this work. How good was something I was keen to find out.

Exploring with my fingertips, I stretched and hoisted myself away from the ravine floor. The rock at the corner was well defined and offered a plenitude of holds. It wasn't sharp like granite but had the granular knobby texture of its coral-type origins. Terrific adhesion. The sequence came easy. Without halt, I went up sixty feet. Charlie Cuvinot, the French monkey, once told me how he had learned to climb by blindfolding himself. At the time I thought he was pushing it. But now I understood what he meant. It was all accomplished by touch, since I couldn't see more than two or three feet in any direction. I didn't stop moving until I had run out almost a whole rope length, then, unfortunately, I had to dance about to find a belay. Belaying on limestone can be tricky. To be on the safe side, I needed a whopper. I got one at last, stepped above it and found another. There were ruddy good ones too. Flakes. I tested them, roped myself on, strung the sling and, on a reasonable sort of ledge, flicked the tail of the rope to tell the Deke to send up the baggage.

This sort of larking about consumed time and tended to sap your energy. I wasn't weary, though. On the contrary. I tell you, mate, what I really wanted to do was uncouple and go straight – solo – for the top. I had an image of myself swarming over the wall of the village with a bayonet in my teeth and a

Service revolver in my hand, yelling blue murder. Taking Khahouris all on my lonesome. But you get court-martialled for doing that. Nobody wants you to behave like Captain Australia, diddle the rest of the blokes out of their share of glory.

I hauled up the sacks one by one and tied them to the rock with slings. Hardware clinked. No help for it. But I did my best to muffle the goat-bell noises. Manhandling heavy packs is always awkward. But the Deke had made them snug and there were no protrusions to throw you off kilter. All done at last, I snapped down a message to send up the Arab.

Deacon had more savvy than I had. He knew that Masud could not be jacked up the face like meat. Masud had to be goaded into helping, into climbing. Didn't matter how unsteady he was, how jittery. He had to propel himself upwards. I listened. There were mutterings below. Then I felt the taut rope slacken a little. I reckoned the Deke had got Masud off the deck.

Nothing much happened for a while. I slid the safety rope tight again. Beneath Masud, still on the ground, Deacon would have the double line in a loop, ready to brace the Arab's every step. If my guess was right, Deacon would climb right beneath him, almost with him, would give him a shoulder to stand on, would put a hand under his boot heel if necessary. It was bound to be necessary. Peering down into the shadows, I was tight as a bloody bowstring myself. I could only just make them out, blots of darkness on grey darkness. The moon was round, though, and rising. Light was coming gradually down the wall to meet us.

It seemed ages before the rope slackened again. Masud had been prodded into making another couple of moves. It was crazy. We should have taken Khahouris, just the Deke and me, and dropped Masud by parachute. He shouldn't have been on that vertical face under any circumstances. But the campaign in Oman was that sort of operation, shot through with amateurishness; not even needful improvisation. Three parts farce. But it wasn't funny at the time.

Masud was grunting. I recognised the sound a bloke makes when his diaphragm has gone rigid with terror, when his chest wall is a sheet of steel, and breath pumps from a sixpenny spot at the top of the belly. He would burn himself out with fear before we got him half-way up. If we got him half-way up. Silently, Deacon was forcing him to move his feet and hands. I kept the rope tight enough to comfort him, but not so tight as to throttle him. Inch by agonising inch, the pair of them came up towards me. There were no eaves or overhangs, so I could watch the shapes thicken. It was like spying on a couple of mating bats, impossible to separate one from another. A rain of pebbles spattered into the ravine. I winced. A stir of wind across the summit made a sound like ocean waves, far, far, far off. Across the face of the moon I thought I glimpsed the pinkish smudge of a flare. Pure imagination.

Grunt. Grunt. Hyperventilating, Masud, a son of the desert, crawled up the vertical rock with knees and knuckles rather than hands and feet. I resisted the temptation to stretch out an arm; he'd have snatched at it like a drowning man and would have had me off. He caught my ankle, though, at last. I'd expected it and was ready. I dipped the knee and let him crawl up my thigh and clasp me around the crotch. Deacon – blowing pretty hard – was up his tail, pushing. Fluidity was all gone from the climb. I would be dragging this lot, like chains, behind me all the way to the crown.

Masud was mumbling wetly. I'm surprised he had enough spit. He was either praying or apologising. I didn't care which. I told him, out loud, to open his bloody eyes. He did. I felt mad and sorry for him at one and the same time. I let him hang on to me until the Deke side-stepped the stance and did something neat with ropes and with a jerk snapped Masud up on to the ledge, spread-eagled against the rock. Deacon put an arm round the Arab's shoulders. The grunting had altered to a thin weeping sound, dry as acacia boughs chafing.

I leaned towards Deacon. 'This won't bloody do, boss.'

'What do you suggest?'

'Lower him down again.'

'You lead, Harper. I'll attend to Masud.'

'And who looks to my ropes?'

'Lead.'

'Is that an order?'

Deacon had the grace to hesitate. 'No. A request.'

'Jesus!' I said through my teeth.

Wind brushed the face, coaxing grit out of crevices and cracks. Moonlight lacquered the route to the mid-point now. I flinched as I studied it. Black blobs might be the heads of rebel snipers. Might be nice chunky bollards of limestone.

'Go on, Aussie,' Deacon whispered. 'Hop to it.'

'Listen,' I said, 'at this rate it'll take us 'til bloody Christmas. I'll use the double rope for a long run-out.'

'What if Masud slips?'

'You'll be right behind him. You'll keep him on.'

Silence, except for Masud's breathing, and the long, soft sweep of the wind. Deacon was still hugging the Arab. Now he changed his grip, caught him by the collar of the linen garment and forced his face round and up. Masud's teeth were clenched even tighter than his fists. The Deke was too sensible to tell Masud to pull himself together. None of that crap. Deacon understood that vertigo was not a lack of courage but a kind of disease, as unwitting and unwelcome as seasickness. Worse, maybe.

Deacon said, 'We're going up, Masud. I will be with you. Hang on to me.'

It must have taken the poor bloke maximum effort to unlock his jaws. But he did it. He spoke sibilantly. One word. '*Yes*.'

'Go on, Dingo,' the Deke said.

'Double rope run-out?'

'Why not!'

I didn't hang about. I had already calculated that a double run-out would take me half-way up that ruddy slab. I would still have the crux section in the middle to negotiate. But there would be moonlight to help me. Maybe Masud would prefer it when he could see where the hell he was going. Maybe not. I buckled down to route-finding.

Kletts were great on limestone. I got almost cocky with friction grips. The angle was only truly vertical here and there, on short sections spaced between slabs. It was mainly balance climbing. There were holds everywhere I set my hands. I could have danced up the bloomin' thing in daylight. My old French mate, Cuvinot, would have run up the Khahouris in an hour. But we were dragging up trouble, and working on long lengths of rope madc it more dangerous. If Masud came off he would swing like a bloody pendulum. I had to trust the Deke to make sure Masud hung on tight.

Where the frayed edge of the moonlight stopped there was a fine fat ledge. Above it, though, was a plate of smooth-looking rock set on a band of crumbling stuff. I eyed it warily, climbing. My hands and feet were imbued with sense of their own. The rope dribbled nicely down, hanging from the knot at my right hip. I reached the ledge and bellied on to it. It was coated with a slurry of heavy grit. I was careful not to dislodge too much of the rubbish. I didn't want the Deke getting an eyeful or Masud thinking that his world was collapsing. Once I was on, though, I had lots of room to walk about. The ledge was three feet wide and about eight feet long, tapering into an awkward corner. I made a quick recce, seeking an easy escape. Didn't find one. Did find a belay, though, another beauty. Roped on. Signalled down to Deacon. Braced myself for another arduous haul.

The packs came up efficiently. I didn't know it, of course, but Deacon had tied Masud to the rock, trussed up like a chicken. It gave the Arab security. It would have taken a charge of nitro to loosen him, so Deacon told me, later. I brought the packs up, hand over hand, sweet and simple, and clipped them to krabs on separate slings. There was a smear of moonlight on the hillside opposite and a wedge nicked across the stone steps at the head of the ravine. What there wasn't was a rebel. Not a sign of guards or scouts.

The air, cold as iced champagne, soon dried the sweat on my face and body once I'd stopped climbing. Up they came, paired like before; Masud, with Deacon right under him. It was the old game, the kind of thing you go through with a raw, rank beginner. Planting their feet, guiding their fingers, plastered all over them, not really thinking of your own security at all. All I'd done was lead the ruddy route. It was Major Jeff Deacon who had the problems and who displayed all the courage and skill for which he was famous. No bubble reputation this. The Deke deserved to be a legend. Believe me, what he did in prodding and goading the fear-stricken Arab up the slab deserved a medal of solid gold. It was one of those episodes which nobody sees and which slips away out of the memory. We had been ordered – more or less – to climb into Khahouris by the back door. And that's what we did. How? Well, that's one of those things you don't brag about.

It took an exhausting couple of hours to hoist Masud al Hasan up three hundred feet of comparatively easy rock. The Deke must have been feeling it. His knees weren't so young and springy any more, and he hadn't been in serious training for this sort of sustained effort. He didn't complain, though. Not a twitter. Masud was making enough noise for a whole platoon of climbers, grunting and gasping, progressing in a series of jerks like he was trying to swim through the air. I was bloody glad of the good belay, a spike, and the fact I could take the strain over my shoulder, with three fat half-hitches round both ropes. Fact is, I'd come up the whole length of the double rope without using a runner. If I'd come off I'd probably have hit the deck before the ropes snapped tight. Normally the Deke would have chinned me for foolhardiness but tonight it was catch-as-catch-can climbing. Again Masud used my legs to get himself over the mantelshelf and on to the ledge. He rolled away from the edge, in a near-foetal position, knees drawn up and head tucked in, face hidden. He must have been bad to sacrifice so much dignity, pride totally submersed in terror. The fine linen suit was ragged at elbows and knees, torn at one sleeve. He was shuddering again, uncontrollably. The ledge didn't seem so large and comfortable any more. There was so much rope around that it looked like an explosion in a spaghetti factory.

Deacon broke out the water bottles. He had a flask of gin too, but, even under stress, Masud would not touch alcohol. He was no True Believer, but old habits probably died hard. He shook his head, pushed the silver flask away. I didn't need a second offer, though. I sipped the spirit from the flask-top, washed down with water. I was still fresh. And I wanted off the slab before Masud cracked up completely. In any case, it was well after midnight and we were running behind schedule.

I went up again, on a single rope this time, with a couple of runners fastened over flakes to protect me. I had to go to the left, a traverse of some thirty feet, to find a line. Above me, very clear in the moonlight, I could see the crack I'd marked on my sketch-pad.

I reached the bottom of it, where there was a block stance and an uninspiring belay. Scant room for three of us. But I was close to the end of my run-out and was attracted by the chimney, wide and deep. I couldn't guess that the chimney would turn out to be the crux. I had misread the angles. The top of the slab slanted away from the exit of that crack, laid at the pitch of a bungalow roof, right to the base of the mud-brick wall that the good folk of Khahouris had built to stop their village sliding down into the canyon. Tucked in under the spout, I couldn't see that far.

I twirled a signal down the rope to Deacon. After an interminable delay, I felt the rope snap and swing as the first of the heavy packs came on it – not on the climbing rope, of course, since it was clipped through a couple of karabiners; on a length of free. The pack wiped back and forth across the rock, then hung steady. I hauled it in. It took a lot of muscle power. By the time I had the three loads secure around me I was beginning to feel the strain. This wasn't the sort of climbing I was used to. It was ugly, functional. There was no exhilaration in it. Besides, I was seriously concerned about getting off.

It took Deacon so long to get the Arab along the short traverse and up eighty feet of slab to my stance that we were way, way out of time.

More gin, more water. I munched a handful of fresh dates which I'd brought in a pocket of my pack. I needed energy. It was bitterly cold now. Occasional draughts of night wind reminded us how high up we were, how exposed. We gave the block stance to Masud, who stood upright on it, clinging to fixed ropes. Deacon and I crouched, supported by rope tension, our Kletts pressed against the base of the stance.

Hand over mouth, I whispered, 'Do you think he'll make it?'

'What alternative has he?'

There was no answer to that. What bloody alternative had we?

Deacon murmured, 'You're climbing very well, Dingo.'

I answered, 'Thanks a mill, boss. But I don't have the gringo standing on my ruddy fingers.'

Deacon gave a funny little laugh. I peered at him. His features were etched by moonlight. Christ! he was revelling in this mess, enjoying himself.

'How far up are we?' he asked.

'Not much more than half-way.'

'Best push along, don't you think?'

I untangled myself from the spaghetti and wiped the stickiness from my hands. I took another long suck from the water canteen. Masud had pulled himself together, though only just. He had opened his peepers and was staring upward. I suppose if you're not used to it, the sight of a vertical crack in solid limestone can be pretty rough on a bloke who has no head for heights.

'It's easier now, Masud,' I told him, lying. 'Once you're tucked into that crack, you can't fall out.'

I was speaking in such a low tone, however, that I don't think he heard me. If he did, he showed no reaction.

I started up again.

A lead off the left took me round the block. After a couple of moves I was into the crack.

It was too wide for hand-jamming, not quite wide enough for bridging. I climbed mostly on its edge, using the inside of the fissure for right-hand holds, and to wedge my boot when necessary. Exposure was considerable. The upper part of the slab was awash with moonlight, bright enough to throw stark blue shadows everywhere, accentuating the verticals. I seemed to be carrying the moon on my back like a steel helmet. Wind too, tugging and filling my jacket, catching me across the chest like a big hand. It was stimulating and nerve-racking at one and the same time. But the climbing was not above severe, if that. After a hundred and thirty feet of rope, I made it into the chimney proper.

More delay, more strain, while the Deke got Masud on the move and up the hairy old section. I was locked into the recesses of the chimney, knees and elbows spread. You couldn't have yanked me out with anything less than a crow-bar. Just as well, since Masud was on the drop and dangle seven or eight times. He must have been petrified. But each time he slipped off and was held within a couple of feet, he gained a shade more confidence. I wouldn't say he relaxed, lost the gut-clamping fear that possessed him, but he did manage to make his limbs work. And that was something to cheer about.

I was shanked on to a monstrous flake in the back of the chimney, with the packs – brought up in advance of the second man, of course – stuffed above me. There was nothing very technical about it. Fact is, it was crude and clumsy by most standards. But the whole idea was to reach the top in one piece, fit to fight.

By now, coming up for an hour before dawn, the SAS Squadrons would be clambering up the ridges and preparing to counter rebel gun-fire. When we reached the plateau, the attack to the south-west should become audible, maybe even visible. I wondered, optimistically, if the Imam's guards had already been pulled out of Khahouris to strengthen the ridges of the Kamah Slab or the tracks from Awabi. Perhaps we'd find the village unguarded.

Some bloody hope!

When Masud and his guardian angel, the noble Deke, were

slotted into the chimney and the ropes had been sorted out yet again, I girded my loins and tackled the last pitch of the widening chimney. It should lead out on to the less steep slabs below the village wall. As I've told you, I was wrong about the slabs. They were easy enough to allow me to walk up them, unroped. But I didn't know that. I figured on another couple of hours' hard slog. I made it out of the chimney, off the breast of the slab, in thirty minutes, with double run-out ropes strapped tight to the rock. Fortunately I had arranged with the Deke not to begin his push until I gave him a clear signal. I came up out of the recess, got my forearms over the rim and heaved myself to my feet. I found I could stand upright. The Kletts gripped like suction pads, a little bend forward gave me all the balance I needed.

The upper slabs ran in waves. They were strewn with rotting garbage from the village, up to the wall, about eighty yards away. It looked fine and quiet, though the shoulder of the mountain cast a sail of shadow over the village itself. There wasn't a bloody sound. Not even a dog-bark.

I checked my watch. We'd made it – or I'd made it – with bags of time to spare. There was just one problem. To bring up Masud and Deacon I would be obliged to squat on the eaves, open and exposed to any stray glance from the village or its surrounds. And in that sheet of moonlight I would be as obvious as an ink-stain on a bridal gown. So I thought to myself, 'Right, Dingo, secure the rope and hop on a bit. Look for a better stance.' I found a tight belay, laid back but stiff, hooked the rope sling under it and fixed the end of the climbing rope to it by two krabs. I was free. Quite free. Feeling confident, I stole stealthily up the slab towards the mud-brick wall at the vee, leaving Masud and the Deke in the chimney.

All I intended to do was have a quick peek over the wall.

I was fifty yards from the edge, thirty from the wall, when the flare jetted upwards in a high arc. It was red, blinding in its intensity at first. I blinked and stopped as the rocket whooshed over my head, rustled away into the sky and burst wide open, flooding the slab with pinkish light. Jesus! Why did they need to waste a flare? They could have counted my ruddy teeth by the moonlight.

I was caught unarmed, exposed in the middle of the slab. Nothing behind me but a thousand-foot drop, nothing ahead except hostile guns. An instinctive reaction, I flung my hands over my head in capitulation. I was standing stock still, like the proverbial spare whatsit, when the shooting started.

The one and only target was me, little Maurice Harper, the Aussie abroad.

'*Deacon*,' I yelled, at the top of my voice, hoping none of the rebels spoke English. '*Deacon. Stay put.*' Then, with bullets stinging and whining around me, my hands raised high, I began to walk unsteadily towards the wall, into the cannon's mouth, you might say.

When the Very flare burst and sent a cascade of rufus light down into the canyon, Deacon wasted no time. The rope that snaked up the chimney had been idle for five or six minutes and the major guessed that Maurice had gone walkabout. He had already sent a tentative twitch up the line. He did not dare snap it in case he was wrong and Dingo Harper was merely resting, precariously balanced on crux holds. But the twitch went unanswered and the line remained inactive, firm but not taut.

Squeezed into the limestone cleft, Masud had begun to recover his nerve a little. Deacon understood the phenomenon of the nervous system. Masud could no longer see what lay beneath him and the crush of the walls gave him a sense of physical security which soothed the inflamed portion in his brain. He was breathing better, his eyes were open and he had even managed to utter a few intelligible apologies for his unpardonable cowardice. Deacon would have patted his arm and told him not to be silly, except that it wasn't over. Masud still had to face the upper sections of the Khahouris slab. For all Deacon knew, they might be even more exposed than the lower parts, in which case Masud's condition would recur, he would again become useless.

It had been hard on Deacon. He was sore and scraped. The

ligaments of his right knee throbbed. Though the grade of rock climbing had been less severe than he had anticipated and Harper had led with great élan, Deacon felt as if he had been on the damned slab for days, not hours. His alertness had not been dulled, however, and the flare prompted him into immediate and positive action.

'They have expected us, Major,' Masud cried, and dug his bleeding fingernails into the crevices.

Deacon had already untied himself from the ropes and performed a neat hop-step-hop out of the chimney. To Masud it probably appeared as if he was standing in space. The Arab's body contracted in tension. Deacon climbed fifteen feet and swung inwards once more.

Masud was saying, 'Do not leave me, Major Deacon. I beg. Do not leave me.'

For the moment, Deacon ignored him. He reached into the cleft, fumbled, found the pack with the long valise strapped to it. He worked his forearm into the strap and, with the fingers of the same hand, thumbed open the gate of the karibiner which held it in its sling. He readjusted his feet, clasped the edge hold more securely with his left hand, and let the heavy pack come away, taking its weight on his shoulder. He manoeuvred, found purchase for hip and knee and hunched himself into the pack-straps, settling the load on his back. The shotgun was a blessed nuisance. He should have left it in camp. He had not anticipated having to climb with it on. In the long pack too, however, were grenades, ammunition and a handgun. He would need all the fire-power he could muster.

There had been a sudden fierce burst of shooting up top. He thought he had heard Dingo's voice but he could not be certain. The empty wind absorbed such sounds, though the volley of rifle-fire echoed sharply across the mountainside. Then, as suddenly as it had commenced, the shooting ceased. It would not be unduly pessimistic to assume that Dingo was lying dead somewhere up there. But the Deke thrust such thoughts from his mind, made no assumptions. He had already decided on a course of action.

'Masud.' Deacon spoke in a normal voice. 'Stay put. Don't move a muscle.'

'Major, *please*.'

'I'll come back for you, I promise.'

'If you do not, Major . . .'

Anger sparked in Deacon; he was sorely tempted to snarl, 'Then you can damned-well jump.'

Instead, he said, 'Somebody will come, never fear. Keep in and you will be safe. Nobody can see you there and you won't fall.'

Masud's mouth opened and closed several times but protest died in his throat. Besides, the SAS major was moving away from him, carrying the cumbersome high-pack as if it was filled with goose feathers. He looked like a demon, misshapen and unhuman, supported in space, a black entity against the waning moon. Masud moaned and closed his eyes again.

Jeff Deacon gave no further thought to the Arab. It had only been a couple of minutes since he had first seen the Very flare, heard the crackle of rifle-fire. He had moved as swiftly as possible. Now that he was out on the slab, though, traversing diagonally across it to its leftward edge, he felt as if he was swimming through treacle. He repressed the urge to hurry on to untested holds, and moved with rhythmic agility, balancing the pack on shoulders and hips. He stepped from hold to sloping hold with the precision of a ballroom dancer.

It had been nine years since last he had tackled hard rock. But he had kept in trim on the mountains of North Wales, 'sitting in' on standard SAS courses from time to time. Though his knees ached, Deacon was gratified to note that his nerves showed no sign of decay. In any case, the Khahouris slab had turned out to be a bit of a fraud, less impregnable than it appeared from below. It was really littered with soft rock hollows which, once one learned to trust them, gave excellent friction holds. He was obliged to hug the slab more closely than he would have wished. He could not stand out from it because of the pack. But he was possessed of enough style to climb naturally with his feet on the long upward traverse.

Moonlight had begun to dim. Even so, it was hardly blind climbing. He had an acute awareness of direction. He was not aiming for the village, of course. He had elected to go out across the slab and seek protection from the buttress which flanked its north-western rim.

Deacon paused only to listen to gunfire from above. It was close now, loud, and not random. Single shots. Had Dingo managed to hide himself in the rocks? To the best of Deacon's knowledge the Australian carried no gun. Puzzled, Deacon pressed on to the fold where the slab connected with the buttress in a band of deep blue shadow. He leaned the pack against the side wall, fingers in a deep crack. He craned backwards and saw, with surprise, how the slope eased above the chimney. The pitch would be classed as the easiest of scrambles. Dingo could have walked it. He could see no sign of the Australian, however, on the slanted slabs.

Melded with shadow, Deacon pulled himself into the angle of slab and buttress and moved up the 'book-end' route which stretched before him. On the alert, he noticed the shapes of men along the wall, heard voices. Urged on by their companions, two tribesmen, bearing weapons, draped over the mud-brick. Tentatively they backed down the grey slab. Though they had lived among the mountains all of their lives, they were uncomfortable on naked rock. Eye upon them, Deacon kept climbing. They were no more than sixty yards from him, a hundred or so feet up to his right.

Had Talib bin Ali put all his eggs in one basket, planted all his piquets along the wall top? There appeared to be no rebels in the ravine or on the hill to the south. Prudently Deacon stopped. Balanced on good sloping holds, he remained motionless in the patch of darkness. Then he noticed something that had escaped his attention. Under the wall, hard against it, was a sprawled figure. A corpse? One of the tribesmen stooped and turned it over. The slope made it roll, flopping, for several feet before it came to rest again. Deacon's mouth was suddenly dry.

The tribesmen were nervous. Their uncertainty was

encouraging. Peering along the breast of the big slab, Deacon made out the curve of the fixed rope. Yes, Dingo had tied off and gone walkabout. Obviously he had been spotted and shot at. But had he been killed?

Wind, whipping over the slab, brought the cold taste of dawn. To the east, the stars had dimmed. There was a stippled rose tint in the sky, behind mackerel cloud.

Deacon watched the two Arabs descend the slab. Unroped, they slid down on their tails, like children on a sticky chute. Jabbering from behind the wall was loud now, querulous. It occurred to Deacon that the guards expected an attack over the edge of the ravine, confirming the fact that they had no sentries posted on the ravine's far edge. In all probability most of the local soldiers had been transferred south-east to man the vulnerable peaks at Awabi. Dingo's abortive first raid had not been taken too seriously after all.

None of this informed guesswork aided Major Deacon. Finding a solution to the present plight would not be easy. Masud was strung half-way down the damned slab. He, Deacon, was balanced like a jackanapes and unable to unpack a weapon. And Maurice Dingo Harper had vanished into thin air, for the corpse by the wall was emphatically not Australian.

Dingo Harper

Blown, I thought. Blown with a bloody capital B. I'd really frigged up this mission. The penetration of Khahouris wasn't going to feature as one of the Deke's success stories. If Nasir or the American did happen to be lurking in that hanging mess of mud huts, they would already be packing their bags and whistling for a taxi-cab to whisk them quietly away. Secret agents and agitators take no chances. The blown mission worried me less, of course, than the safety of my skin. All it would take to wipe out old Maurice was one twitchy tribal finger. Hands above my head, I trudged up the slab towards the wall.

I could see the rebels now. There didn't appear to be more than eight of them. What would have made them difficult to dislodge, if we'd been planning a frontal assault, was their defensive position. Four SAS troopers and a Bren could have held that nook against ground attack for ever and a day. The wall was about eight feet high, brick plastered with limewash. There were two drainage holes, like nostrils, on the base and a shaggy shrub glowering over the left edge. The village seemed to balance on the wall, houses piled like cardboard cartons on a garbage dump. A haze of wood-smoke, faint as breath, gave outline to the rebels on the wall.

They were shouting at me. Naturally, I couldn't understand a word. I kept right on going. Somebody fired a shot. I didn't flinch. If you heard the report, the bullet had missed. Anyhow, it was only a warning. If they'd wanted to plug me they'd have done so as soon as they spotted me. I prayed to God that the Deke hadn't abandoned Masud and come up the chimney after me. All it would take to send the guards into a panic would be the appearance of one more soldier. It was the fact that I was alone that made the snipers uncertain. I kept my hands high, waggling my fingers.

'*Kamarad*,' I shouted. '*Kamarad*.'

If they didn't savvy plain Aussie, flashing a little German wouldn't do any harm.

I reached the base of the wall and stopped, looking up. Crack shots those tribesmen may have been, but they sure as hell weren't soldiers. They bunched above me, swarthy, curious, puzzled. Beards and moustaches jabbering to each other. Leaning over that wall.

Eight feet? Well, I may not be Wilt the Stilt but I could dunk a basketball off a short run. I reckoned I could make eight feet.

I said, 'Where's the headman? I want to talk to the headman.'

There was a glimmer of comprehension. A consultation.

I said, 'Come on, mates. Which way to the boss-man?'

Then I had a flash of inspiration. This was it. There *was* no headman. What I had before me was the full military might of Khahouris.

A bloke leaned over. He had a weapon, a Thompson

submachine gun, in his right hand, resting on the wall top. I took a couple of steps closer to the wall, forcing him to lean out.

'Woo yoo frim?' he asked, scowling.

I gave him my most alluring smile.

'Sanitation department,' I said.

'Plise?' The mug leaned out further.

I filled my lungs with air. Jumped.

I caught his head with both hands. I hooked my fingers round the nape of his neck and fell backwards. I heard something crack. He teetered and came over. The submachine gun clattered to the rock. I flung the Arab to one side and went for the Thompson like a bloody terrier. I got it, rolled, braced and fired, spraying the wall top. I was on the roll, of course, because of the steepness of the slab but I had three or four seconds in a kind of stasis. That was enough. I stabbed my right hand down and stopped myself before I could gather any momentum, fired one more burst, the weapon stuffed into my left armpit, left hand around the butt. I thought the recoil would rip off my shoulder, since I wasn't prepared for it. But the suprise attack did the trick. And bloody how!

The bloke who'd come over the wall tried to lift himself up. He was moaning. I hit him a right good roundhouse with my forearm. He waned away and flopped down the slab a piece and only stopped because his clothing gripped on something. I didn't hang about to watch. I went off like a streak. I had the gun. I had the drop on that contingent of rebels. I had a decent enough position on the outside of the high wall. There wasn't even any firing for the first minute. By that time I was almost at the buttress, left of Khahouris. They got off some shots, but only a scattered handful. I expected them to send up another Very flare, illuminate me against those towering rocks and pick me off. But there was no flare. Jesus, how I danced over the roof of the slab into the wide scarf of shadow that wrapped the shoulder of the north-east buttress. I kept the Thompson on my arm, held snug, left hand against my chest. I made the buttress just as gravity began to grab me. My fist closed on a jug-handle. For the moment, I was safe. I was breathing like a rip-saw. Still leery of being caught by a sky-candle, I recced the situation p.d.q., and started up, not down, the joint of slab and rock wall. I was looking to get myself above the roofs of the village on the side of the limestone sugar-loaf. I climbed soft, with fists and feet, the Thompson slung on my shoulder. I went up the fold for about forty feet, then on to the buttress proper, wending up it for another thirty or forty feet until I reached a ledge big enough to accomodate me. I stretched out on my belly, snuggled the Thompson into firing position, and covered the crest of the Khahouris slab and a fair piece of the wall.

If I was flushed out I could get myself into the village, striking down and right-forward; or I could go for the out-facing side of the buttress. So far this part of the Jebel had been a novice's paradise, riddled with good friction holds. For the time being, I elected to lie doggo. I waited, growing cold.

It took the Deke only a quarter of an hour to traverse from the stance below the chimney. His sudden appearance didn't surprise me. God knows how he'd shaken off Masud, though. Maybe he'd pushed him over the bloody edge or clocked him one with the butt of the shotgun. I spotted the major as soon as he hove into view. It cheered me no end to see him. Particularly as the rebels, having done bugger all for ten minutes, had finally shoved a couple of reluctant heroes over the wall to investigate the slab. It was still a bit too dark for me to make out whether or not the bloke I'd dragged over the wall was alive or dead. But his brothers left him where he was so I guessed his neck was broken after all. The Deke had picked up sight of the loose rebels too, so I'd no need to warn him. He came fast across the upper part of the slab. Soon he was crouched against the buttress not far below me. I could have sent a blob of spit on to his beret if that had been my style. Like me, the major waited. It was just as bloody well. Just as well for Masud al Hasan, I mean. If the Deke and I had worked our way higher, into the village, say, then our handsome Arab agent would have had his head blown off.

What possessed Masud, I'll never know. For the best part of

six hours he'd been paralysed with fear. It had been like shoving a window dummy up the limestone. Now, left to his own devices, the little rat suddenly finds enough volition to drag himself up the chimney. Maybe he was scared of being abandoned seven hundred feet from the deck. Whatever, he was abruptly there on the edge of the slab by the rope sling. His head looked like a soccer ball, waiting for somebody to boot it into space.

Climbing again, Deacon had worked his way up the upper corner of the slab, probably hoping to find me. If two rebel soldiers hadn't been out in the open I'd have given the Deke a verbal sign that I was alive and well. But I'd no opportunity. With a fierce yell, one of the blokes behind the mud wall spotted Masud's nut and began firing. The pair on the slab, who had been sliding tentatively down to the edge, flung themselves flat as a volley of rifle fire boomed over their heads. Masud had got his elbows on the edge and was trying to hoist himself up. He looked as awkward as a lungfish on a marble floor. Couldn't get the leverage needed to make the final surge.

I shouted, '*Boss, I'm here.*'

Then I started firing. I had no spare ammo for the Thompson so I didn't let off a rash of shots. But I got the pair on the slab. I saw them flop, one of them rise to his knees then plunge headlong over the top of the slab, missing Masud by inches. Masud's head disappeared below the rock lip. I reckoned he was hanging on to the fixed rope for dear life, boots kicking thin air. Served the bastard right.

I shouted, 'Deke, are you mobilised?'

'Yes.'

'Armed?'

'To the teeth.'

'I'll cover you.'

'Most kind.'

Then I lost him.

I didn't have the leisure to peer about for him. A couple of tribesmen had obviously sussed us out and were triggering shots at the buttress. Rock chipped and the bullets made noises like tracers but they didn't seem to have exact aim. I held fire, anxious not to give my position away. I elbowed forward and peeked over the side of the ledge. Deacon was moving up the fold like a jet-propelled crab. He had shed his pack, hooked it to the buttress, and was going on towards the wall's end with only the shotgun. Or so I thought. I couldn't see the four grenades in the sack at his side. I should have realised that the legendary Deacon would have the same instinct as me. We were being stalled by a very small rearguard force, only a handful of rebel guns. Some shrewd *tamimah* or local sheikh had ordered Khahouris evacuated during the night. I'll say this for those Arabs, they had guts. They could have cut out, whizzed off into the wilderness; we'd never have run them to earth. But they had been told – and paid – to hold the wall at Khahouris, and, by the Beard of the Prophet, that's what they were going to do. The fact that they weren't too good at it is beside the point.

The first grenade startled me, never mind the enemy.

The Deke had passed out of sight, left around the base of the buttress. Rifle fire was desultory, just enough to make me keep down. It appeared that Deacon was intent on taking the target all by himself. Nobody ever made better use of two HE grenades and a loaded shotgun. He flung the first grenade in a long, high toss over the breadth of the wall. It exploded in white light, and a shattering outward blast that knocked a huge hole in the mud-brick barricade. The major was on the move before the explosion. He went over the left corner of the Khahouris village wall so fast I didn't even see him do it. Me, I got myself off that bloody ledge a split second after the blast. If there was going to be action I didn't want to be stranded and left out of it. I wanted my fair share. I had a Thompson with a few shells still in the magazine and a honed bayonet in a sheath by my shin. What more could you ask for?

Just as I dropped from the vertical buttress on to the slab, another grenade burst deeper into the tiers of the village. I heard the shotgun bark. It was weird, the abrupt flash of light, the Deke silhouetted astride the wall. The dry leaves of the shaggy tree were stippled with glare. I saw the vivid spurt of the Vaughan as debris pattered from the heavens. Nobody came out of the hole in the wall. There was nobody left to fight.

I clambered up to Deacon and grabbed his ankle.

'What's in there?'

'Precious little,' he answered.

'We'd better clear it,' I said.

'Of course.'

I found holds and hoisted myself up on to the wall top. There was a hot stink of explosive, the charred-rope smell of stone. Something was smouldering among the rubble where the wall had collapsed. The miasmic mist on the floor of the village had been thickened by fumes.

'Don't tell me you got them all first go, boss?'

'How many did you estimate, Dingo?'

I shrugged. He had a hand on my shoulder, steadying me. We might have been double-up on a charger. 'Eight at the most,' I said.

'Three on the slab. Four there.'

'So there's one on the loose.'

'Wouldn't it be nice to find him?' Deacon said.

'In that warren?'

We could see the village clearly in gathering daylight. Warren it was, too. The houses, about thirty of them, weren't of mud, but of stone. They reminded me of crofts I'd seen on remote Scottish islands, only they didn't have the snug, rounded shape of those close-to-the-earth dwellings. They were angular, with unglazed slots for windows, palm-trunk roof poles, and thatch made of leaves, straw and general litter.

The houses were built along the sloping sides of a bowl above the base wall, at the back of which was a stone reservoir fed, probably, by a spring. Rising above the habitations were terraces. On these narrow shelves some cultivation was carried out, scanty crops of cereal grains, stunted fig and apricot trees. The ledges were linked by rock steps. There was only one track, which looked as if it had been scrubbed out of the limestone. It wandered over the shoulder of the buttress behind us, presumably on to the wind-swept plateau where the herds grazed. I had visited some pretty dismal holes in the Outback, but this place took the bloody biscuit.

'Perhaps,' said Deacon, 'we should rescue our Arab friend first.'

I said, 'Hell! Leave him where he is.'

'It wasn't his fault he went to pieces, you know.'

'Are we going to turn our back on that wall again?'

'Come now, Dingo. How would you like to be dangling from the end of a rope?'

'My Ma always said that'd be my eventual fate.'

The Deke gave me a nudge. 'Cover me. I'll go down on to the slab and enquire how it is with Masud.'

'I can cover you better from the front,' I said. 'Besides, it might take two of us to lug him to the surface. I've played about on that ruddy slab too long to push my luck any further.'

'Very well,' Deacon agreed.

I understood what was in the major's mind. He was a humanitarian, sure, but he was also responsible for Masud. It wouldn't look good if we had to square up to the Sultan and tell him we'd lost his agent before we even got into Khahouris. We needed Masud. We hadn't a clue where to start once we got into the village and began our search for information about the American connection. Like the Deke, I was ninety per cent certain that we'd have no shooting-type trouble now.

Masud was clinging to the rope with both hands. He had found a convenient sloping ledge and had rested his knees on it and bowed his forehead. He resembled a bloody gargoyle that a careless builder had cemented to a roof the wrong way round. Oddly, though, he wasn't in as bad a state as he was when the climb started. I imagine he had used up all his adrenalin, that his kidney organs or whatever had gone hard as golf balls.

Keeping a weather eye on the village, the Deke and I managed to bring him over the edge. Even on the easy slope of the slab roof, though, he would not stand up straight. He crawled before us on all fours. He was sick, that Bedouin, with wounded pride. Fevered with rage. The rage was at his own weakness, of course, but no Arab was going to admit that. Hissing breath was no longer a sign of hyperventilation but of fury. I almost expected him to fall on the corpse that barred his way off the slab and rip it limb from limb.

It was light now, pale and cold and milky. The village looked incredibly drab. We didn't try to hoist Masud to his pins but followed him away from the edge. Then I went back and abseiled down the rope and rigged the packs, climbed up again, and the Deke and I brought up the rest of the gear. Masud, Deacon informed me, had been left in safety behind the wall.

It cost us thirty precious minutes to retrieve the packs. But we had need of them. Deacon, though at a bit of a loss, still had hopes that we might pick up Nasir's trail, find the end of the string that would lead us to the American. I couldn't see how, myself. For my money, the operation had foundered.

To judge by the din from the south-east, the SAS squadrons had attained their objectives and were storming the rebel nests, flushing out resistance. In three or four hours they would be here. Aircraft. Choppers. By then, according to plan, we three were supposed to be miles away, bloodhounds on the trail. No chance, mate. We'd hauled our arses up that bloody great chunk of rock for nothing. The birds had flown.

3 A hawk in the hand

The thirst which possessed Masud al Hasan consumed his reason. It was like a manifestation of the rage that scorched his heart and soul. When the major left him safe behind the broken bricks of the wall, to go down to the edge of the great fall again, Masud could find no rest from his torment. He had lost respect in the soldiers' eyes, in his own too. Shame consumed him and out of shame was born a red-winged hatred. Hatred created the thirst. He rose unsteadily to his feet and padded towards the reservoir, passing the contorted corpses of the rebels without a glance. Major Deacon had warned him that there might be rebels lurking in the houses but Masud no longer cared. He had passed through fire and would have rejoiced, at the moment, in the coming of an honourable death.

On reaching the worn stone slab which mounted to the rim of the pond, Masud paused to glare at the slotted windows, defying them to spit death at him, showing he was not afraid of *that*, whatever else. Stained by cowardice, he lowered himself to his belly on the stone and dipped his head into the water. Fine dust coated the surface and the water was cold, cold as ice, crimping his skin and clinging like honey to his beard. He swallowed gulps, sucking them whole into his mouth with his head under, too cold to taste the chalk of the spring water. He extended his arms and slipped them beneath the surface. His flesh burned and throbbed where the rocks had torn it, his fingers ached wonderfully. For a half-minute he lay, head, shoulders and arms submerged, then he pulled into a sitting position and, squatting on his heels, supped more water in his cupped palms, clothing soaked and dripping and the stone slab darkly-splashed about him as if he knelt in spilled blood.

Slowly Masud rose to his feet. He held his arms straight out in front of him, clenched fists over the water. Trembling had ceased. He fanned his fingers. They were as steady as rods.

Slowly he brought his hands to his face and stripped water from his beard, then he stepped from the slab and lifted his eyes to the ledges where the stunted fig trees clung like imps immobilised by daylight. Breath came from his lungs with a low growling sound. He drew the short knife from the pocket at his waist and stropped it across his palm, letting it sample the seep of blood. He could not put shame behind him. Nonetheless, he would atone for it. He would regain stature in the eyes of the British officer. Masud al Hasan walked across the narrow neck of the square to the nearest dwelling and kicked open the door.

A fowl clucked and flapped away into the roof trees. The one-roomed house was otherwise empty. But the embers of the evening fire still glowed on the earth hearth and he could smell the warm *'eish*, crushed wheat porridge, in its pot by the stones. He could smell too the pungent vinegary stench of palm-wood fuel which told him that the family had been poor, or starved by the long siege. A timber saw and flail were against one wall. Worn mats and a single clotted sheepskin. There were no garments on the pegs. Motionless on the threshold, Masud sniffed. Women, yes, he could smell women. But they had gone in the night like dreams. He backed out and went to the dwelling next door which, like the first, was deserted. It was as he crossed the arc of the upper part of the village that Masud's black eyes detected the bloodstains.

Six stone steps had been hewn out of a band of limestone, lifting the village up by a man's height towards the terraces. One of the stains was almost as large as a fig-leaf, thus shaped, and when Masud knelt and dabbed it with his fingertip, proved to be wet as water still, without thickening. Masud's upper lip peeled from his teeth, and the tip of his tongue made a faint triumphant *yallowing* against it. He had no thought to summon the major. He had the knife, needed no gun to expedite his search, only cunning and stealth and the darts of fresh blood to lead him to his prey. He growled and moved on, hugging the ancient steps.

*

Rashid had stolen his name. He did not belong to any of the septs of the noble family of the Rashidi but was the son of a lowly hide-dealer of the wild tribe of the Qara, who called themselves the Hakli. The Hakli differed so greatly in character and appearance from true Arabs that they were generally classed as heathens. Rashid had been dropped into the world among the dung-baubled hoofs of starving oxen in a cavern at Dirbat one bitter winter night about twenty years ago. It seemed that he might be fated to drop out of it through the dirt floor of a house of strangers on the cliffs of the Jebel Akhdar.

Rashid was no stoic. He did not accept the tenet that all men must die and time and place had no consequence in Allah's scheme of things. They had much consequence in Rashid's scheme of things. There was a girl of the Nidabi whose virgin thighs tormented his dreams with their length and smoothness and who had been promised to him as soon as he could raise the bride price in riyals or dollars. It was beginning to seem that it would be another man's member which would eventually summon the dew of ecstasy from the Nidabi girl and taste joy upon her belly. Rashid was wounded, trapped and alone. To escape death by bleeding he would have to surrender himself to the English who had stormed the wall of the village in great weight of numbers. He had heard, however, that the English were merciful to prisoners and they would surely have doctors who could cauterise a shattered hand.

He held the blood-glistening stump of his left fist to the light from the window and examined it again. Would Julnar despise him for being less than whole? Would he be cast out from the service with Nasir Salim Azzi? Reduced to theft or beggary in the *suqs*? After all, it was not as if his trigger finger had been ripped away by the piece of the English grenade.

Squirming, Rashid poked his thumb and forefinger into the pulp to search for the end of the cords from which his life blood trickled like water from a broken *falaj*. He had wrapped a dirty scarf around his wrist but the knot did not bite deeply enough to hinder the flow. On the dirt floor, between his knees, there was already a dark pool.

Rashid might have surrendered at once if he had known how to go about it. But he was undecided and, stirred perhaps by the blood of the quarrelsome Hakli, pondered on the necessity of making a fighting exit. After all, he still had a weapon, the magnificent American carbine which fired .30 calibre round-nosed bullets from a little box under the action. The carbine had been given into his keeping by Nasir Salim Azzi in person, drawn fresh from a crate at the fort in the desert, at Ashfra, where he had been taken along with thirty of his brethren. There he had learned how to strip the semi-automatic rifle, how to clean it, how to aim and fire it. It was his true friend. But even the carbine would not save him now. He might die bravely with it in his remaining hand, but die he would if he pulled its trigger just once.

One of a small squad of mercenaries brought into Khahouris Rashid fought for money not principle. He did not much care whether the Sultan or the Imam held sway over the peoples of Muscat and Oman. He was not ignorant of the purposes of the war but did not believe that the wealth which would ensue from the pumping of oil would affect him one way or another. Nasir Salim Azzi had not tried to sell him that dream; the smooth, plump Egyptian was wise. When Nasir talked of power, however, the mercenaries from the caves and squalid huts of the hinterland of Arabia fully understood the essence of it. Equating political power with fire power was simple and, in the chambers of the fort at Ashfra, there was power in plenty. When Rashid thought of what might be attained, he imagined Venom aeroplanes piloted by tribesmen, heard the singing snarl of those massive engines. He thought too of shiny trucks and of long guns, and hoped, faintly, that he might be found a place in Nasir Salim Azzi's army of the future, an army which would rule with a fist of steel. Now, it seemed, he must be prepared to die for a nebulous ideal. He wound the scarf tighter around his elbow and crawled on his knees to the slot in the wall of the room.

The house in which he had sought refuge had been chosen entirely at random. He had become too weak to drag himself further up the terraces, to escape over the top of the steps on to the plateau and to follow the women, boys and old men of the village into shelter among the flat rocks where they had gone with their livestock in the hour after dusk, going away suddenly when Nasir arrived.

Nasir had come on horseback, riding a fine big stallion, accompanied by three other men also on horseback. They had come from the south-east and the horses were lathered badly. It was at Nasir Salim Azzi's command that the village had been cleared. Nasir had spoken with Ghanim, who was the leader of the mercenaries and Rashid's friend, and had told him what to do, how to hold the wall until one hour past dawn and then withdraw down the track to the head of the Wadi Yafayn where transport would be waiting.

It had been Ghanim's opinion that there would be no trouble, that it was only a precaution. The eight rebels had felt light-hearted and had eaten and drunk well as the night came down over the mountain.

Nasir had led the ancient headman of Khahouris away. The little chieftain's name was Julanda, and the fool believed himself to be holy, a late descendant of the first Imam of Oman, all on the strength of the link of the name. He held the boxes, though, those metal chests in which letters and papers were kept, the property of the Imam and all related to this war and other wars. Rashid, the hide-dealer's son, did not understand what was in the letters but, being an Arab – in spite of slanders to the contrary – he appreciated that the documents within the metal boxes represented a potent source of power.

The boxes would not be taken from the mountain until the mountain itself was lost. The Jebel Akhdar was the last bastion of power, the paper treasure part of that power. The removal of the metal chests would weaken the Imamate and dilute the rule of Suleiman bin Himyar, the Lord of the Green Mountain. The boxes were removed from the village by two of Julanda's sons and, Ghanim speculated, would be hidden in a cave nearby, perhaps in the narrow-mouthed slit on the rock of the Young Deer, the *ghizlan*.

Rashid was not aware that he had become the repository of vital information. He was one of only six men who had an inkling where the documents were hidden. One of those six men lay dead on the slabs; Ghanim. Three others, old Julanda and his grizzled sons, were lying low in the rocks among the goats. And Nasir Salim Azzi, riding his lathered stallion, had vanished again during the night.

Papers and secret caves were far, far from Rashid's concerns as he crouched, shivering, in the house on the third level of Khahouris. He did not expect the English soldiers to be concerned with mere papers. Surely they would be more interested in finding fresh water, fresh meat and the whereabouts of desirable women.

In this confusion of knowledge and ignorance, Rashid floated like a feather on water. He was uncertain what he could do to save himself. No final decision was required of him, however. Even as he propped himself and his carbine by the window slit and peered blearily into the daylight, the enemy came upon him, not a brisk English soldier, but a Bedu with a savage heart.

Masud had glimpsed the glint of daylight on the muzzle of the carbine before he reached the third level. Even without that tell-tale, he would have tracked the wounded man. The trail of blood drops was obvious and unbroken. With so much blood shed from his body no human could hope to find the strength to climb the steps to the open ground. Besides, the houses were all deserted. There were no rifles hidden anywhere, of that Masud was sure. It would not have deterred him much if there had been snipers on the terraces. He would have prowled after his prey in defiance of the bullets. A wounded man was a weak man. And Masud needed another's weakness to help cancel out his own.

The house looked exactly like all the others, except that the door had not been closed properly. It swung on its rope hinge, giving him an invitation.

Cautiously, but without pause, Masud had crabbed left,

passing the front of the house on a lower level. He had come up eight stone steps on his belly, slithering, and completed his approach at a crouching run. He ducked under one window and flattened himself against the wall by the half-open door. He listened. From within he could hear soft rasping sobs, the breathing of a man in pain. Masud grinned and, mouth open, stuck the knife between his teeth to free his hands. For all he knew, there might be ten rebels hidden inside the house, but he doubted it. He glanced back down the terraces, over the flat rooftops to the crescent shape of the wall. He could not quite see the edge of the slab from here, or the broken section of the wall. Nor could he see Major Deacon or the Australian. Looking down brought a slight queasiness to him, though he was anchored to solid ground now. The queasiness caused reaction. Biting on the knife blade he slammed his left forearm against the door and flung himself into the house, pitching on to his shoulder and rolling upright, as he had been taught in the gymnasium at Barthorpe.

It was dark within the fetid apartment but he saw a shadow by the window and concentrated on it. The young man was wallowing, one arm held girlishly away from his hip, the other hooked awkwardly into the rifle sling. Masud hit the rifle barrel with his foot and the weapon, torn from the rebel's grasp, clattered against the hearth stone. The rebel had long greasy hair and a skinny face. He wore baggy khaki trousers with canvas straps just above the ankles and a quilted jacket, open to the breastbone. Two straps of ammunition crossed his body and another belt was wrapped around his waist. He could have fought a war by himself, so well equipped was he. But a child could have taken him now, without the carbine.

Masud planted one foot on the rebel's breast and pressed him back against the wall, then leaned into him and grabbed the suspended stump of the man's left arm just above the wrist and jerked it violently.

The rebel did not scream. He throttled his cry, though his cheeks bulged hideously and his eyes widened until they seemed to be standing out from his skull like two blunt horns.

Masud dropped to one knee, twisting the wounded hand again.

'Are you alone?'

'I am alone.' The answer came instantly, gasped out.

'Who are you?'

'I am Rashid.'

'You are of the Hakli?' Masud said.

Rashid did not answer this question. He asked one of his own. 'Are there no soldiers, no English?'

'Yes, there are soldiers.'

'I . . . I . . . wish to be a prisoner.'

'You are my prisoner, Rashid of the Hakli,' said Masud.

'Where are the English soldiers?'

'They will be here in two hours.'

'I require medicine.'

With sinister gentleness Masud al Hasan lifted the wounded arm and turned it this way and that, admiring the shattered hand which still flowed with blood.

'Medicine will not save you,' Masud said. 'It will be too late before the doctors reach here.'

Major Deacon and the lieutenant had field dressings in their rucksacks. One or other of them would be able to bind the Hakli's wound and halt the bleeding, save his life. But Masud knew of another way, the way with which the young man would be familiar, the traditional method of dealing with such injuries. Clearly the Hakli was bemused by loss of blood, and had not been too bright-minded in the first place. It suited Masud's purpose well. He settled by the rebel's side, holding the arm up so that the blood fell with a patter on to the floor.

'Why,' said Masud, 'have you not fired this wound?'

'Fired? I have no fire.'

'If you had a fire, a clean flame . . .'

Rashid swallowed. His Adam's apple bobbed in his scrawny gullet. If this event had happened to him while he was deep in the Great Desert, protecting caravans against thieves and raiders, then he would have thought at once of burning. His companions would have bound him and held him down, would have found a plug of hashish for him to chew upon, and they would have scorched the stump with a brand, sealed the bleeding orifices and cleansed the flesh with the flame. It had not occurred to him to do this; he had been thinking of other things. Besides, it was known that it took a man of mighty strength to plunge his limb into fire by himself. The stranger, the elegant bearded Arab was right, however. The wound had to be fired.

'Do it,' said Rashid.

'I have no inclination to waste time upon you.'

Rashid grabbed a handful of the loose linen suit and begged. 'Make a fire. Do it, I beg of you, in the name of Allah the Merciful, the Creator of Mercy and All Favours.'

Blood droplets continued to plop to the floor. Rashid stared at them, mesmerised by this soft ebbing of his life. He could not make a fight of it for weakness had stolen over him, a loss of all will. On the flat hearth stone there were embers with a faint glow in the coals. In the corner, however, there were straw ties and a few chips of wood, not palm but *ghadha*, from the goosefoot bush which grew here and there in sandy pockets at the head of the Wadi Yafayn and was hauled uphill by women who were fastidious housekeepers and did not like smoke clouding their homes. It had clean white bark and burned hot and well. By the smell of it, there were also some twigs of tamarisk, which would be acceptable.

Glancing round, Masud followed the line of the young man's gaze. The dwelling was identical to the others in the village, a single apartment. There were no chickens, though, and no implements of cultivation, only a cradle of carded wool and a two-spoke spindle on a frame for spinning.

'A fire,' said Rashid. 'I ask you for a fire.'

'Can you walk, man of the Hakli?'

'I . . . I . . . cannot.'

'Crawl?'

'Where would I wish to crawl to?'

'You would not make much distance,' said Masud al Hasan, with a note of sorrow. 'Can you talk?'

'I am talking.'

'Can you hear my words?'

'Yes.'

'I will talk, and you will talk, and if we are quick there will be time to stop the blood flowing and to save you for your punishment.'

'Punishment?'

'What that will be,' said Masud, 'is not my concern. The Sultan and the British officers will decide what is to be done with the likes of you.'

'Will I be shot?'

'No.'

'Beheaded?'

'Time will kill you sooner than the axe.'

'Axe?' muttered Rashid, drowsily.

When the stranger left him for a moment, Rashid's arm remained suspended in the air. He could feel it floating away from him and wondered if it had emptied, as the neck of a goatskin water-bag will empty.

Listlessly, without panic, Rashid watched the stranger stir the embers on the hearth stone with his knife and set twigs upon them and, stooping, blow. The sound was like that of the breeze sighing in the cavern at Dirbat, like a girl's laughter behind her veil. Like most Arabs, Rashid of the Hakli had little sense of time, yet an instinct for survival told him that he had, at most, fifteen minutes before his body dried out and he slipped into darkness and a long sleep. His eyelids sagged. He saw a muted sun before each eyeball, round and golden.

Flames danced through the dried kindling. The scent of tamarisk filled Rashid's nostrils and brought remembrances of nights on the trail with the Imam's caravans of arms; of the taste of moist Turkish tobacco and American coffee, of the voices of women in the cool date groves round village wells, the sweet-sharp tang of a lime bitten by the teeth.

The stranger shook him roughly.

'I will speak. You will speak, Hakli.'

Rashid nodded.

'How many soldiers were here, last night?'

'Thirty.'

'Paid rifles?'

Rashid nodded.

Masud shook him again. 'When did they go away?'

'Evening, after sunset.'

'On whose instruction?'

'Nasir Salim Azzi . . . came . . . horseback . . .'

'When did Nasir Salim Azzi leave?'

Rashid's skull bobbed like a heavy flower on a dried stalk.

'When, Rashid?'

'The village people . . . go . . . hide . . . Nasir . . . goes. We . . . we stay at guard posts on the wall.'

'How many?'

'Eight. Ghanim is dead.'

'Do you know of papers, in a chest or in a box?'

Rashid sighed and closed his eyes as if he was bored by it all. He had stopped feeling pain at all now. The throbbing in the nerve endings of his hand had reduced to a slow pulse. His lap was wet with spilled blood, his blood.

'*Rashid. Rashid.*'

'In . . . taken . . . in . . . cave.'

'Where?'

'Here.'

'*Where?*'

'No deer. I see no deer.'

Masud's lips curled with impatience and his fingers balled into fists by his thighs. He was kneeling forward, seated on his calves and heels like a devout Muslim at the hour of prayer. Had he arrived too late, tarried too long? Had the rebel slipped from him?

'What is this talk of deer, Rashid?'

'Ghanim say . . . Deer . . . Rock of the Young Deer. Above.'

Masud's voice was quiet but insistent. 'It is a marked place?'

'Cave. One cave . . . one only. Ghanim . . . say.'

Masud inched closer. Behind him the chips of white wood had caught alight and blazed. He could feel the heat on his back and buttocks and flickering light shadowed the apartment and etched the pain deeply on the rebel's features. Masud felt a pang of sympathy. In an impoverished country the bearing of arms for gain was not an enterprise to be despised. Did he not do the same, after a fashion, in the name of the established ruler?

'Do you still listen?' Masud asked.

Rashid mumbled, his Qara accent too thick to be comprehensible, the words slurred. Masud shook him vigorously.

'Rashid, see, the fire burns.'

'Do it then. Do it, please.'

'Soon, very soon,' Masud promised. 'Who paid you to bear arms for the Imam's cause?'

'A man, an Egyptian . . . has the skin of an Egyptian.'

'What is this Egyptian's name?'

'Nasir . . .'

'Nasir Salim Azzi?'

Rashid nodded.

Masud said, 'Where did he take you to give you your guns?'

'Fortress.'

'Where is the fortress?'

'Ashfra . . . Ashfra.'

Rashid's eyes were closed now, but whether from fear or pain or that drowsiness which precedes death, Masud could not be sure. He realised, however, that he had very little time remaining, no more, in fact, than Rashid, the Hakli warrior. To his surprise, Masud found that he did not want the rebel to die. In spire of the quality of his hatred, and the lurking sense of humiliation in his breast, he knew Rashid was just a simple soldier, a grain of the desert sand.

With urgency, Masud said, 'The fortress at Ashfra has been abandoned these many years, Rashid. Do you lie to me?'

Rashid said, 'I do not lie. It is our place, where the rifles are kept and our fighters are assembled.'

'Under the leadership of Nasir Salim Azzi?'

'Others . . . others . . .'

'Is there an American? Have you seen an American there?'

'Yes.'

After all it had not proved too difficult. All that had been required had been a dying soldier too stupid to know what he was giving up. It had almost been worth the hours of terror on the rock. Masud had heard of the dilapidated fort at Ashfra, eighty miles to the north. He had a vision of it in his mind, though he had never clapped eyes on it personally. It was in the territory of several small quarrelsome sheikhs, nomadic and irresolute, and lay close enough to the scythe-edged dunes of the Empty Quarter to be safe from patrols and air reconnaissance.

The young rebel murmured, 'Lorries . . . for us . . . Wadi Yafayn. To . . . to . . . take us . . . back.'

Across the gravel desert by the old camel track to the well at Ifram and then north, by some uncharted route among the rebel tribes, to Ashfra: Masud grunted. If Nasir had left Khahouris at dusk, or shortly after, he would be in Ashfra in ten or twelve hours, though the route from the well at Ifram was across a dry and barren tongue of the Great Emptiness. There was so much more that Masud wanted confirmed but he doubted if the soldier would have answers – or be fit to give them.

Rashid's lids flickered. Masud stared into the moist, sad, dark pupils. If he stopped the bleeding, cauterised the wound, then Rasid of the Hakli might survive long enough to be treated by the incoming British troops. There were helicopters, at least one, and Captain Pemberton would be sure to arrive here, perhaps with Pig Bressol, and they would take the wounded rebel away. A transfusion would be necessary, but first . . .

Masud lifted Rashid's head with his fingertips and held it, chin raised and slightly turned. With the blade of his right hand Masud chopped neatly down upon the muscles which protected the base of the man's brain. Rashid slumped immediately. Masud al Hasan sucked in a deep breath and dragged the rebel towards the fire. He stretched him out with his head towards the hearth, drew out the left arm and, seated astride Rashid's back, extended the bloody stump of the hand into the high white flames.

Rashid twitched but remainded insensible while the stink of burning flesh filled the house and wafted out into the daylight, along with a wisp of greasy smoke.

Dingo sniffed the clear morning air. He said, 'By the smell of it the crafty little wog's found himself some breakfast.'

'I hope there's enough for all of us,' said Deacon.

'Yep. I'm ruddy starved.'

Burdened with packs, weapons at the ready, the SAS officers advanced into the village. Deacon had made a point of checking the dead men to ensure that none was alive and in pain. Meanwhile Dingo had scanned the tiers of houses and terraces of trees in search of the missing Masud.

'There he is,' Dingo pointed. 'What the hell's he lugging on his back.'

'It isn't a side of bacon,' said Deacon.

'A prisoner?'

'Probably the missing rifleman.'

Cautiously the officers moved past the well towards the steps. Above them Masud al Hasan was picking his way down. He seemed to have lost his fear of heights and the body slung casually across his shoulder appeared weightless. Within minutes he had reached the major. He did not deposit the rebel at Deacon's feet, like a dog might a bone. He continued to hold the young man firmly. The rebel's left hand was blackened, hardly more than a stump, his forearm scorched. Dingo glanced at the Deke, an angry but unspoken question in his eyes. Masud's expression gave nothing away. Torturers were notoriously implacable.

Deacon said, 'I see that you've recovered your equilibrium, Masud.'

'This man is of the Hakli.' Masud ignored the jibe. 'He is a hireling, who fights for Nasir Salim Azzi.'

'Been a busy little bugger, haven't you?' said Dingo. 'Is he alive or dead?'

'Alive. I saved him.'

'Don't look like it to me,' said Dingo. 'Who stuck his mitt in the fire?'

'He had a gushing wound. The fire cleansed it.'

'Oh, sure!' said Dingo. 'Pull the other bloody one.'

'Wait, Dingo,' said Deacon. 'Masud, put the boy down, please.'

Obediently Masud lowered the rebel to the ground. Deacon went down on his knees and examined the young man. 'Cauterisation. Crude but effective. He's very sick, though. Much blood lost, by the look of it.'

'He would have died,' said Masud.

Deacon dragged a pack to him, opened its straps and rummaged inside. He found the field-kit and opened it. Maurice Harper noticed how dexterously the Deke worked, with the assurance and authority of a trained medic. As he dusted the wound with powder and dressed it with gauze and bandages, Deacon rapped out questions.

'Masud, how do you know that this boy fights for Nasir?'

'With his own lips he told me.'

'I see,' said Deacon. 'What else did he tell you?'

'The documents we seek are hidden in a cave only a short distance away.'

'What of Nasir and the American?'

'Nasir was here, in Khahouris, last evening. He rode out again.'

'How?' put in Dingo. 'Magic carpet?'

'Dingo, put a sock in it,' said Deacon.

Masud said, 'On horseback.'

'Jesus!' said Dingo. 'Horses, now!'

'There is a truck awaiting the soldiers, to take them to the meeting place where the guns are stored,' Masud went on.

'The arsenal,' said Deacon. 'Do you mean to say that this chap told you where Nasir's arsenal can be found?'

'It is at Ashfra, in a ruined fortress.'

'How far is Ashfra?'

'Eighty miles.'

'North?'

'Towards the Great Emptiness.'

Deacon bit off a tab of sticking plaster from a roll and strapped the bandage tightly. So far, the young rebel had remained unconscious. He was pale, sweating lightly, but had a regular pulse. Like most desert-born Arabs, the mercenary was vulnerable more to disease than injury. Gently, Deacon smoothed the dressing and laid the arm flat by the boy's side.

'Did you hit him hard, Masud?'

'He will not die of the blow, Major.'

Dingo Harper had quit protesting. He had not relaxed his vigilance and had continued to scan the terraces while Deacon doctored the rebel.

'If you take the kid's word for it, boss,' he said, 'then we've done our bit.'

'Tired, Dingo, are you?'

'No, just hungry.'

'Masud,' Deacon said, 'can you find the cave where the papers are hidden?'

'I can do it, Major.'

'And, in the light of what you've learned, do you think the cave will be guarded?'

'It will not be defended, Major. The people of Khahouris have travelled on to the plateau to hide with their flocks.'

Deacon got to his feet. He stretched his back, flexing then bending. His knee joints cracked audibly in the stillness. He checked his wrist-watch.

'It's six thirty-five now. I don't anticipate that we'll see anyone from "A" or "K" in this area until nine or nine-thirty. If, that is, the operation has been successful.'

'So?' said Dingo.

'I want to be on the move by seven-fifteen at the latest.'

'On the move? The move to where?' Dingo asked.

'Ashfra, of course.'

'Ashfra? It's eighty bloody miles. Some walk.'

'Walk?' said Deacon. 'Who said anything about walking?'

'I don't get you.'

'I'll explain,' said Major Deacon.

'It better be good,' said Dingo.

'Oh, it is,' said Deacon.

Four military prototypes of the Fairey Ultra-light helicopter had been built under contract and one had been demonstrated at the Farnborough Air Show in 1955. Bill Bressol had been at the show and had been awfully impressed by the tiny utility flying-machine and very disappointed when HM Government withdrew support for production a year or so later. Bressol had grafted through Woolwich College and had spent years with REME before being seconded to Military Intelligence and posted, under duress, to the Middle East.

Never the type to deny himself pleasure, Bressol had soothed his irritation at the posting by using his new-found authority to trace one of the little Fairey Ultras. He had eventually located one, a civil model, which was in service as an inspection vehicle with the Royal Canadian Mounted Police. These gentlemen, Bressol supposed, were more used to gee-gees than sophisticated machinery and had recently put the aircraft into store; in fact it had proved too susceptible to the roaring winds of the Rockies. The Mounties were happy enough to sell the Ultra to the Felix Oil Company and shipped it in three stout crates via the Royal Canadian Air Force base at Joppa to an RAF station in Bahrain where it was assembled by amused British mechanics. From Bahrain it was flown, in four hops, to Zambat with Hector McKellar, oil company employee, at the controls.

In Old Bill's opinion the Fairey Ultra was a beautiful unit. Fifteen feet in length, it had a cruising speed of ninety mph and a hover ceiling that could hold it over the Jebel's highest summit. Its payload, though, was limited to pilot and passenger. Its range was under 200 miles, though Hector could nurse it along on seemingly empty tanks for another thirty miles or so if the occasion demanded. Hector had also personally modified the door and observer's seat so that Bill Bressol could survey the passing scene in comfort and not back-to-damned-front like an army skivvy.

Hector McKellar was a withered, lugubrious-looking Scotsman who had been invalided out of the RAF with a bad case of peptic ulcers at the age of forty-three. Seven years later he was still flying round the hell-holes of the Middle and Far East, wherever he could pick up a charter or contract, and seemed to thrive on a diet of whisky, cream crackers and antacid tablets. Hector was at the controls that morning, 27 January, when the Fairey Ultra fluttered over the foothills above the Wadi Yafayn with the risen sun glossing its plexiglass and its rotor blades whirring silver like a dragonfly's wings. Old Bill, togged in full combat rig, was strapped into his padded armchair with a chart and compass on his knees, items which McKellar scorned.

'We're looking for Khahouris, the village,' Old Bill shouted.

'Aye, I know what we're lookin' for,' Hector McKellar snapped.

'It should be somewhere just over the ridge.'

'Hey, who's flyin' this crate; you'r me?'

'You are, old chappie, you are, of course.'

'Right, then.'

'Watch out for snipers.'

'Christ!'

'Sorry, old chappie. Sorry.'

Hector McKeller had already homed in on the wall and its flanking buttresses. He had been here before, piloting for Bressol's photographer, a kid from the RAF squadron at Aden who chattered like a fuckin' idiot all the time, as if he was taking snapshots for *The Scots Magazine*.

'I say, what's that?' Bressol jerked forward against the straps.

'Smoke,' said Hector.

'It's a signal.'

'Aye, I know it's a signal.'

'Move in, move in.'

But Hector McKellar wasn't as green as his boss. He lifted the Ulta and veered south-east, sweeping quickly away from the spiral of brown smoke which ascended from the dead centre of the mountain village. He had seen lures before. He doubted if the Omani rebels were that cunning, but you couldn't be too careful. He heard there were Gyppos and Yanks involved in this uprising, stirring the broth; they would know how to tempt a wee heligyro down so it could be shot at with .303s.

'Go in, go in. Closer. Closer, old chappie.'

Not on your nelly, Hector thought. He lowered the little craft behind a lump of wilderness, a raking ridge which ran for three rugged miles to the head of the Khahouris ravine. Snipers and rebel piquets tended to dig themselves into caves and could not be readily spotted from above. There were usually a few shepherds around. They could be spotted with ease against the patched scrub or on the stony paths that latticed the upland. Nothing doing today, though. Bressol was right; the long slender feather of smoke was a signal, not a lure. Hector hoisted the Ultra high over the village, swung the craft round the smoke in a clockwise direction while Old Bill leaned out and tried to make sense of what he saw.

'Bodies,' Hector shouted.

'Quite! Quite! I see them.'

'Your lot?'

'I don't think so. Actually, no. No, not mine.'

'Rope.'

A single rope still draped the face, like a pencil stroke against the pale rock. Bressol had not noticed it. He fastened on it now, as the Ultra wheeled and settled lower. But there was nothing to be made of that single strand, relic of the SAS climbers' presence on the mountain. What puzzled Bressol was that neither of the officers had made an appearance. By now they must have noticed the Ultra; yet there was no signal, apart from the smoke column, that the three-man team had taken Khahouris and that it was safe to land.

'Down?' asked Hector McKellar.

'By all means, yes. Yes, down.'

The rotor blades chopped up the smoke as the helicopter dropped. It had an acrid stink, tasted of vinegary palm-wood. Through it, as it dispersed, Bressol could make out the body of a man lying on an arrangement of boxes by the well's stone steps in the centre of the 'village square'. It was into the 'village square' that McKellar dumped the Ultra. The French turbo, slung under the boom behind the cockpit's shell, fanned up a storm of grit and chased wavelets across the still, dark surface of the pond.

The man lying on the boxes raised one arm, feebly. Greeting or threat? Bressol could not be certain. When the skids bumped to the ground and the machine settled, Bressol's first action was to haul out his trusty Webley .45 service revolver, a heavy piece, and thumb it to full cock. Unstrapped, he lowered himself to the dirt, stooped low under the beat of the blades. McKellar had a gun too, an old Luger, which was stuffed into the bosom of his scuffed leather jacket.

Old Bill Bressol may have been pompous but he wasn't stupid. He approached the young Arab with caution. There were two boxes, metal, like pre-war cash-boxes; each would have held a pair of size nine shoes. They had been padlocked but the locks had been jemmied off and hung like cheap ornaments from the latches. A mattress of straw had been slung between the boxes and it was on this bed that the Arab sprawled. His left hand and arm were bandaged. He was clearly in a bad way, though conscious. To the left of this grisly tableau was a wooden cross, roughly whipped up out of kindling. It was three or four feet high, with a small cairn of stones at its base. Exactly like a grave, only in miniature. The fire had been set and lit on the far side of the pond, a typical smoke-pile strewn with bits of cloth and lumps of thatch torn from a house roof. He pointed the Webley at the Arab's chest as he advanced. In spite of the cold, flies buzzed around the young rebel's head. He looked very near to death.

Bressol tried a question in plain English but got no response.

He formulated a simple sentence in basic Arabic. 'Did the English soldiers put you in this place?'

The rebel nodded his head and managed a slight smile.

'Dok . . . dok . . . tar. Doktar?'

'No. No, I'm not a doctor,' said Bressol, uncaring, in English.

McKellar leaned from the cockpit of the Ultra.

'Where are they, then?'

Bressol turned on the pilot. 'How the devil should I know?'

'Look in the letter box.'

'What?'

'Somebody dead?'

On this advice, Bressol gave his attention to the mock grave, while Hector McKellar kept the helicopter's engine ticking and his eyes peeled for ambush.

The message was under the little cairn of stones at the base of the cross. It was printed in a neat hand in soft pencil on the back of a sheet extracted from Harper's sketch pad. Revolver in one hand, the letter in the other, Bressol read it, his lips moving. The message was concise.

0718/27th. This to Major Wm. Bressol. Urgent. All well and moving on. Targets at fort at Ashfra. Send support. No assualt before dawn 28th. Repeat. Hold off attack. Targets may be in residence. Documentary evidence in boxes herewith. Take to Major Bressol. Important. Please ensure prisoner receives immediate medical attention. Repeat immediate. Deacon (Major).

Bressol checked his wristlet watch. 0956. Deacon's team had been gone for two and a half hours. But what did *moving on* mean? Where was this fort – Ashfra – and how in God's name did Deacon intend to reach it? What was he using for transport? Three captured donkeys? Everything else in the letter was explicit.

Bressol nodded his satisfaction. The targets were at Ashfra. It was immaterial how Deacon had discovered this vital fact. Ashfra, too, was a fort. One of the half-buried, forgotten stone heaps out towards the Rub-al-Khali. Eighty to a hundred miles away, probably. If, as the letter suggested, Deacon was in pursuit of the targets, then it would be prudent not to scare them away. To hold off the attack. A detailed map would show the best disposition for an assault force. It would be necessary to pull thirty men off the Jebel, of course, or to use units from the Sultan's forces. Bressol sniffed and wiggled his moustache. Perhaps an air strike on this fort would be the best medicine. Purging the arsenal. He could have done with three minutes' conversation with Jeffrey Alexander Deacon. But the Deke had gone, of that there was no doubt.

Stepping back, Bressol lifted the lid of one of the metal boxes with the barrel of his revolver. The box was crammed with letters and documents. The silliness of the Imam and his supporters in hoarding such incriminating evidence never ceased to astonish Old Bill. But sheikhs and chieftains didn't trust each other; hard facts in deals and contracts had to be committed to paper, to seal them for the future. With any luck at all there would be written evidence of the American's intervention in the rebellion.

Clear sunlight bathed the village now. By this afternoon, this evening at the latest, the columns of the SAS would reach Khahouris. The night attack on the peaks above Wadi Kamah had been completely successful; Bressol had skipped in to check on the 'official' operation before taking off for Khahouris. The tribesmen were surrendering in droves and the march across the plateau to Sharaijah was under way. Venoms had made a supply-drop, and 'victory' was secure, as far as it went. The regiment had added another short chapter to its history. But the activities of the victors did not touch Khahouris yet, nor Major William Bressol. His business was to set up a victory of another sort. To do it he needed not only the evidence that the boxes might contain but the instigators, particularly the American agent, George Seback.

The wounded tribesman groaned.

From the Ultra, McKellar shouted, 'What about him?'

Bressol hesitated. He did not have to examine the prisoner

to realise that the man's life depended upon speedy medical attention. The Fairey Ultra could whisk him back to the field hospital at Nizwa in less than an hour, though it was in the lap of the gods if the injured man would last out the trip. On the other hand it was essential that he, Bressol, get back to Zambat as soon as possible to set up, with Gore's assistance, the next phase of the mission. Besides, he was very keen indeed to dip into the boxes, to see how damning the letters might be. There was no possibility of the Ultra bearing three men plus the boxes. Bressol hesitated. McKellar could ferry the prisoner to Nizwa, refuel and be back here in a couple of hours at the outside.

As if reading the major's mind, Hector McKellar said, 'He's got no belly wound, has he?'

'No. No, I don't think so,' Bressol replied, shouting above the clack of the motor.

'Stick him in the seat. I'll come back for you.'

'I—'

'Christ!' McKellar snarled.

'Yes. Yes, you're right, old chappie.'

So Rashid, mercenary and fighter, was hoisted over the shoulder of a portly English officer and, biting his lips against the pain, put into the tiny aircraft. He closed his eyes as the straps were cinched about him and a sling draped about his neck to keep the stump of his arm comfortably immobilised.

'Right?'

'Off you go, McKellar. Don't dilly-dally, please.'

'Ach!' Hector McKellar squinted up at the terraces. 'It's as quite as the grave. You'll be fine here 'til I get back.'

The helicopter throbbed, skids lifted vertically from the ground, turbo engine roaring and rotor blade slashing the air. Bressol stepped back and clamped a hand to his combat beret, then shuffled anxiously forward again, waving.

Hand to mouth, he shouted, '*McKellar, tell HQ about Deacon. Deacon at the fort at Ashfra. Ashfra, old chappie, do you hear*?'

But if Hector McKellar picked up the last-minute message

over the din of the Ultra, he gave no acknowledgement.

Bressol watched the Fairey Ultra skim over the buttress to the north and swing wide, changing direction. It came back close to the village, whirling low over the lip of the terraces and on to cross the Khahouris ravine.

Bressol was still watching when the tiny aircraft bucked in mid-air, tilted snout down and crashed into the rocks. In sundry smoking parts, the remains plummeted into the chasm, taking with them one dyspeptic Scotsman and a poor Hakli rebel who, in the end, never even knew what hit him.

Sheikh Julanda's beard was stained with the dribblings of the dried apricots to which he was addicted and which he chewed as other men chew green-leafed *qat*. He held a great swollen cheekful of the golden mush and smiled round it as his sons, men in their forties, patted his shoulder and muttered approval of his prowess with the new Remington Magnum sporting rifle.

It was the first time that Julanda had fired the powerful weapon in earnest, though he had taken it out on to the plateau and shot at quail and wicker targets and had even succeeded in killing a lame old ewe at a hundred yards. But that was as nothing compared to the single shot which brought down the soldiers' aeroplane.

It had been his sons' idea to fire upon the helicopter. Julanda had silently disapproved, not wishing to draw attention to their position on the cornfield's edge. The corn had not thrived along that high and exposed strip for a decade but it was nonetheless 'the cornfield' and gave the best vantage point over the village. From there, Sheikh Julanda and his three sons had watched the capture of their village and all the things that had happened thereafter. They were confused by the behaviour of the English soldiers and, though they did not believe in sorcery as such, had a superstitious dread of returning to that tethered corpse by the cross. The fire and its wand of smoke seemed symbolic to the cowardly old provincial and he had restrained his sons, and their henchmen, from descending the paths to the well. Wild horses would not have dragged Sheikh Julanda from the safety of the open country that spread across the summits.

For all that, the old man had an astute perception that he had lost face. The boxes of letters which he had been instructed to keep safe had been found in the cave and brought out by two of the English soldiers. Julanda's sons had urged him to recapture the boxes but the old man appeared to have lost interest in them, though inwardly he was smitten with shame. None of this would have happened if it had not been for Nasir Salim Azzi who spoke with the authority of Ghalib bin Ali and Suleiman bin Himyar, Imam and Overlord, men who could not be ignored. But the men of Julanda's tribe were not warriors and soon there would be lambing and kidding and earth to be broken and spring seed to be sown.

When the first of the soldiers had gone and nothing remained but the smoke pile and the cross and the corpse, Julanda had moved closer to the cornfield's edge and had looked down upon the centre of his domain with doubt and apprehension. For two hours he had sat upon a rock and stared, while his sons grumbled behind him and their henchmen stirred restlessly. Then the aeroplane had appeared, winging close, and they had lain flat upon the earth among the rocks, even Julanda, until the aeroplane had settled. Then they had watched again.

Whatever level of comprehension had been touched in the Sheikh of the people of Khahouris, it was insufficient to rouse him to retaliation. It was his eldest son, Amair, who fetched the Remington rifle from the lots by the women three miles away and who desired to fire it. But the American rifle was not his to use. It had been given into Julanda's hand by Nasir Salim Azzi, in the name of the Imam, and it was for Julanda to strike the blow, or not, as he might, in his wisdom, choose.

Amair was jabbering, poking his father rudely in the back, when the aeroplane took off. The hawk-sized flying-machine was so utterly unlike the big aeroplanes that zoomed over the plateau and scared the animals that Julanda was moved to retaliatory optimism, to a belief that the Remington would perform a kind of magic. He had taken some minutes to settle himself on the earth, seated, legs out, spine supported by a rock, before he signalled to Amair to put the Remington into his hands. He had still been fiddling with the adjustable sight when the aeroplane had risen and swooped away to the north. Amair and his second son had howled. And Julanda had gone on fiddling, ready to blame the recalcitrance of the rifle for a lost opportunity. But then the aeroplane tilted and swooped back across the summit of the great buttress and everybody around dived for protection – except Sheikh Julanda who found that he had raised the rifle and was tracing the flight of the tiny aeroplane with it, though the image was blurred in his old, tired eyes.

He plucked the trigger cleanly enough, however.

And struck something vital.

Open-mouthed, Julanda and his sons and their henchmen watched the aeroplane crash into the far wall of the ravine. And the old Sheikh, dribbling apricot juice, smirked as if he had meant it and the lucky shot had been pre-ordained. But when his sons suggested charging down into the village, Sheikh Julanda drew the line.

Within minutes of the destruction of the Fairey Ultra, the headman of Khahouris and his tail of dependants were hustling away from the cliff edge to hide themselves with other innocents in the rolling acres of scrubland from which the SAS patrols, in due course, would flush them out in amicable surrender.

If only Major Bill Bressol had known what old Sheikh Julanda was up to, it would have made that long, tense day much easier to endure.

Major Bressol did nothing to protect himself for fully a minute after the fragments of the beautiful little helicopter clattered into the ravine. He gaped. He wasn't, at that moment, thinking of poor Hector McKellar, whose string had at last run out, and certainly not of the unknown prisoner. He was stunned by the realisation that he was alone in enemy territory and that it would be hours before the SAS reached this far to the north along the Jebel Akhdar, particularly as their primary target was Sharaijah, many miles away. He, with Gore's aid, had rather marked Khahouris as private property. Now he would suffer for it.

Bressol swung slowly to face the amphitheatre of limestone terraces. He had no idea from which direction the shot had been aimed. The whole hillside might be bristling with unredeemed, unrepentant rebels, mad factions of the Imam's army. Old Bill's hand began to sweat on the butt of his revolver and he held the gun up, nobly, ready to fire. Naturally, nothing happened. After three or four minutes of exposure, Bressol's common sense returned and he ran to seek shelter in the nearest house.

Crouched inside, by the window, Bressol watched the wind shake smoke out of the fire and flap the mat that the prisoner had been lying upon.

After a quarter of an hour, Bressol became bored with caution. Tempted by the sight of the two metal boxes, the major crawled out of hiding and, with much scanning and squinting, crabbed across the open square and retrieved the boxes, carrying them one by one back into the safety of the house. He made a third run, armed with a large earthenware pitcher, which he filled from the well.

For another hour or so, the portly major kept watch by the apertures in the dwelling at the base of the village. He spied from the windows and from a hole picked in the thatch and, latterly, from the roof itself. But the lofty panorama of stone showed no signs of life. Bressol began to wonder if there had been a shot at all, if McKellar had not simply misjudged altitude and had, at last, got too cocky in handling the lightweight aircraft. Bressol strove to recall if he had actually, positively, heard a shot. He could no longer be sure. He supped water from the pitcher, ate a handful of cold meal mush from a pot by the hearth, and smoked his pipe.

About noon he sneaked out of hiding and made his way

stealthily to the corner of the wall where a brushy plant overhung it and gave him a screen. From there he looked down into the ravine. There were corpses on the slab and black birds, like carrion crows, at them. And the frail vertical line of a climbing rope. There was no trace of the Ultra or of McKellar, except for a dash of greasy oil on the adjacent wall and two deep scars, like slashes made with a whitewash brush. The ravine was too deep, too narrow, to allow him to see the bottom.

By now Old Bill was convinced that there had been no rifle shot, that the Ultra had simply crashed. Even so, he was a model of caution and did not expose himself to full view as he returned to the dwelling house. He drank more water, smoked another pipeful of St Bruno Flake, and, for a few brief moments, toyed with the idea of slogging across the open plateau to meet the SAS patrols. Quickly he discarded this option. The plateau would be crawling with tribesmen and they would not all be ready to surrender. He might vanish there, vanish without trace, and he had no fondness for the thought of being buried under stones in an alien country.

At length he decided that he must wait it out, trusting to the thoroughness of Deane-Drummond's boys to reach the spur of the Khahouris before nightfall. He must hide, and wait. And if the SAS did not reach Khahouris until tomorrow, what of Deacon? Deacon would be at Ashfra. How he would get there and what he would do when he arrived, Bressol hadn't a clue. If things went wrong, however, it would be put down to ill luck, not incompetence on his part. After all, he had the boxes which in themselves might be enough to satisfy his masters in far off Whitehall.

Yes, Major Bressol decided, Deacon must look after himself.

4 The swords of Islam

Dingo Harper

Sounds simple when you say it quick. But the Deke's plan for getting the three of us to Ashfra wasn't for Boy Scouts or the faint of heart. It was, however, just the sort of number in which I'd been trained, by no less a person than Major Deacon himself, so I didn't baulk at it. Anyhow, it was a bold idea, bold as bloody brass, and would catch the rebels napping.

We shed all the climbing gear, except one length of rope, and repacked the rucksacks, toting weapons and ammo, food and water and warm clothing. We had 'hockey boots' with us but kept on the kletts which were comfortable enough and quiet on the rocks. Masud seemed to have a fair notion where we were, in relation to other parts of Oman, and gave Deacon's maps only a cursory glance.

It was the Arab who led off, keeping clear of the vertical cliffs on our left. I was feeling pretty chipper, in spite of the hard night. We'd had breakfast and drunk tea, and had got through the preparations for departure in short order. It was Masud who found the cave, Masud and I who brought the metal boxes back to the village. They were really very light and portable and the cave was only three hundred yards away, though well hidden. By that time the Deke had built and lit his fire and acrid smoke was purling nicely heavenward. He had given the rebel prisoner a shot of dope from the medical kit and the poor bloke was out cold again. Away to the south-west we could hear the growl of guns, heavy stuff, and glimpsed a couple of Venoms, like black paper darts streaking across the sky, though they were a long way off. Deacon didn't bother to look into the letter chests. Intelligence of that sort wasn't our business. Our business was trailing and nailing Nasir Salim Azzi and our American, discovering for definite if Ashfra was the site of the rebels' secret arsenal. What was this startling plan of Major Deacon's? Well, he figured that Nasir wouldn't have left more than one lorry to transport the rearguard back to base, and that the lorry wouldn't be too far from the track that straggled down from Khahouris. The Deke was dead right.

We all thought it would be one of the ubiquitous Dodge pick-up trucks but it turned out to be a good old British Land Rover. Stolen goods, I expect. It was a long wheelbase, soft top and was fitted with long-range fuel and water tanks. What's more, Nasir wasn't wasting manpower. There was nobody with the Land Rover except one driver. He wasn't an Arab but a black African. He had made himself comfortable by the front of the vehicle, with a tiny fire and cooking pots and the like, and a coloured blanket. Obviously he hadn't been warned to expect trouble, though how come he hadn't heard our gunfire I don't know. Perhaps he was just lazy.

The Land Rover was tucked close to the foot of the little path where it came down off the hillside. It was easy going here, now that all the piquets had been withdrawn. There were rocks and a couple of bushy trees to give the Negro shade and to screen the Land Rover from air attack. We stopped and reconnoitred through the Deke's field-glasses.

Masud said. 'I will take him for you, Major Deacon,' and Deacon grunted, 'Very well.'

Masud I figured, was trying to make up to us for his poor show on the slabs. It was no skin off my nose who did the dirty on the black driver, though I don't know that I'd have killed him. I didn't hate the Omani rebels, not the way I'd learned to hate the Communists in Malaya. The game element never quite went out of it, at least not until later.

Masud al Hasan was gone like a shot. Deacon and I crouched on the path, watching. Our Arab was visible for a couple of minutes, jinking down the path. The Negro was fussing with his pots, bent over the fire, then he swivelled round, as if he'd heard a noise. The Deke and I pressed ourselves flat to the dirt. We kept our noses down for three or four minutes, then Deacon lifted his head for a recce. He tapped me on the shoulder. I looked too.

The black driver was dead. Masud was waving us on

'Jesus!' I said. 'Where did he learn to do that?'

'We taught him,' said Deacon.

'Who? The SAS?'

'Lord, no. MI5 or MI6 or somebody of that ilk,' said Deacon. 'He was hand-picked by Gore to be trained as a spy.'

'You're kidding me?' I said.

'It's true. I don't know the actual details. But I expect he was put through six months' intensive at one of those gaunt country houses we never hear about.'

'Being taught to kill?'

'Among other useful skills.'

'Pity they didn't teach him how to climb.'

'I don't think it's on the curriculum.'

By the time we got to the bottom of the path, Masud had cleaned up the mess. There was a stain of blood on the sandy soil and you could see where he had dragged the corpse into the shade of the bushes. I guessed that Masud had come on the driver from behind the Land Rover and had cut his throat. Knife was cleaned and sheathed again, though, and there was nothing left for us to do except climb into the cabin of the Land Rover and head out for Ashfra.

Masud showed no flicker of pleasure when Deacon touched him on the shoulder and said, 'Well done.'

Deacon took the wheel and fired the engine, checked the gauges. The petrol tank was half full. I had already squinted under the big buggy and discovered that there were indeed a couple of extra tanks welded there. Not the best place for them, considering how it lowered the clearance height, but maybe this particular vehicle wasn't earmarked for rough country. Interestingly, the bonnet of the buggy was painted with two broad red stripes, dusty but discernible. The soft top was packed down and stowed in the rear. There was a metal drum with a tarpaulin over it which, when I prised off the lid, contained drinking water. To Deacon's disappointment, though, there were no steel tracks on board, only a couple of shovels. If we bogged down anywhere en route then Deacon's

North African experience wouldn't do us much good; it would be dig and be damned, at best.

The Deke wasted not one minute. As soon as I climbed into the passenger seat he revved the engine to a healthy roar and drove off, heading across a ribbon of scrubland towards the camel track at the head of the Wadi Yafayn.

'How far is this place, Ashfra?' I asked.

Masud answered me, 'It is between eighty and one hundred miles.'

'So we've enough juice?'

'Lots,' said Deacon. 'But we will undoubtedly need it. We daren't go through the oasis at Ifram. A detour will be essential.'

'All of this,' I waved my hand at the landscape, 'is hostile territory?'

Masud said, 'It is a place of small tribes. Some have no enmity towards outsiders. They are neither for nor against the Sultan, for nor against the Imam.'

'But the others?'

'Ah, they are ferocious in their loyalties. They will kill a stranger for his wristlet watches.'

'Shouldn't we dummy ourselves up to look like Arabs, boss?'

'Later, perhaps,' said Deacon.

But we never did get around to it. After twenty minutes or so rocked about in the seat and crooned to by the engine, I fell asleep.

When I wakened again, four and a half hours later, we were almost there.

When Masud al Hasan also fell into a doze, head resting lightly against Deacon's shoulder, the major did not waken him. He had no need of navigational advice. Besides, it might be the last opportunity that the men would have to catch a little shut-eye, uncomfortable though it was in the cramped and overheated cabin. Deacon did not feel drowsy, though he was sore and would have appreciated stretching out flat for an hour or so to relieve the stiffness in his back and limbs.

Folded square and clipped against the windscreen, the map was of very little help. Deacon ignored it. Masud had set him bearings and he drove by the compass which was slung on a thong around his neck. The area covered by the map, though by no means vast, had been inadequately surveyed. Not even the Sultan had exact charts of his kingdom. God knows, there was nothing to record on flat paper, though the infinite variety of the scene, a kaleidoscope of textures and colours, intrigued Deacon. He had a good sense of direction, of where he was going, and drove the sturdy Land Rover at a steady lick, without fear of the surfaces beneath its wheels.

There was no soft sucking sand yet to bog down the vehicle. The limestone bed supported hard red sand in contrast to the flanking dunes which were the colour of clover honey. Here and there were hollows dotted with bushes. They were out of the Wadi Yafayn, having crossed the gap at the wadi's head, at two or three hundred feet, up a well-trodden ramp of the same sandy red earth. Low dark hills danced in the rear-view mirror, the hazy heights of the Jebel Akhdar behind, distant now.

Masud had chosen the route to avoid the wells and the large oasis through which, he speculated, the 'trade route' to Ashfra would dog-leg. Running flat to distant dunes beyond the little arid wadi in which he now travelled, there was a plain of land which was no longer cultivated. It had touches of green to it and clumps of stunted growth, echoes of a more prosperous past. There was something sad in the sight of the wasted plain, a display of the results of centuries of violent bickering among communities, of wars between neighbours. Religious fanaticism and unadorned greed had eroded the peoples' priceless heritage, water and agriculture. Now there would be oil. But that commodity would not be left to the tribesmen, to the Imam or the Sultan or the brigand chieftains. Nor would it last for long. In the interim the swords of Islam would be whetted by avarice and selfishness, and unscrupulous governments would use idealism for gain.

The area was not deserted. Here and there were camel trains, a camp, a tiny melancholy grove of date palms with a hamlet embedded in it. But the dusty red-slashed Land Rover sped past and caused no flurry of worry or excitement. If there were rebels here, spies for Nasir or the Imam, they did not realise that the enemy was in their midst or that they had anything to fear from the familiar machine tabbed on to the wilderness by a tail of dust.

Deacon weaved the Land Rover between stunted shrubs, avoiding the obvious crumbled ditches through which water had once fed the plain. He aimed at the dunes, at the scalloped nether edge which, according to Masud, marked the overlook of the Zambat Sands. Ashfra lay outward, twenty or thirty miles to the south-west, if memory and calculations were accurate.

It was strange to realise that a helicopter from Nizwa could have covered this trip in one hour, a Venom in ten minutes, and that a camel caravan would plod on for almost three days. The locations were mathematically so close each to the other, yet so distant and remote in actuality. Slowing now and then, Deacon let the wheel of the Land Rover rest in his left hand and took the map from its clip and studied it. He was aware of a rough triangulation between Nizwa and Ibri, very rough, and the fact that somewhere to his left was the oil installation at Fahud. What he could not figure out was the location of Gore's prefabricated oil outpost, which had seemed much closer to the coast at Muscat; yet this area was called Zambat, and there were on the map little hints that the name existed here, in a wadi, in a hamlet, in the name of a hill. If the jigsaw did not fall into place soon, in Deacon's mind, then he might crash into the fort at Ashfra unaware. Distance, like time, was relative to all Arabs, and Masud, his training in England notwithstanding, was an Omani born and bred.

Gradually the plain dipped, below sea level Deacon reckoned, and hissing sand whisked off the dunes and changed the tune of the tyres. The dunes were low but on the flatland seemed huge. Out to the right, to the north-west, lay the camel route through the oasis at Ifram and the angle of the dog-leg. Nasir Salim Azzi would be on it, might be taking a bite of lunch, if that was his habit, in the shade of a date palm; might – more likely – be spurring his driver to reach Ashfra as soon as possible, to draw swords against the Sultan and his British henchmen. What would there be at Ashfra? A community of trained warriors or just another gaggle of inferior tribesmen bought and paid for by Nasir and the American agent? Deacon had no idea. He could not even visualise the outpost on the tongue of the mighty sands of the Empty Quarter.

Suddenly there was resistance beneath the wheels.

Deacon slowed. From far back in his memory he recognised the drag of fine sand. Not axle-deep yet, nor anything like it, but enough to retard the Land Rover's progress. He slowed again, the vehicle slightly tilted. Finally, prudently, Deacon braked to a halt.

Masud and Harper wakened at once.

Dingo made sounds like a bath emptying and, groggy, reached for the water bottle between his feet.

'Sit tight, Maurice,' Deacon said. 'Don't let anyone steal the Rover. Masud, come with me.'

Carrying the map, compass, field-glasses and a rifle, Deacon got out of the cab and, with Masud at his heels, headed up the slope of golden yellow sand towards the crest of the dunes. The sand, he noticed, was fine but impacted. He reckoned that the Land Rover might make it without recourse to spading the wheels every few yards. Four-wheel drive would be a boon on this terrain.

The day was hot now, nearing noon. Sweat started out on Deacon's body. His knees still ached and he had a nagging pulse of a headache behind his right eye. He struggled to the top of the sandhill and lowered himself to his stomach. Masud slithered up beside him.

'It is the sands of Zambat, Major,' the Arab murmered.

There was no reason, except habit, to keep voices low. There would be no piquets this far from the fort, if there were piquets at all. Deacon doubted if Nasir had enough men to post lookouts along the dunes in any case. One long, ribbon-like dune reached away on the left, like a fold of satin, smoothing out into flatness. The range of sandhills on which the major and the Arab lay was no more than an interruption on the plain, though it marked a change in the texture of the land. Beyond it there was no evidence of cultivation, of green growth, except for a thumbprint of khaki in the distance.

'Is that Ashfra?' asked Deacon.

Masud al Hasan hesitated to commit himself. 'I believe it to be Ashfra. If the bearings of the compass are correct, Major, it can be no other place but the fortress.'

Deacon said, 'How far is it, do you imagine?'

'It is not so far as it appears.'

'Six miles? Seven?'

'Seven, Major.'

Deacon used the field-glasses.

The magnified image gave him little information; there was damned little to be seen. A handful of flat-roofed houses huddled round the base of a square fort with a round tower above it. The tower was similar to the magnificent edifice which dominated Nizwa, though it was not nearly so large or so grand. No flag fluttered above it and there were no signs of occupation. The khaki daub was a planting of palm trees.

Disappointed, Deacon passed the glasses to Masud who studied the image for a considerable length of time, while Deacon rolled on to his back and stretched out, the beret over his eyes.

Masud said, 'I am sure it is at that place we will find the armaments.'

'We've come this far,' said Deacon, noncommittally, 'so I'm not going back without a proper reconnaissance.'

Masud too turned his back on the sands of Zambat and, with his arms around his knees, contemplated the scuffed leather of his boots. 'You cannot ride in on a donkey this time, Major.'

'Nope. And we daren't drive any further. Once the Land Rover comes into view then friend Nasir will be moved to investigate.'

'No man could hide a large vehicle,' said Masud. 'Not even you, Major Deacon.'

Deacon lifted himself up from the sand with his elbows and squinted from under his beret as Dingo toiled up the hill towards them, then, dropping, cautiously crawled the last few yards. Below the Australian, the Land Rover stood in isolation, all too obvious. Dingo shaded his eyes and scrutinised the horizon.

'Jesus! Is that it?'

'That – we think – is it.'

'Well, at least there's fair cover.'

Masud glanced at the Australian while the Deke swung himself round and surveyed the flatness. 'Yes, Dingo, I believe you're right.'

'Course I'm right, boss. You could work a cavalry platoon through that lot. Might look like a concrete car park but I'll bet you a quid it's littered with good cover.'

'Walkies?' said Deacon.

'Walkies, sir,' said Dingo Harper.

Dingo Harper

Come May or June I wouldn't have been so ruddy cavalier about taking a hike across the pancake. It was hot as it was, and this winter. Inland, about a couple of hundred miles from Muscat as the crow flies, the temperature in daylight didn't vary much and the seasons were less marked. I hardly knew Oman from a hole in the road but I had enough experience of sunburned wastes to make a feasible analogy. Even if we were out there for thirty hours or so, we wouldn't fry. Fact is, there was more danger of us freezing to death at night.

The Deke was a shrewd bloke. He reined the Arab and me in, made us light a Metabrick fire and brew up cans of tea, eat a couple of tins of lousy patrol rations, generally rest up.

It was about then that I asked him how long before the SAS back-up units moved in.

'Tomorrow morning.'

'Sure they'll come, boss?'

'I see no reason why not.'

'Supposing nobody finds your message.'

'Somebody will.'

'Maybe one of the villagers will use it for bumf.'

'Are you always so pessimistic, Dingo?'

'Could happen.'

'In that case . . .'

'In that case – what?' I said.

The Deke was smoking a cigarette. He held it like Noel Coward, very English elegant, a smile of reassuring sincerity on his chops.

'We are only going to scout, you know,' he said.

Masud said, 'What if our enemies are there, Major?'

'It's all rather moot,' said Deacon. 'The back-up units will arrive.'

'And if they don't?' I insisted.

'We'll just have to hold the fort on our own, won't we?'

'You're not bloody serious, boss?'

'Of course not,' said Deacon.

But I knew he was.

With this threat or promise weighing heavy on my head, I hooked into the pack and hoisted up my rifle. The whole bloody shebang felt like a couple of tons of lead. It was the water that really tipped the scales. But we had to budget for a couple of days. Even the Deke conceded that.

'All set, Dingo?'

'Anytime you like.'

I slithered down the sandpaper dune on my bum and scuttled across to a big boulder and used it as cover. I'd advanced fifteen yards. Nobody had seen me or shot at me. So far, so bloody good. Another twelve thousand, four hundred and forty yards and I'd be at the door of the fort at Ashfra, ready to ask them for a glass of water and the time of the next bus to Buraimi.

I moved on, Masud and the Deke behind me, picking up the same fragments of cover. Relentlessly I kept going across the plain. There would be plenty of time for rest once we had the fort under our noses and could set up a shift watch. The only concession I made was to Masud, keeping him in sight in case he conked on us again. But he seemed able to hold his place.

After a couple of hours of duck and scuttle, I laid up and let Deacon and the Arab join me. The fort was now about a mile ahead, much of its detail visible to the naked eye. But the reason I'd stopped was the quality of the cover. A long edge of stone fluted with drift-sand gave a crescent of shadow to tuck down into and a comfortable bed to lie on. Fact is, though, I'd have tried to work in further if it hadn't been for the activity along the parallel. Dust clouds trailed vehicles off to my right, and Deacon would want a look at them. He did his bit with the field-glasses.

'Land Rovers. With striped markings,' he said.

'Nasir Salim Azzi,' said Masud, itching for a shuftie through the lenses.

'Hasn't exactly hurried himself, has he?' I said.

'It is a longer travel,' said Masud.

'Three, is it?' I asked.

'Yes,' Deacon confirmed. 'God knows where they acquired three – four – long wheelbase British machines.'

'I'll bet you'll find the contracts in the boxes,' I said.

'Purchased by the Americans,' said Deacon. 'Perhaps. There's absolutely no embargo on the sale of Land Rovers, of course.'

You could hear the engines clearly. We lay and watched the three vehicles approach and enter the fort. In particular, Deacon kept an eye on the battlements – we'll call them that – and the tower. Two or three heads appeared up there, high above the sands. So they did have lookouts. Useful information. The Land Rovers entered the fort by a huge front gate. The bloody place had hardly an aperture on its façade, apart from tiny slots, more like pores than windows. With the lenses I could see how desolate Ashfra was and why it had been ignored by our air patrols. The square mud-brick houses were badly decayed, half crumbled, the walls eczemous, even the scanty line of palms looked as if it was diseased.

'Where does the water supply come from. Pipes?'

Masud answered, 'It will be a well, Major.'

The Arab explained that the fort was very ancient, one of a chain that had existed here centuries ago, when the local tribe – the Beni Shawekah – had been numerous and warlike and had maintained armies to dominate the other chieftains and to fight against the Sultanate and the ambitious tribal leaders who surged in from the south. Masud disgorged history like a litany, droning away while Deacon and I, in turn, kept rigorous watch on the fort.

Once the Land Rovers had been admitted through the wooden gate, however, nothing else happened. Heads were gone from the battlements. The houses at the skirt of the walls of the fort remained deserted. It was a fair guess that Nasir had all his boys inside, and had made damned sure nomads didn't camp on the doorstep to give the game away.

It wasn't all that close to sunset but you could feel the deepening of the afternoon, shadows enlarging on the sands. Sands was a misnomer. More ruddy gravel than anything. It would be noisy going across the stretch to the fort.

'All right,' the Deke said, 'so far we have no hard data to take back to HQ. Three Lands Rovers and some faces on the walls hardly constitute a rebellion in high gear. Now, I admit that if we go in to the fort we may have a problem getting out again. On the other hand, if we secure the targets, we might be able to hold them until a back-up units arrives.'

'This Yankee, we don't even know . . .'

'One thing at a time,' said Deacon.

'Sorry, boss.'

'We'll move out in a quarter of an hour. I'll take the guide-dog position this time and look for a hide close to the houses. After dusk we'll try to find an entrance to the fort itself.'

I said, 'I'd got the impression that Nasir was shipping out a terrorist unit to blow up one of the oil installations.'

Masud said, 'It is an army attack. Many men, not few.'

'So when'll this band of warriors hit the road?'

'That,' said Deacon, 'is something we don't know.'

'Supposing Nasir's mob's on its way before our lot show?'

'Come off it, Dingo,' Deacon said. 'You've worked off the cuff before now.'

'That's all I want to hear,' I said. 'Off the cuff it is.'

Deacon gave me a hard stare, not much toned down by his smoked glasses. He wasn't keen to take my muzzle off, let me rush in and savage those wogs. What bothered me most about Ashfra was not knowing what sort of battle we were supposed to be fighting. I hadn't got used to having my hands tied by 'political considerations'. In ten years we'd all be adjusted to that queer way of soldiering. Nobody who wore an SAS uniform would feel confused or frustrated by the edicts of Whitehall and Westminster. But it was my first taste of a half war, and it made me nervous. I mean, was I supposed to go for the rebels if they showed signs of mustering? Was I empowered to shoot Nasir bloody Salim's balls off if I bumped into him in the dark? The Deke issued no instructions. Because the Deke didn't know either. He was groping towards solutions, hoping that a correct course of action would open up along the way. If the worst came to the worst, we had done our best.

'Follow me,' said Major Deacon.

I hopped to obey him.

Shelter was minimal. There were some large boulders strewn among the shingle and, dotted sparsely here and there, twisted little trees with hardly any foliage. Then there was a road, if you could call it that. This was the track that the three rebel Land Rovers had whizzed along and it ran in a straight line from the fort's only visible door, due east. At least, I think it was east. In the rays of the afternoon sun it, the track, had a slick macadamized appearance but, of course, it was only gravel flattened by the passage of trucks and camels.

The three Land Rovers had been swallowed up by the fort. There wasn't the whisper of any sort of traffic, not even pack animals. If the mercenaries at Ashfra were preparing for a big show, an all-out attack, then they were being bloody quiet about it. Unless they, too, were waiting. But for what? Nasir, as far as we could surmise, had arrived in the Land Rovers.

Belly to the dirt, I creep-crawled after Masud. He resembled a sand-flea rowing along under the pack on knees and elbows, tearing lumps out of his fancy clothes. I had buttoned my shirt sleeves at the wrists and thanked my stars that I hadn't toddled out on this operation in an Aertex.

It was all too ruddy exposed for my liking. If we were spotted we'd have no chance of retreating or of making much of a fight of it. But I'd been trained in techniques of escape and evasion by the best in the business, including Deacon, and even Masud had the appearance of a bloke drilled in invisibility. We got within a hundred and fifty yards of the fort and found a margin of cover in a stand of twisted, leafless trees. The fort loomed over us. Ashfra was no showpiece like the defences at Nizwa. It looked rusty, not pink-white. One round tower was erected above the rectangular walls. There were window slots, forty feet above the ground, broken embrasures round the battlements. This was a derelict, not a monument.

Hand over mouth, I whispered, 'Now what, boss?'

'Wait and watch.'

This we did, for more than an hour.

It would have been difficult to keep awake if the situation had been less keen. Here we were up Nasir Salim Azzi's nostrils and he was too bloody careless to notice us.

The air cooled. Breezes rustled through the trees, stirred the dust. In a half-hour it would be full dark, for the sun had dipped low into the line of the western hills. Draped in the yoke of tree branches, Masud al Hasan hissed. Deacon and I followed his pointing finger.

The light in the sky looked like a star at first, then we made it out to be a helicopter, flying at about three hundred feet, a hefty transport craft. A Sikorsky H-19 variant of the old S55 type, it was a common enough utility chopper used by most US armed services. But it didn't look right out there in the sands, hanging over the fortress. The engines made a hell of a row and Deacon and I were able to have a conversation while the aircraft manoeuvred and dropped, like something on a cable, into the walls of the fort.

'Jesus, it's big.'

Deacon told me the type, adding, 'It can carry about a dozen troops.'

'What's its range?'

'Probably about three-fifty to four hundred miles.'

'Somebody coming in on it,' I said, 'or somebody going out?'

It was Masud who put his finger on the truth. 'It is both things that happen.'

God, how we would have loved a squint over the wall right then. The arrival of such an aircraft opened up all sorts of unpleasant possibilities. The Deke didn't have to underline them for me. I had heard how big, long-range transport choppers were used in South East Asia. Strike forces. Raiding parties. None of us, though, had figured on finding anything so sophisticated in Oman. Though the chopper had no markings it wasn't hard to guess that it was another 'contribution' from the Americans. It was just the sort of baby a US oil conglomerate could purchase by the dozen and no questions asked. For all we knew, the Saudis had a fleet of the bloody machines.

The parade-ground square of the hollow fortress amplified the sound of the engines and we could hear exactly when they were cut, when the babble died away. The silence was uncanny.

'That settles it,' whispered Deacon.

'Over the wall?'

'Absolutely,' Deacon answered.

Masud, I thought, looked slightly sick.

Allah would have to take care of our Arabian spy. The Deke and I no longer had the leisure to jolly him along. We would have our work cut out getting into the fort. We had a positive end, though; to make sure that the big Sikorsky didn't wing again. If it did, then the oil boys at Fahud or Zambat would be eating dirt not steak for breakfast, and the SAS 'victory' on the Jebel Akhdar would pale beside the rebels' triumph in obliterating the foreign imperialists who were in league with the Sultan. I needed no lessons in propaganda or diplomacy to understand how that would bite into the British government's credibility.

Deacon, without more ado, unpacked his shotgun from its travelling valise.

Me, I decided to take the Sten.

SAS Sergeant Buz Campbell had left the Vaughan shotgun to Deacon in a scribbled but valid will. The gun had been retrieved from a sodden paddi-field in Malaya where Buz had used it only a split second before he met his death. The Vaughan was an expedient version of the Canadian Arms Company's 12 gauge Model 774 sporting gun, with the barrel cut to 20 inches, and a riot-grade bore. As a robust, five-shot semi-automatic combat weapon it was almost without equal. Deacon squatted behind the tree, filling his belt with cartridges. He had laid out six HE grenades and would clip them to his webbing. Maurice, he noticed, was assembling the 9mm Sten Mark VI, a special model with a silencer, the gun balanced perfectly to the integral suppressor. This type of weapon had been around a long time, was part of SAS history, really. It still functioned beautifully, though it was gradually being replaced by Sterlings from the Royal Small Arms Factory at Enfield. Masud had an identical weapon in his pack but he was less adroit than Harper – naturally – at rapid assembly.

Masud was going to be a problem. The short stiff climb up the fort wall would present no serious problem to a climber like Dingo Harper. But Masud could not be hauled up. There simply would not be time for 'antics'. Dingo and he would have to be over the wall and into action instantly. He could not count on the battlements being undefended. He touched the Arab who, as if guessing what was in the major's mind. nodded.

Deacon drew him down and, heads together, said, 'I want you to stay outside. Here's as good a place as any.'

'I will climb.'

'No, Masud.'

'I will be all right. You have my word to it.'

'I need a man on the outside. What if we don't make it? What if something goes wrong?'

'I will come into the fort for you?'

'Absolutely not,' said Deacon. 'If there's shooting, you buzz off.'

'Buzzing . . .'

'Retreat. Go back. In the darkness. It's flat enough. You shouldn't have too much trouble. Find the Land Rover and the moment it's light get back down the—'

Masud smiled smugly. 'No petrol to make Land Rover run.'

Deacon suppressed his anger. 'There's enough to take you into the Wadi Yafyn. Come on, Masud, you're not a fool. You know we've got to report this. When you get into the wadi, and *if* the Land Rover stalls and won't go any further, then you will set fire to it. There should be aircraft, RAF spotters, in the vicinity of the Jebel Akhdar. If there isn't, perhaps somebody on the plateau will notice the smoke.'

'What if they do not?'

'Walk, damn it.'

'What's he moaning about now?' Dingo Harper asked in a whisper.

'I will await you here. You will find a way to let me into the fort, Major Deacon. I have business with those who are within.'

'All right, all right. But if there *is* shooting . . .'

'I will obey you. I will go to the vehicle, for aid.'

'Settled, boss?'

'Apparently,' said Deacon.

The final quarter of an hour was a tense time for the major and the lieutenant. Crouched side by side behind the gnarled trees, they watched the afterglow rapidly diminish in the sky. The fortress became a silhouette, the breast of the round tower the colour of fox-pelt, while the grove of date palms darkened threateningly. Stars emerged in the stainless sky. Light appeared in a couple of the windows high on the wall. From within the fort, though, the silence remained complete. Prayer, perhaps, occupied the rebels. Masud might have given a clue here but Deacon was in no mood to talk with the Arab again. He was not at all sure he had made the right decision, though no other seemed possible under the circumstances. At length, twilight having thickened into night, Deacon tapped Dingo Harper on the shoulder. The Australian did not even turn his head. Gripping the Sten in both hands, he darted across the stretch of open ground into the gloom of the walls. Deacon followed him. Both men left their rifles behind.

Thirty seconds later the SAS officers were together again, pressed into the fold of the wall of the fort. Here they wasted no time. Dingo Harper slung the Sten over his shoulder, found holds and swiftly climbed the vertical. Deacon gave him twenty feet of a start. The stonework was rough, weather-worn, the climbing even easier than the slab at Khahouris.

Dingo hoisted his chest over the edge of an embrasure, hesitated then vanished. Deacon completed the climb carefully, not rushing it. He adjusted the tilt of the shotgun on his back before he thrust himself through the embrasure. Dingo was kneeling on a broadwalk, eight or ten feet in width. Above them, to the right, was the tower, going up another twenty feet or so. There was no visible means of entry to the vantage point, no ladder or steps. But there was nobody up there that Deacon could see, and no guards at all on the broadwalk. Dingo made a hand sign, drawing the major's attention to the scene below. Deacon made a purring noise in his throat, like a cat who has stumbled on a crock of cream.

The Sikorsky filled the 'square'. It was no square in true geometric terms but a huge oval, for the broadwalk which bordered it fashioned a curve that planed out the corners. The helicopter looked huge and out of place. The contrast between the rebel stronghold and Bressol's nest of spies at Zambat was marked. Apart from the incongruous flying-machine, Deacon might have been gazing down on a scene from the last century. Approximately forty tribesmen were nestled under tents around the arches of the walls. Their cooking fires were tucked under the walk and would be invisible to an aircraft. The Land Rovers, four in all, were similarly screened. Whatever else Nasir Salim Azzi had learned in Kiev, or in MIT for that matter, he had mastered the rudiments of camouflage. Deacon and Harper moved stealthily forward to the edge of the broadwalk and, lying flat, studied the arena intently.

Apart from the glow of the fires there were torches on some of the inner walls, and three or four workers with hand-held lanterns. There were no animals within the fortress, not even chickens. The army must be fed from supplies brought in by the Sikorsky or by truck. Perhaps local chieftains supplied cereals and mutton from their meagre stocks. Anything could be bought at a price. The well was in the far corner, shaded by palm-frond planking. There was no guard upon the stone trough so there must be no shortage of the precious liquid here. Nose over the edge, Deacon peered down. Oil and petrol drums and a column of spare tyres were stored under the broadwalk, almost out of sight.

Omani fortresses tended not to have deep chambers beneath them, so Masud had told Deacon. Building techniques did not incorporate digging down into rock. What was visible, more or less, was what there was. In the lighted room just below the officers' present position, would be an admin. office or its equivalent. It seemed odd that Nasir hadn't posted lookouts. On the other hand, everything that Deacon had so far seen indicated that secrecy was the number one priority. In daylight the fort would 'go to sleep', with tribesmen and equipment under cover. How long had Nasir been entrenched here? There was no means of telling. Given finance and know-how, the fort could have been established as a strike base in a week or less.

It occurred to Deacon that Nasir and his American backer had expected the plateau of the Jebel Akhdar to fall. In a sense, their plan required it. Four Land Rovers laden with armed tribesmen, and one Sikorsky transport helicopter with a dozen trained terrorists inside it would wreak havoc at the oil installations. Nasir would not have to choose between Fahud and Zambat. He had the means to take them both. If Seback, the American connection, had arrived with the chopper then he was somewhere indoors. On the other hand, Seback might have done his work and be safe in Saudi.

Dingo nudged the major with his elbow.

From under the broadwalk below the SAS men two figures came out into the square. Each emanated a kind of proprietorial arrogance. George Seback was easy to mark. He wore a linen suit and a broad-brimmed, unblocked Stetson-type hat. He was lean, lantern-jawed and walked as if he was floating on air, like other Texans that Deacon had encountered around the world, a breed difficult to forget. Nasir Salim Azzi was recognisable by his bulk and thin, Egyptian moustache. Also by the fact that he wore a camouflage jacket, baggy pants and calf-length para boots. Webbing belt and a field-cap completed the portrait of a soldier, but in the throat of his shirt he sported a scarf which was as white as driven snow and would have made an excellent aim-point for a sniper on the darkest night. Behind Nasir came two other men similarly dressed, each toting a Thompson submachine gun. Was it necessary, Deacon wondered, for Nasir to be protected within the fort? Probably the armed escort was only for show. Passing into and out of the light pools, Nasir and Seback went to the Sikorsky. For one horrible moment Deacon thought that they might be about to board the helicopter and take off. Dingo obviously had a similar thought and the Australian's hand reached for a grenade at his belt.

Tense now, the major and the lieutenant watched the area around the Sikorsky carefully. There was no light within the cabin, no sign of a pilot. To Deacon's surprise, the sound of voices, speaking English, rose up from the amphitheatre below, Nasir's booming and guttural tones and Seback's drawl. Unfortunately, the substance of the conversation was inaudible. Perhaps they were discussing the payload of the transport craft, how many troops it could safely carry.

After ten or fifteen minutes, the American broke away and

strolled, alone, under the broadwalk, leaving Nasir to talk at considerable length with his armed adjutants.

When Nasir too returned to the shelter of the apartment, out of sight, Deacon drew Dingo back from the edge, as far as the outer wall. Shoulder to shoulder like monkeys on a rock, the SAS men conferred in whispers.

'Is that who I think it is, boss?'

'Without doubt.'

'What about the others, Talib and the Imam; think they'll show up here?'

'Absolutely not,' murmered Deacon. 'They'll be making their own way into hiding. This isn't their raid.'

'But it'll look like it is, since nobody knows about this pair.'

Deacon nodded. 'It smells to me as if two raids are planned. One by tribesmen in the Land Rovers. The other by trained guerrillas in the Sikorsky.'

'Where?'

'Oh, they're not going to attack the army. It must be the oil sites.'

'Zambat and Fahud,' said Dingo. 'Which is nearer?'

'Zambat.'

'Land assault there. Air strike at Fahud. Christ, it'll be slaughter.'

'We can prevent it, you know.'

'I'd rather we didn't have to,' said Dingo.

'We can easily sabotage the Sikorsky.'

'And the trucks?'

'Blow the magazine, if we can find it. And the fuel dump, which is directly below us.'

'I thought orders were to capture Nasir and the Yank?'

'Needs must when the devil drives.'

'Come off it, boss. It's a fair cow, and you know it. Sure, we can demolish some of this place. But we'll be carved to pieces soon as the first grenade explodes. I'm not wagging the old white feather, sir, but I don't fancy being a martyr when I don't have to be,' whispered Dingo Harper. 'I'd hate to make the grand bloody gesture and then have the RAF turn up five minutes later and obliterate the joint anyhow.'

'I agree,' said Deacon.

'I suppose Intelligence'll have got your *billet-doux* by this time?'

'I sincerely hope so,' said Deacon.

''Cause Masud isn't going to bring in the cavalry in time.'

'Nasir won't take the helicopter out until daybreak.'

'Yep,' said Dingo Harper. 'But the trucks might shove off in the dark.'

For almost a minute Deacon sat against the wall, kneading his tired eyes with his fingertips, his beret tilted back and the Sten across his knees. Harper had the sense not to press him.

At length Deacon murmured, 'All in the name of the Imam. The swords of Islam. A Holy war.'

'I'm not a religious bloke, thank God.'

'All right, Dingo. I'll tell you what we'll do. We'll compromise.'

'How?'

Major Deacon spoke softly for three or four minutes, the plan fully formed. When he had finished, Harper said, 'That's a compromise?'

'What do you think, Dingo?'

'I think you're bloody crazy, boss.'

'But will it work?'

'It might.'

'All we need to find is a quick way down to the ground, and a safe place to hide out.'

'What about the tower?'

'Ah-hah,' said Deacon and glanced upwards at the circular stonework bulked black against the sky.

Two big male scorpions were fighting furiously over the corpse of a meal-worm not three feet from Bressol's right leg. It was the dry, wire-brush din of the conflict that had wakened him and he would have remained puzzled by the noise if the scorpions had not been illuminated by a wedge of moonlight which cut through the half-open door. Bressol flinched and drew his leg back from the creatures, heard the whisper of another by his hand and, scared, leapt to his feet. He swayed giddily and the sheaf of papers that had been in his lap when he fell asleep spilled and wafted across the floor. Bressol closed his eyes, fought to regain his balance, then steadied. He breathed slowly, deeply. All around were night noises, whisperings and creakings, the chirrup of rats or mice in the uninhabited houses, in the gutters and the thatch. Even this high on the mountain, nature was both alien and profligate.

Old Bill's mouth tasted like a recruit's sock, thick, hot and fetid. He held his wrist to the fan of moonlight and blearily peered at his watch. It was 2022 hours. After eight o'clock. He had been asleep for the best part of five hours. Anger at such stupidity, such weakness, consumed his nervousness. Fumbling in his breast pocket, he found his cigarette lighter and thumbed it. By its yellow flame he collected the papers from the floor and put them back in the metal box. It was very, very, very valuable stuff. Inflammatory, really. The chappies back home would have a jamboree with some of the letters. He would like to be present – a fly on the wall, say – when the Americans were hit with copies of selected missives; informal, underground pacts, contracts and bills of sale for quantities of brand-new arms.

That done, Old Bill directed his hand to the water pitcher and checked to see that there wasn't a damned snake floating in it or another scorpion practising the crawl. He lifted the pitcher and tilted it across his shoulder like a Somerset cider swallower, drinking expertly, spilling hardly a drop upon his sweat-stained shirt. Satisfied, refreshed and with his heartbeat back to its normal rate, he studied the door for a moment – had it been left ajar? – then tiptoed across the threshold.

A cold quiet night in the mountains, yes. No mutter of gunfire tonight. And not a snifter of sound from the village. Outside the house, Khahouris was as dead as Old Trafford in mid-February. He scanned the hillside and terraces, hoping to see signs of a British patrol. But there was nothing. Was it possible that a patrol had come through, missed him, and gone sweeping on? No, not possible. Not even remotely. For a start, there was nowhere really for the SAS to sweep to. Khahouris was the end of the line. They simply hadn't reached here yet. Nor would they tonight.

Conscience pricked Old Bill's heart a little at the realisation that Deacon would be expecting a military back-up, come morning. There would be no chance of that now.

He, Bressol, would not have been missed. Gore would assume that he had spent the night at Tac HQ and the officers at Tac HQ wouldn't much care where Old Bill had got to. It was fortunate indeed that Gore had seen fit to evacuate the installation at Zambat. If friend Nasir swooped on the station he would find nothing but a few empty buildings. Fahud, however, was another kettle of fish. Gore had not deemed it wise to alert the crews there to the possibility of rebel action.

Major Bressol contemplated the dark ring of the mountains once more. Perhaps he should light a signal fire, as Deacon had done. But he was afraid of attracting the tribal elements. He had no notion of how close, or how far away, SAS sweepers might be. With no tricks up his sleeve, he had no alternative but to sit tight.

He shivered. The temperature was dropping. There might be snow before morning, a touch of frost. He returned to the dwelling to find a blanket and make himself as comfortable as possible for his long, solitary vigil, and put poor Deacon out of mind.

Unlike Major Bressol, Masud al Hasan had no patience at all. He was angry at being excluded from the raid. He had every right to be there, to breach Ashfra along with the SAS officers. He too was a soldier of sorts and had proved himself efficient in killing. But the walls, though not high, daunted him and he could evolve no plan for gaining admittance otherwise. Deacon and the Australian had been gone for less than an hour when Masud ran out of scruples and, flouting Deacon's orders, left the shelter of the stunted trees on a reconnaissance of his own.

In fact, Masud was in search of a means of entry, one which did not involve climbing anything much higher than his head. He moved swiftly and silently, navigating around the fortress and its derelict houses. It was no mystery to the Arab as to why nomads had kept clear of Ashfra. The only water supply was within the walls of the fort. A generation ago, when the fort was in use as a defensive position, the ground around it would have been swarming with tents. Bedouin and sects of the Bedouin – the Beni Khalid, the Hirth, the Beni Riyam too, perhaps – would have congregated here, drawn by the promise of profit and arms, and by curiosity. But Nasir Salim Azzi had warned them off.

It took Masud some forty minutes to travel round the area of the fort. He did not come too close to the walls. He was not quite so foolish as to risk detection. He found nothing of interest outside and no means of entry save by the narrow south-facing gateway which was barred by wooden doors. A rat or a viper would have difficulty in finding a way inside. Whatever hand had designed and constructed the Ashfra fortress had been skilled. The place was impregnable.

Masud returned to the trees, slumped against a trunk and sucked water from his canteen.

It was well into the fore part of the night now. From beyond the walls came a few sounds and no indication that the major had been discovered. Masud rolled on to his belly and glared at the gateway painted by moonlight. He remained in that position for twenty minutes, then, drawing himself to his feet, headed into the darkness, back across the gravel sands of Zambat under an icy moon.

Dingo Harper

To tell you the truth, I was a bit pissed off with all that climbing. Not that the round tower of Ashfra was much of a challenge or even particularly strenuous. I traversed the base then went up the outer wall and over the top. There was a drop of about four feet to a wooden floor which made an unfortunate thump when I landed on it. Cat-foot Harper got a bit careless there. The floor was solid enough, no danger of it collapsing or anything, but the kiln-shaped tower was like an orchestral drum and magnified every little sound. When the Deke's head and shoulders appeared over the top I gave him a frantic signal to hold his horses and braced myself under him so he could step on to my back and down from there.

Though it was pretty dark within the tower, we made out a trap in the floor. The place was thick with dust and crawling with tiny spiders which attached themselves, painlessly, to my hands as I got down on all fours to have a look at the hatch.

The Deke swept an area of the floor with his forearm then hunched over with his ear to the woodwork.

There wasn't a dicky-bird to be heard from below. That didn't mean that the place was deserted. For all we knew it might be the dormitory for sixty wild Arabs, early bedders. One thing, though, it was a bloody sight warmer inside the tower than out. On the parapet it had become cold enough to shrivel off your tiny parts. If we were doomed to spend a night in hiding – and the alternative wasn't much cop – then this was the place. It was high above trouble and snug and even the spiders had taken the hint and were buggering off in all directions.

An iron handle was sunk into the trap. I brushed away a layer of dust and picked at it with my fingernails. It lifted on primitive hinges, stiff but workable.

'Open sesame?' I breathed.

Deacon unslung the Vaughan and stood behind me, the gun slanted past my left lug ready to blast the daylights out of anybody who might be lurking below.

'Lift,' the Deke whispered.

I hoisted up the trap and laid it flat. We looked down into a pitch-black hole. I stretched on my stomach with my head over the opening. It was a pretty narrow opening. Only one bloke at a time could wriggle through and it would have been a tight squeeze for anyone with a beer belly, though there were few of those in Oman. I still couldn't see very much. There were no stairs. Deke sniffed. I smelled it too, a pleasant, familiar odour, a mix of clean new wood and oil.

A thin beam of light struck past me; Deacon's pocket torch. I saw a wooden cross-piece with a rope knotted round it and two or three steps, like platforms, affixed to the side of the tower not far below the trap. But the beam petered out long before it reached the floor, and the steps did not descend far.

It took me a moment to work it out. The tower was a last line of defence, not for 'modern' warriors like Nasir Salim Azzi but a relic of the bad old days when sieges were rife. That stout hempen rope was the only method of getting up on to the tower. It probably dropped right to the ground. If the fort was breached then die-hard tribesmen and their sheikh could make a stand here, drawing the rope up after them. Even with gunpowder it would have been bloody impossible to winkle them out.

I shifted back and, squatting, whispered, 'Are you thinking what I'm thinking, boss?'

'Absolutely,' said Deacon.

It was so bloody perfect, it might have been built to accommodate us and seal the Deke's idiotically risky plan.

All we had to do was immobilise the Sikorsky and the Land Rovers, blow up the fuel dumps and the magazine, kidnap the American, and retreat with the prisoner to the tower. Nasir wouldn't dare shoot lumps out of the tower in case he nobbled Seback, and we could sit it out until the SAS galloped over the hill to capture the fort.

All we had to do? Simple, what?

Deacon whispered, 'Do you think there's anyone down there?'

'Only one way to find out.'

Deacon flicked on the pencil torch. It showed me the cross-piece with the loop of rope around it. I strapped the Sten to my back and stepped out and down on to the wood. Deacon handed me the torch. I explored with it. The steps or shelves jutted out of the stonework. More spiders on them, big fellows too. But I could see how it worked now, how anybody climbing the rope would have support to make the last haul through the trap on to the platform of the tower. I assumed that supplies were hauled up by rope too. But where the climbing rope went to, and whether it was intact, were questions which didn't have an answer.

I groped for the shelves and lowered myself down from the wooden cross-piece on to them. They felt solid as rock. I had one hand on the beam, waved about, found the rope and brought it to me, gave it a hearty tug. Seemed okay. I shone the torch down it. It wasn't just a rope. It was a ladder. Spars of wood had been woven through the hemp at regular intervals. I stepped down on to one. The rope twirled slightly, steadied. I glanced up at the Deke, visible against a crescent of sky cut by the angles and curves of trap and battlement. He nodded, and I began to descend, the pencil torch in my teeth, like a pirate's cutlass.

I hadn't gone down more than twenty feet when I realised that the rope wasn't anchored at the bottom. It swung and pendulumed and I had difficulty in holding it steady enough to find the rungs with my feet. Every so often I had to stop and wait for the hemp to ravel round and straighten out before I could carry on down. I counted the rungs. I reckoned them to be about thirty inches apart, maybe a little more. Thirty-five or forty of them should bring me to the ground. I shone the torch intermittently on the walls of the tower. To be truthful I didn't expect to find anything, except maybe nests of bats. I was worried about bats, had bats on the bloody brain. What if they took fright and went squeaking and shrieking out across the courtyard and alerted Nasir's boys? I didn't find any bats, though. Found a wooden platform about twenty feet down and, set into the wall, a door.

A gentle swing carried me on to the platform. I rested my weight on it, found it as solid as the rest of the construction. I stuck my hand out and winked the torch, hoping that the Deacon would understand. Seconds later the major began to climb down too.

When he joined me I gestured to the door. It was square, not arched in the Moorish style, and only about three feet high. I passed the torch to the Deke and pressed against the door with my palms, then gave it a touch of the shoulder. It creaked and yielded reluctantly. I ceased at once. But I had broken an opening and could feel cold air seeping through.

No doubt Masud would have been able to give us a run-down on these frills of Arabian castellated architecture. Fact is, you didn't have to be a genius to figure out the function. The system, if you could call it that, had a simple purpose. It was an escape hatch to the sanctuary of the tower. Dry desert air had preserved the parts for centuries. Maybe there had been repairs done in living memory, though, since the tribes had been baiting and quarrelling right through the twentieth century.

When I applied more weight to the low door it swung outward with hardly more than a murmur.

The Deke switched off the torch.

Before us a wooden balcony stretched the length of the southern wall. Propped on the arches it was roofed by the battlements. The balcony gave access to apartments built into the wall. A flight of stone steps went down to ground level and a wooden ladder went upwards on to the broadwalk. We could see this much by the spillage of light from one of the chamber windows and the flicker of torches in the courtyard below. The balcony was almost level with the blades of the big Sikorsky. Whoever had piloted the helicopter into the yard sure knew their business and had dropped the bird as neatly as a chicken into a casserole.

I hesitated. I didn't know what the Deke would want to do. Recce the chambers off the balcony or carry on down the rope ladder to the bottom of the tower. While the boss was making up his mind, I listened to the jabber of conversation from the yard. Though the voices were low they had that excited quality which is characteristic of Arabic intonation. If only there had been a few more of us in the raiding party, we could have wiped out this rebel nest entirely. As it was, the lie of the land was much in our favour. Deacon reached past me and drew the door shut. The balcony could wait.

I went back on to the rope ladder and climbed down. It was inky black at the bottom, though a faint chink of light indicated another door there. The rope did not stop short of the floor but had a coil on the flagstones, slack. I didn't drop but went right to the bottom before I let go. I stepped to the left, bumped into something edgy and solid. When the Deke joined me with the torch we saw that the circular space at the base of the tower was being used as an armoury. Crates and boxes were everywhere. Hence the pleasant smell of new-cut wood and gun oil.

The crates were unmarked, though some of the ammo boxes bore stencilled letters and numerals. Deacon gave me the torch. I followed him while he prowled about the area. It was cold down there, a perfect site for an arms store except that it was too ruddy close to the fuel dump which, if I had my geography correct, was just outside.

We followed the wall, clockwise, searching for open crates. Six were laid out directly in front of the door. Bedded within the crates were Springfield M1 rifles and Thompson submachine guns, cartons of ammo plus HE hand grenades, compact brown Dopplers. Obviously the weapons had been set out for issue. On rough estimate there was enough hardware to arm fifty rebels. God knows how many mines had come through here in the past months, how many sniper rifles now in use in Oman had arrived through Ashfra. Somebody had spent a small fortune on the acquisition and allocation of sophisticated weapons. Toted up, though, I don't suppose it was much of an investment when you consider that it might win oil contracts worth millions of bucks.

Deacon nudged me. He pointed upwards. I hesitated, making gestures. Fact is, I found all that shooting stuff hard to resist. I reckoned we might find a use for it ourselves.

Deacon whispered, 'Let's find our American.'

Tracking Seback within the fort proved easier than we thought it would be. Looking back, it seems Lady Luck was luring us on. Nabbing Seback wasn't the problem – hanging on to him was the tough part.

We climbed back up the rope to the door in the side wall,

went through it on to the balcony. We hugged the outer wall and stole towards the lighted windows. We could see tribesmen in the courtyard. If they strained their eyes they could certainly see us too. But they were busy feeding their faces. The reek of mutton was in the air. A festive murmur came from the groups gathered round the pots. There wasn't a scrap of cover on the balcony. It was little more than a wooden gallery. It creaked like a man o' war, though, and I was so keyed up I imagined I could feel it swaying. If somebody came clipping up the steps at the far end, Deacon and I would be spotted instantly. I held the Sten ready. But nobody came up the steps.

The Deke and I got to the first lighted window. It was glassed and had a fly-curtain on the inside so we couldn't make out much detail. We flanked it. I took the far side, my back to the door situated between the windows. We listened. Heard gutteral laughter.

Hazily I made out four Omani soldiers in battledress seated round a wooden table. There were water pitchers and, on a little petrol stove, a bubbling coffee pot. It appeared cosy and comradely within the small, low-ceilinged chamber. I couldn't make out whether there were cots or bunks in the room. I gave Deacon the 'head on pillow' sign. He shook his head, motioned me on. We skirted the doorway and arrived at the next lighted window. There was no fly-curtain. Perhaps Seback preferred to have an uninterrupted view of his Sikorsky. Seback and Nasir Salim Azzi were also having supper. They ate from plates. Seback was drinking whisky and Nasir had four bottles of Coke ranged in front of him. Chatting, the pair appeared relaxed.

From the edge of the window, Deacon and I watched and listened. We could have killed them both there and then. I wish we had. But the cohorts in the adjacent chamber would have used us for target practice. Anyhow, the Deke was no kamikaze officer. It wasn't in his nature to fling his life away if he could help it. For two or three minutes we pressed ourselves against the wall.

Seback was younger than I had imagined. Nasir was older. The Egyptian had an unhealthy complexion and bags under his eyes. His hair, now that he had removed his beret, was streaked grey. He was slow-moving, deliberate. Seback was deliberate too, but quick. He ate with a fork, spearing the meat lumps from his plate with a striking motion, chewing with rapidity, his lantern jaw grinding efficiently. I noticed that he kept his eyes on his food, didn't once glance up at his companion, as if he was shy.

Maddeningly, we couldn't make out much that passed between the men, just a word now and again. The walls of the fort of Ashfra were thick enough to absorb the voices, the window too far from the table.

I heard, 'Fahud' and 'British forces', a drawled but emphatic agreement from Nasir to something that Seback suggested.

At length, the Deke touched me with the Vaughan to draw me down and away. We pressed no further along the balcony but returned to the door in the tower and hid ourselves behind it. Seconds later the uniformed squadron leaders came out on to the balcony and shouted orders to the men in the square. There was sudden activity. Deacon and I crouched by the door, squinting through the crack, then Deacon closed it gently.

'If they eat there,' said Deacon, 'they'll sleep there too.'

'Yep.'

'It appears to be a question of timing.'

'If we take Seback now,' I said, 'we'll have to hold on to him until the squadron arrives.'

'Precisely,' said the Deke. 'We'll leave him for a while.'

'So, what do we do in the interim?'

'Personally,' Deacon said, 'I'm going to catch a little sleep.'

'Where?'

'Upstairs.'

I had catnapped that day but the boss had been on his pins for forty hours. I couldn't blame him for wanting a snooze before diving into another bout of strenuous activity, especially at his age. Anyhow, there was nothing we could profitably do before three a.m., or thereabouts. We lugged ourselves back up the rope ladder and through the trap into the top of the tower.

It was cold and clear. You could see forty miles in any direction, across oceanic dunes towards the Saudi border and all the way to the serrations of the Jebel capped by a wisp of creamy cloud. The moon was as bright as an RSM's button. Deacon didn't waste any time. He pulled on a woolly sweater and settled himself into a corner, seated not sprawled. Within minutes he was fast asleep. He hadn't asked me if I'd mind keeping scout, nor did he give me any instruction about when to wake him. He didn't have to. I wasn't a trooper fresh out of training – though I behaved like one.

Fact is, I got bored. The prospect of action made me restless. I stuck it out for a couple of hours then I decided to be smart. It wasn't that bad an idea at the time. I told myself I was showing initiative. Looking back, I guess I was just impatient. I opened the trap carefully and lowered myself on to the ladder. The interior of the tower had lost all heat too now. It was like lowering yourself into a well. Where was I going? To the armoury, of course. I intended to bring up a bunch of grenades, a couple of the Thompsons and a quantity of ammo. If we were going to shoot it out, then the ammo on our belts wouldn't go far. It wasn't much of a drag up and down the ladder, only sixty feet or so. I had a vague notion that I might be able to sabotage the magazine by spreading petrol. Horse sense prevailed on that one, since the Deke, Seback and I would be perched on top of the tower. I was too cocky by half. It had all been comparatively painless so far. I had no respect for the wogs or for a bloke like Nasir Salim Azzi who would set up an elaborate base then neglect to post guards.

I shinned down the rope ladder and with the pencil torch shaded by my fist picked up a dozen Doppler grenades and two unwrapped Thompsons. I carried the weapons up to the platform by the door to the balcony and unloaded them there. I went down again, nicked another Tommy and as many thirty-round box magazines as I could carry in my shirt and toted them up to the platform. Now I'd got the hang of it, shinning up and down the old rope ladder was a piece of cake. I had quite a pile of hardware on the platform when I went down for my third trip.

I was ten feet from the bottom of the ladder when, without warning, somebody flung open the door at the base of the tower and two wogs stomped into the armoury. Thirty feet further up and I'd have been fine. But there I was hanging like a bloody old spider just above their noses. Even Nasir's desert scourings weren't that dumb. What made matters worse was that I had left my Sten on the platform. I fumbled at my belt and found a grenade. I whipped it out and armed it. One of the startled wogs shouted. I pitched the grenade at him, aiming for the pool of light that showed through the open doors. They were like the doors you find in country churches, pretty high. Fortunately for me, the grenade bounced and hopped out of the doorway. If the bloody thing had gone off within the armoury I would have been blasted skywards like a fucking rocket. One of the wogs let off a shot. I hadn't even seen the gun in his hand. I heard the bullet wasping about within the kiln. Practically before the grenade had left my fingers I was monkeying up that rope ladder, chased by the yells of the tribesmen. I was ten feet under the platform when the Doppler exploded.

It must have bounced a fair long way into the yard. One of the wogs took the blast full on. He came sailing into the tower, screaming, and pitched on to the coffin-like crates. I heard only a vague, unconvincing *whum*. By that time I was muscling myself on to the platform and the Deke was at the trap above. Perhaps some of the Deke's instinct for doing the right thing had rubbed off on me. I don't know. Maybe I was just so shit-scared of being cashiered for crass stupidity that I ran into instead of away from the mess. Fact is, I knew exactly what I was doing. My intention was crystal clear. I kicked the litter of weapons to one side and barged the square door wide open. I snatched up my Sten and dived through the door on to the balcony. I was possessed by one purpose, had but one single thought in my mind – to grab that bloody Yank.

George Robert Seback had been dead for the best part of four years. He had died along with seven other troopers from the US Army's Air Mobile unit during a training exercise in the mountains of Nevada when the medium-lift transport chopper in which they had been flying crashed with no survivors. Unlike his seven companions, however, George Robert Seback was not given a military funeral. He was buried discreetly in an Inyo County cemetery, with the permission of his only living relative, a bibulous elder sister who lived in LA. Within the month, papers had been processed transferring George Robert Seback from the 1st Cavalry Division to a Signals base in Washington State. Only in the records of the US Army Paymaster Corps was the truth to be found; G. R. Seback was paid not a penny for serving his country now. In the spring of 1957 George Robert Seback was granted an honourable discharge and, according to records, returned to Houston, near which city he had been born and raised, raised for the most part in a state institution for orphaned boys. Nobody really wanted G. R. Seback much when he was alive. But after his death the scant reality of his life was moderately valuable to certain agencies whose business was deception and disguise.

The man who assumed the identity of George Robert Seback was, and remains, unknown. Unsubstantiated rumours suggested that in another guise he had been active during a hectic period in Middle East politics, particularly in the Lebanon. The man who was now George Seback was certainly not warranted to an official US government department. Consequently, he had no scruples about climbing into bed with Communist-trained agitators like Nasir Salim Azzi. Mr George Robert Seback was the kind of guy who gets the work done as best he can, a devoted exponent of the philosophy that the end always justifies the means. Nutshelled, in this operation the end was to prevent the British government establishing monopoly over highly promising oil rights in Muscat and Oman.

Seback had dined well and was in process of turning in when the grenade shook the fort. Initially, Seback was not too startled by the sound. Tribesmen were careless and unused to quality arms. Seback was standing in front of a square mirror which unfolded from the top of his dressing-case which he had placed on the chamber's one and only shelf next to an oil lamp. Stripped to undershirt and pants, he had been tenderly applying a lotion to an angry rash which had recently appeared around his throat at collar line. The tumbler of scotch on the shelf trembled with the vibration. Seback paused, listening to the scream of pain from outside. He listened again, cotton swab in one hand, to hear if Nasir reacted, if there was a thunder of Egyptian feet in the adjacent room. But there was nothing. Seback, though not quite settled, went on with doctoring his fair skin.

Minutes later, however, further alarming sounds accumulated. Quickly Seback tossed away the cotton swab. He raced across the little room to the peg by the door where his shirt, coat and the harness containing his Colt Automatic hung. Nasir was moving now okay. Shots. Three loud bangs impacted with a soft, plangent volley which Seback instantly recognised as the report of a silenced machine-gun. He snatched at the gun harness. He dug for the butt of the automatic, tearing it from the bundled coat.

The door burst open. A voice yelled, 'DROP THE BLOODY POPGUN, MATE.'

Surprised but not panicked, Seback froze.

'THROW IT AWAY.'

The soldier was Australian. He looked wild, with blond stubble on his chin and his hair spiked with sweat. His uniform was filthy and torn, but his webbing had a fringe of hand grenades, and the weapon in his fist was a reliable Sten, fattened by a repressor. Seback would have been happier if the soldier had been laconic. But the Aussie was bellowing like a poled steer. The young man's excited state caused Seback to be cautious. He flipped the bundle to one side.

From outside, close to the door, came the bark of a shotgun fired several times in rapid succession. Another grenade went off. Rifle bullets whined. Zoo-chatter rose from the courtyard.

'NOW, OUT.'

Seback asked where the soldier intended for him to go.

'OUT.'

Seback passed the soldier, through the doorway on to the balcony. He glanced left towards the steps that led to the courtyard. There were no allies to be seen. He raised himself on to the balls of his feet, stretched his neck and tried to discern what was happening in the square. How many British raiders had invaded Ashfra? The snout of the Sten dug into his spine. Seback spun round, reaching. The muzzle dashed agonisingly across his wrists.

'BLOODY BEHAVE, BUSTER.'

Steered by the Sten, George Seback turned right and began to walk along the balcony. He had never really noticed the low door in the base of the tower.

'*Look out, Dingo*,' somebody yelled.

Instantly, Seback's escort dropped to one knee. The Sten at his shoulder, he pumped six shots through the glass into Nasir's room.

It wasn't Nasir, though, who died. A uniformed rebel named Abukir, handpicked from a training camp in the Nejid, caught the bullets in the chest and throat. He crashed through the frame of shattered glass and, with blood gushing from his mouth, reached towards Seback like a supplicant. Seback was in no position to offer salvation. He gripped the handrail of the balcony with both hands and bent his legs. He would risk the drop into the courtyard rather than capture by the British. Seback was no slouch but the soldier was twice as fast. The Sten's skeleton stock caught Seback's ankles. He tripped and stumbled to the balcony, narrowly missing the rail with his jaw. The soldier planted a knee on the nape of his neck and, resting weight there, blasted again with the Sten. Prudently, George Robert Seback kept still. Resistance from the rebel commanders was broken within thirty seconds. A grenade pitched through the window finished it. Seback felt a hand on his undershirt, felt himself being lifted and placed on his feet as if he weighed no more than a sugar bag. It was like being picked up by an orang-utan. Hustled from the rear, he shuffled forward.

When the Australian bawled, 'RUN, BLOODY RUN,' he ran.

When Seback reached the low doorway he bent from the waist, expecting a boot on the ass to help him along. Instead, he was grabbed from the front and jerked through the opening. Seback did not resist the fists that flattened him against the wall inside the tower.

'George Seback?'

George Robert Seback did not answer.

'You are, I know you are, George Seback.'

Neither confirmation nor denial crossed the American's lips. He expected the English officer to strike him but there was none of that. The English officer had a blue-chip accent and an emaciated appearance. He was blond, white blond, and wore, even in the half-dark of the tower, a pair of gold-rimmed, smoked-glass spectacles.

Meekly, Seback kept his back to the wall. There seemed to be little retaliation from the tribesmen clustered in the courtyard. He would have expected this sort of thing from some of the ethnic groups he had worked with in the past but not from the Arabs. They had a justified reputation for courage.

Before his eyes Seback saw the rope, like the pull in a bell tower. One leap and he could be on it. The platform was strewn with Thompsons and grenades but there was no rail. He could thrust himself out, catch the rope, slide – .

'I wouldn't advise it,' said the English officer.

'Right,' said Seback.

'Shan't keep you long,' said the English officer.

'How many in your unit?'

'Enough,' said the cadaverous major.

George Robert Seback had no reason to doubt him.

Dingo Harper

I had a prickly sensation that at any moment some bloody wog was going to hurl himself off the broadwalk and slit my throat with a *khanjar*. But once you're into something you have to reject fear and doubt and push through with your plan. Sure, we had the Yank. But Nasir still had Land Rovers and the chopper. The Deke or I wouldn't have another chance to nobble them. Another couple of minutes exposed on the balcony weren't going to make much difference, so I told myself.

If the Arabs had any inclination to rush out of the room firing like cowboys then my work with the Sten put paid to it. To be on the safe side, though, I unhooked another grenade and underarmed it through the broken window. It bounced on the buttocks of the dead lieutenant and vanished. I flung myself to the deck with the Sten held like a dumb-bell over my head. The grenade went off to the sound of screaming. The screaming stopped very quickly. Before the debris had stopped falling I was on my feet. I rolled another grenade along the balcony. Its wide-open explosion ripped away the railing and a chunk of the deck. Spikes of timber sailed into the courtyard. I had forgotten about Nasir. In the heat of the action it slipped my mind that he had been in one of the rooms. Uppermost in my thoughts was the need to immobilise the Sikorsky before the marksmen got themselves sorted out and the balcony became like a fairground shooting gallery with me the tin duck.

Let's not exaggerate; the chopper was only twenty yards away and ten feet below me. I could have bitten off the blades with my bloody teeth. Destroying the Sikorsky was no great feat of daring. I simply let off a whole clip, switched, and let it have another. So long as I was warmongering with the Sten I had no knowledge of what was happening elsewhere. I could hear nothing, though the submachine gun was silenced. I was as hot as the muzzle itself. The Deke, apparently, was yelling at me to clear off. I didn't hear a dicky-bird. I followed the second clip with three grenades. I remember leaning over the rail and plopping them at the rotor, like feeding sprats to a dolphin. When they went off the blast knocked me backwards against the wall and practically stripped away my sun-tan. I felt my beard charring and my eyeballs beginning to congeal like raw eggs on a skillet. By sheer fluke one of the grenades tore a hole in the Sikorsky's fuel tank and a rain of petrol flared among the cooking fires, causing the tribesmen to dive for cover.

Reeling, I limped towards the tower, basted with ruddy light. Grinning, the Deke looked like the devil welcoming me to hell. Shaking, I waggled through the door. I expected the Deke to slam it shut. But he had other ideas. He wasn't going to be left out of it. He had already stashed Dopplers into his pockets and loaded the Vaughan to capacity. Seback was pressed against the wall, a look of slight disdain on his face. I glanced below into the kiln but found no signs of rebels down there. Perhaps they thought we had taken over the armoury with a force of soldiers.

'Watch him, Dingo.'

'Yep,' I answered, and clipped a new box on to the Sten.

I pointed the muzzle at Seback's groin.

The Deke slipped out of the doorway and ran along the balcony. I could see him well enough from my position inside the tower.

'He'll never make it,' said Seback.

'Don't bet on it, mate.'

I had half an eye on Seback and the rest on the Deke. He didn't appear to be hurrying, moved with gliding steps, the Vaughan in his left hand. In his right hand was one of the pilfered US grenades. I reckoned the boss had gone out after Nasir Salim Azzi. But he wasn't that ambitious. His targets were more accessible. He knew enough not to go prying into those closed apartments. Nor did he go too far along the balcony. Abruptly he dropped a grenade over the rail. I heard the explosion, an oddly softened *woof*, preceded by an audible clang, like a hammer striking an anvil.

The Deke was still in view. I saw him drop another grenade in the same place, then run out. He stooped, laid down the shotgun and pitched two more Dopplers far into the yard, then turned and came back towards me, scooping up the shotgun as he did so. By that time the grenades were doing their work. The Deke had plopped one into the fuel dump. The drums went up in a cacophony of metal and a rip of igniting fuel. I saw a rubber tyre rise higher than the pock-marked Sikorsky and bounce wickedly down again. Black smoke and pretty blue flames thickened under the balcony. The Deke sprinted through them and dived through the door.

It was the best we could do under the circumstances. If you can't make sure of knocking out the transport then you wipe away the fuel. Besides, we needed breathing space to make our retreat. The chaos caused by Deacon's grenading would buy us a few precious minutes.

Deacon shouted, 'Up the ladder, Dingo.'

I slung the Sten and one Thompson and stepped on to the ladder. I climbed like crazy. Seback would be next, prodded on by the major. On the ladder we were vulnerable to shots from below. But the Arabs were still shy of rushing into the tower.

Shoving the guns before me on to the circular wooden floor, I hoisted myself through the trap. Kneeling, I peered down. The Yank was alone on the rope. Through the doors at the base of the tower I could see the hue of flames from the fuel dump. The stink of oil and rubber rose like smoke up a flue. Seback climbed neatly, hand over hand. I could only just make out the boss on the platform. I wondered how many guns and how much ammo the Deke would be able to haul to the top. We would need every Doppler, every bullet we could muster, in the coming hours.

I inched back, giving Seback room to come through the trap. I offered him no aid. He would have dragged me on to him if I put the notion into his nut. I let him come all the way through. He stood. He stared at the sky, iridescent with stars. Moonlight painted the rim of the desert and defined the distant mountains. Seback sighed, I remember, took three or four big breaths as if he was as relieved to be here as we were.

I motioned with the Sten. 'Back up.'

He backed up, raising his hands. His head and shoulders were outlined against the sky above the circular battlement. I kept a fix on him as the Deke clambered through the trap. He had brought two Thompsons and a bunch of clips and pushed them through ahead of him. Far below there was the hiss of burning and a noise like combers on a coral reef. But the sounds died very quickly. Grenades weren't that powerful, not even the latest HE Dopplers. We could be sure that we had grounded the Sikorsky but not that we had immobilised the Land Rovers or done more than superficial damage to the fuel dump.

'Give 'em a couple for luck, boss.'

'Why not?'

Holding the trap with one hand, Deacon dropped two grenades down into the shaft, then, before they went off, slammed the door on them. We felt the shake through our feet. It seemed pretty puny, to tell the truth.

Funny, it didn't occur to me that we might have done for old Nasir Salim Azzi. True, he had been in the apartments off the balcony when we had blasted those rooms. For all that, I had the feeling that the Egyptian was charmed, that the best of our luck had run out short of an accidental kill.

We had one thing going for us, though. We had Seback, the moneyman, the American influence. Nasir Salim Azzi would not permit us to fly away with such a damning piece of evidence. He would want Seback returned, preferably in one piece.

It made things very simple for Major Deacon and Lieutenant Harper, it surely did. All we had to do was hold on until daybreak when, so we believed, relief would come rumbling out of the west.

No problem, Maurice?

Ho-ho-ho!

5 Prisoner and escort

Woven with wooden struts, the weight of the rope was considerable. It taxed Deacon to haul it hand over hand, yet he waved away Dingo's offer of assistance. Unlike Harper, Deacon did not speculate on what had happened in the courtyard, nor did he try to read the mind of Nasir Salim Azzi. Too often the major had been caught out by wrong-guessing an enemy. On this occasion there was no need for it.

Seated, shoulders against the wall, Seback studied the SAS officer speculatively. When Deacon finally bundled the great hairy snake of rope on to the floor, Seback said, 'Where's it gonna get you?'

'It's my job.'

'Taking me back to Old Bill Bressol?'

'Absolutely,' said Deacon.

'Whyn't you kill me now?'

'Because I'm not a murderer.'

'You could've fooled me.'

'Make no mistake, old chap,' said Deacon, 'I'll do it if I have to.'

'The Arabs'll try to get me back, you know.'

'I'm counting on it.'

'Meaning?'

'Meaning that your comrade-in-arms, Nasir, won't dare blast us out of here while you're with us.'

Seback shrugged. 'You never can tell 'bout Arabs, my friend.'

'I thought Nasir was an Egyptian.'

'God knows what he is. Arab's close enough.'

No signal passed between the major and the lieutenant. The Australian stuck a steel-bladed knife into the woodwork unasked. Deacon plucked it out and, shanking a length of rope between fist and elbow, began to saw at it.

Seback said, 'You must be goddamned confident that your mob will show soon.'

Deacon went on sawing at the rope without a word.

Seback stirred. Dingo laid the muzzle of the Sten gently against his chest. Propped against the wall, Deacon's shotgun was tantalisingly close to the American.

'Easy, mate,' said Harper.

'There's a hundred and ten armed warriors down there,' said Seback.

'Minus the wounded,' said Harper.

Seback nodded. 'How long do you figure you can hold this position?'

'Twelve hours, anyway,' said Harper.

Seback said, 'I'll say this for you guys, you've got guts.'

Deacon tugged at the strands of rope, which finally parted. He ripped the ladder from the beam below and pulled the final few feet on to the floor. Kicking it away, he closed the trap door.

Harper said, 'Hey, boss, I think we should tie this bloke up. If things get hot I don't want him clubbing me on the nut unexpectedly.'

'Would I do that to you?' said Seback.

'Bloody right you would.'

With a length of climbing rope which Dingo had tied about his waist, Seback's hands were fastened together. Dingo threaded the rope through the American's belt and led it down to a second length of nylon with which he linked the man's ankles. 'That should hold you.'

Cautiously, Seback seated himself one more, making himself comfortable against the swaddle of rope in the corner. On the surface, he seemed resigned to being a prisoner.

He said, 'I don't know what you guys want with me.'

'My superiors have a few questions that they'd like to ask you.'

'I'm an American citizen. Private citizen.'

'I suppose you just happened to be passing in your

helicopter when you thought you'd drop in for supper?' said Harper.

'My company aren't going to like this,' said Seback.

'Which company is that?' Deacon enquired.

'Bayfield Oil.'

'Bayfield Oil?' said Dingo, with sarcasm. 'My, my, my!'

'You may have legitimate business in Saudi Arabia,' said Deacon. 'But this is Oman.'

'Guess you could say I got lost.'

'Not as lost as you're going to be, buster,' said Harper.

'Quiet, Dingo,' Deacon broke in suddenly.

Dingo hoisted the reloaded Sten into his arm and cocked his head, listening.

'Jesus, they didn't hang about, did they?' he said.

'Where?'

'Inside wall. There.'

Deacon stole to the outer battlement and flattened his back against the stonework by one of the embrasures. From the round tower, twenty feet above the broadwalk, the view extended outwards over the sands of Zambat but precious little of the interior of the fort could be seen from that height and angle. He swung the Vaughan over the rim and shifted his head behind it.

'An attack?' muttered Dingo.

'In the bud,' Deacon answered.

In the shadow of the fort's outer wall scuttled Nasir's chosen team. Ten of them were strung out along the broadwalk beneath the parapet. Deacon took them to be trained guerrillas for they moved swiftly, seeking a position below the breast of the tower.

Deacon whispered, 'Check the trap, Dingo.'

Harper knelt and lifted up the heavy wooden trap and, with his Sten propping the door, pushed his face into the gap. Bullets *thocked* into the woodwork. Dingo ducked backwards, letting the trap fall. Behind him, Seback chuckled.

'If you surrender, Major,' he said loudly, 'I'll guarantee you both safe conduct out of here.'

'Shut your face,' Dingo snapped.

Deacon paid no attention to the exchange. The gunfire from within the tower did not distract him. He kept his gaze fixed on a line of raiders who were moving along the broadwalk. Provided the moon stayed up, there would be light enough to spot attacks from that quarter. If the sky clouded towards dawn, however, defending the tower would become more difficult.

Another spray of bullets from below rattled into the trap door. But the tower and its appurtenances had been built to endure and even heavy ammo did not penetrate the woodwork. It would be awkward firing from below, rifle butt pressed against collarbone, sight wavering, forearm without a rest. Harper dragged the rope ladder across the floor and coiled it over the trap. Seback chuckled once more as if the whole operation had degenerated into a huge joke.

Next, Dingo stepped to the north-facing side of the tower and peered down. Moonlight washed the wall there and against the planes of light he saw no sign of movement. So far, it seemed, Nasir was content to try an obvious mode of capturing the tower. Dingo checked the connection of the north and west walls too, where a section of broadwalk and a flight of stone steps were illuminated by the glare of burning from the yard. He saw tribesmen with guns but they were in the courtyard, not on the walk.

Turning, Dingo called across to the major, 'All clear.'

'After me,' Deacon shouted. 'But don't waste it.'

'Yep.'

Deacon brought his shoulders square to the embrasure. He pumped out the Vaughan's five shots, sawn barrel tilted downward, then he flung himself to one side.

Retaliatory fire winged into the sky and chipped the stone as Dingo replaced the Deke in the gap and released half a clip from the Sten. Acrid gases floated like ectoplasm in the cold night air. Dingo inhaled, intoxicated by the spasm of fighting. Below, the guerrillas were sprawled like lead soldiers in a museum tableau, kneeling, canted back, three or four already stretched across the narrow band of moonlit stone edged by the drop to the courtyard. There was firing from the yard too. The circular cavity at the top of the tower hummed like a hive. Dingo discharged the rest of the clip and dropped. The Deke's knees crushed his shoulder as the major assumed position and tugged at the shotgun's trigger. The boom of the autoloader was loud in the enclosure. The Deke dropped, stayed the lieutenant with a hand. Dingo noticed that the tinted glasses had been removed, almost as if the boss had finally emerged from hiding to show his naked face to the enemy.

'How'd we do?' said Dingo.

'I believe they're backing off.'

Dingo whispered, 'Think he's telling the truth, that there are a hundred of the buggers down there?'

'It wouldn't surprise me.'

'Would I lie to you?' shouted Seback.

'He's wearing on my wick, boss. Can't we gag him?'

'Later, perhaps.'

'Water,' shouted Seback. 'I want water. Under the Geneva Convention I'm entitled to—'

'Fuck off,' Dingo shouted.

Seback laughed.

Deacon reloaded the Vaughan from his already dwindling supply of shells. He had taken an inventory of weapons. The Thompson submachine guns that Dingo had stolen from the armoury would be essential to survival. There were eleven Doppler grenades, plus six of their own stock.

'Dingo, how many clips for the Sten do you have left?'

'Three.'

'Aim carefully.'

'Always do,' said the Australian.

'After all, it won't be daylight for another seven hours.'

'Hey, guys, how 'bout singin' me a lullaby?'

'A kick on the ruddy skull will send you to sleep.'

'Give him some water, Dingo.'

Without protest the Australian fed water from the canteen to the prisoner, holding the big metallic bottle to the man's lips. Seback drank greedily; more than he required, Dingo reckoned, and drew the bottle away.

'Keep an eye on our friends out there, please, Dingo,' Deacon said. He got down on one knee by Seback's side. 'I want to have a little chat with Mr America, while there's a lull.'

Seback, smiling, closed his eyes and snored.

Deacon said, 'I assume that you are responsible for delivering the arms stored here?'

Seback snored loudly.

Deacon went on, 'What sort of weapons are they?'

Seback emitted a blubbering noise through pursed lips.

Deacon said, 'I advise you to co-operate.'

'You sound like a cop.'

'What sort of weapons? Are there mortars?'

Seback closed his eyes once more.

Deacon said, 'Don't you realise that your only hope of getting out of here alive is to trust me?'

Then play-acting was gone. Seback snapped his eyes open and his head back and glared at Deacon angrily. 'You shit-mouthed colonial,' he hissed. 'You think you got a goddamned God-given right to be here. This ain't your country any more'n it's mine. Sure, I know how you lousy English bastards work, with treaties and smiles and ten-gun salutes in Buckingham Palace yard.'

Deacon said, 'Are there mortars?'

'At least we give value.'

'We?'

'America. We have a conscience, you know.'

'So much conscience that you'd deal with a Communist?'

'Nasir's a Nationalist.'

'He's Moscow trained.'

'Go friggin' whistle.'

Deacon said, 'Your safety depends—'

'Don't you understand a goddamn thing?' Seback shouted. 'Unless Nasir gets me out, I'm cooked.'

'Nasir won't get you out, I'm afraid,' said Deacon. 'You will be handed over to British Military Intelligence.'

'Goddamned Bressol.'

'Probably,' said Deacon. 'You'll be – what? – swapped or traded back or simply sent home. No harm will come to you.'

Calm again, Seback lifted his bound hands in a gesture of defiance. 'Nasir will write me off, if he's forced to. I've done my number, chum. I'm the disposable American.'

'So far as I'm concerned,' said Deacon, 'you're just another prisoner.'

'And you're just a simple soldier, right?'

'Not that simple,' said Deacon.

Abruptly Seback decided to answer the original question. He said, 'No mortars. No bazookas. Nasir won't be able to blast you off this perch by sheer firepower. Wanna know what Nasir'll do? I'll tell you. He'll give rescue a whirl until dawn, then he'll make sure none of the three of us gets out of Ashfra alive.'

'How will he do it?'

'He'll burn us out.'

'Really?' said Deacon.

'Yeah, really.'

'You too?' said Deacon.

'Me too,' said Seback 'I told you, as of now I'm the disposable American.'

'Boss,' Dingo growled from his stance at the embrasure, 'Here they come again.'

Dingo Harper

It was a long night but not a dull one. Nasir and his mates kept us from shut-eye by mounting a series of assaults on the tower. After the fourth attack had been rebuffed by the Deke and me, just as easily as the first, things quieted down for a couple of hours. I'd heard what Seback had told the boss, though, and I was inclined to take the Yank's word for it. The only thing Seback hadn't explained was how Nasir intended to make his pass at the oil stations, now that the chopper was defunct.

It was around two a.m. when we heard the Sikorsky's

engines tick over. They sounded very sick and, leaning over the wall of the tower top, I could see that there was no more than a quiver through the rotor. The engines gnashed and grated for a quarter of an hour, growing weaker with every revving. So we knew we'd done for the chopper good and proper. Even Seback couldn't pretend that Nasir was going to get it to fly again. The Land Rovers were a different story, however. They were tucked out of our sight but we could hear their engines. You didn't have to be a mechanic to tell that at least three of the British-made machines were working.

It was odd being stuck up there on top of the old fort. We were safe enough from serious assault, provided we kept our heads down. Only a lucky shot would take one of us out and the Deke and I were too cautious to give the snipers targets. Every quarter of an hour I would shift the rope and lift the trap and take a swatch into the depths. There was activity in the armoury below but nothing on the platform that we could see and Nasir certainly didn't have a squad of human flies suckering a route up the inside of the tower. Given enough water and food, you could've held the tower for weeks with a dozen blokes, jury-rigging some kind of shade from the sun. We weren't going to be there that long. One way or another the show would be over by lunchtime. Nasir would either run for the Saudi border, abandoning Seback and the raid on the oil boys, or he would push through with the raid more or less on schedule, make the big gesture of rebellion, the demonstration of defiance which was supposed to put the wind up the Sultan and rally the allies of the Imam, liberationists, freedom fighters and all the other ragged fanatics out there in the desert.

Fact is, it was petty and messy and a bit vague; same as the origins of most revolts against government. I suppose if the British had had a treaty with the Saudis then we might have been backing the Omani guerrillas, doing funny little deals with the rebels. It wasn't the principle of dictatorship that the Deke and I were supporting up there in our tower. We were countering the expansionist element. Big talk for a low-echelon SAS officer, maybe. But it was all plain at the time, the action measured out in ounces, without heavy numbers or tanks or artillery. How many campaigns in how many famous battles in history had been fought like this? If ever I had trouble sleeping some night I would start counting them over. Not at Ashfra, though, since I was one of those little grains of sand in the wasteland of minor wars.

The moon waned. The air was sweetly cold but not, happily, like it was on the heights of the Jebel. God knows what was going on in the courtyard. All we could see were torches and shadows. It was a fair guess, though, that Nasir Salim Azzi had rallied his most experienced fighters and was reorganising them into squadrons for an attack, as planned. Three Land Rovers could carry thirty armed men. If there'd been a hitch and the SAS hadn't received Deacon's message, then somebody, somewhere, was in for a nasty surprise. If Nasir managed to run clear of the fort before the SAS, or the RAF, arrived, then there would be no hope of cutting off the raid on the oil installation.

The Deke and I discussed it. We decided that Nasir was smart enough to head for Zambat, which was a whole lot closer than Fahud, and smaller. There was no oil at Zambat, of course. Come to think of it, there was no oil at Fahud either. But there would be a slaughter of the innocents, the British crew, and it would make a fat splash, hit the world's headlines, and there would be cheering in the streets of Cairo and flags raised in Riyadh. Dummy station or not, decoy or not, what would happen at Zambat a couple of hours after daylight on the morning of 27 January would not be awfully nice. It would overshadow the taking of the Jebel Akhdar for sure. It was frustrating for the major not to be able to do anything to prevent it. We were prisoners too, trapped on the tower by our own cleverness.

If the Yank had an inkling exactly what Nasir would do, then he kept it to himself. He had blabbed enough. He would blab no more, not to Major Deacon, not to Old Bill Bressol and not to any of the grey-garbed men who ranked above Bressol, whoever they might be. Strange as it seems in the context, Mr

Seback was quite prepared to die to protect his masters. I suppose capitalism too is entitled to its heroes and martyrs.

About 0540 hours the ruckus in the yard increased.

I was fagged out, my eyes aching, my neck sore. I wasn't sleepy, though, just rubbed thin by tension and the long vigil. It had been several hours since the last band of Arabs had sneaked along the broadwalk and had been dispersed by the Vaughan and the Thompson. We hadn't even used up too much ammo. The attempts at rooting us out had been half-hearted. It hadn't occurred to Nasir to try to take the tower by another route. Fact is, there was no viable route, not for desert tribesmen who had no skill in scaling walls. There had been other things to do, traditional chores to keep the rebels occupied. Ancient siege tactics, venerable and effective, with a few modern frills to enhance them. Since Nasir couldn't recapture the tower and hadn't time to starve us out, he resorted to the tried-and-true method of smoke and flame. He didn't merely dump some kindling down there at the base of the tower and put a match to it. He builts carts. Fire carts. What's more, he made bloody certain we weren't going to slip out by the door to the balcony. Under cover of the night he had had his boys shore it up with oil drums and other junk.

Seback struggled to his feet. The half-light made him look ghastly, with his lantern jaw, sunken eyes and a cynical grin that showed his white teeth. He hadn't spoken for hours. He didn't say a word now, just settled his shoulders against the wall and braced his feet as best he could while the Deke and I stared over the wall into the yard and watched the rebels wheel the second of three carts out to turn it for the run into the armoury.

'Jesus!' I said, with a lot more reverence than usual.

Down through the angles of stonework by the squat shape of the Sikorsky we had a fleeting glimpse of Nasir Salim Azzi as he accepted a torch from a cohort and plunged it into tinder mounded on the cart. The cart was small, two-wheeled, with long shafts. It was hauled by two men on each shaft and was heavy enough, under the weight of combustibles, to require manoeuvring. Straw and dried palm leaves, drenched with petrol, caught with a spurt of blue flame. The rebels started hauling it, shouting. Their mates urged them on. The cart went out of sight, blazing nicely. But it wasn't the first of the three. The first fire cart had already been shoved through the door in the base of the tower.

I hauled open the trap in the floor and dropped two Dopplers down into the void. I fired the Sten, dropped it, gave the Thompson a go, in a kind of panic. The grenades did more harm than good. I should have realised it. The explosions spread the burning fuel and blew the cart apart. I dropped the trap double quick and backed off, the Thompson still in my hands.

At the arc of the wall to my left the Deke had been sniping at the fire-raisers in the courtyard and had driven them into cover. But it was too late, far too late. Beneath us, working in the darkness, Nasir's troops had cleared out the guns and ammo and had packed in tyres and boxes and any junk they could find that would ignite and throw out smoke. We could hear the pop and snarl of flames eating into dry timber, and the bloody wogs hollering with delight. It was hard to get a clear shot past the bulk of the Sikorsky. After a minute or two the Deke was driven down by return fire. Our sanctuary had become a death-trap. Seback had been right; Nasir Salim Azzi intended to barbecue the three of us before he lit out for Zambat.

The fort at Ashfra had served its purpose. Whatever arms were left in the magazine would be sacrificed to the bonfire. Mines, flares, grenades, God knows what all. I don't know what Seback thought of it. I assume he had gone to a lot of trouble and expense to build the arms dump. Now Nasir was letting it all go, the Sikorsky included. I wondered ruefully which particular insurance company would have to foot the bill for the helicopter and what sort of fairy-tale would be invented to cover its destruction.

I dived to the outer wall and looked down. I had a wild idea in my head about slinging the hairy rope ladder down it and bailing out. Once we were on the sands, though, we would be easy meat, especially with daylight spreading from the east. I tried the other side, peering down the vertical wall.

Nasir had a rifle squad there; six robed tribesmen. They didn't even bother to hide from us, though they had protection of a sort from a sand-pit. The palm grove was on the other side of Ashfra, as were the houses. We would have to run the gauntlet of the broadwalk to dive off into the trees. Out of the question. The tribesmen knew we were cooked and set up a kind of chant, a jabbering, tongue-tickling hymn of triumph, made all the more eerie by the fact that we could see so few of them.

The floor of the tower top was made of wood. And it was growing warm.

Brown smoke seeped through the cracks and exuded from the edges of the trap door. Though we couldn't see them, we sensed that the rebels were still stoking the bloody furnace. All noise balled into fire sound, a ravenous, salivating snarl. The floor grew warmer still. The trap vibrated with the heat rising from below. Suddenly we were sweating. Our eyes stung with the vapours that rose from the punctured fuel drums that Nasir's boys had trundled through the doorway below. Soon, though, they wouldn't be able to get near enough to shove any more kindling into the doorway. We clutched at the faint hope that the fire would devour itself and dwindle before we were roasted to death or suffocated by heat, fumes and thickening smoke.

Deacon shouted, 'Watch the battlements, Dingo. They may try to storm us one final time.'

I hiked the Thompson into a gap in the stonework and snuggled my cheek behind it. A fusillade of bullets from a stance behind the Sikorsky caused me to shrink down again. Somebody whipped a grenade at the tower. It splashed some twenty feet below me, sending a peculiar sheet of light, lime dust I suppose, into the sky. Smuts of soot dithered like snowflakes. The interior of the fort had taken on definition from the glow of the fire.

I shouted, 'We can't stay here, boss. We've got to run for it.'

'Run where?' Deacon answered.

'Untie me,' Seback cried. 'Cut me loose, for Chrissake.'

The sweat on my body felt like oil oozing out of the pores. The planking was beginning to smoke and shrivel and my feet felt like loaves in a baker's oven.

The Deke pushed the barrel of the Vaughan against Seback's throat.

'*What will he do*?' the Deke bellowed. '*Tell me, or I'll throttle you*.'

'Untie me,' Seback demanded.

'Give me the knife, Dingo,' said Deacon.

I handed over the knife. As the Deke's fingers closed around the haft, we were shaken by a series of explosions. The tower vibrated like a mixing-machine. The intense heat had detonated mines. The guerrillas were very fond of mines, used then for booby-traps along the roads where the Sultan's soldiers travelled, also to impede the oil transport towards Fahud. Now the bloody things were flinging the fire about. Cold air was sucked into the doorway and fanned the mass of melted rubber, wood and explosives, drove the heat and smoke upwards against the underside of our platform. Sixty feet was nothing. Maybe men couldn't make the ascent but fire couldn't be stopped by Dopplers and Stens.

Deacon hewed through the ropes binding Seback's ankles. I had the Thompson on the Yank all the while. His was a dirty business and I doubted if he had any scruples about taking one or both of us out. Deacon ripped away the rope that manacled Seback's wrists.

'*Now*,' Deacon shouted, pressing again upon the Vaughan.

'He'll take all his trained men out in the Land Rovers.'

'*Go on*.'

'And leave the tribesmen around Ashfra.'

'So we can't get out?'

'Fat chance,' said Seback.

It didn't happen all that rapidly. Nasir had no real need to hurry it along. The blaze was contained within the tower. Maybe he thought we'd panic and hurl ourselves off the battlements and he'd be able to rescue Seback after all. He probably had it timed. So many miles to Zambat, couple of hours in the Land Rovers, strike at eight a.m., murder and mop up and be away along one of the snaking camel routes to the Saudi border to safety. Deacon had never told me exactly how many British oil boys were in residence at Zambat. I had gleaned the fact that that's where Bressol had his hide-away, but not much more. It was too late now for us to do anything about saving those British engineers.

It was too hot to stand on the deck now. The stonework had become warm to the touch too, though more slowly. I hooked the Thompson under the trap and, craning away, prised it up a little. The fire seemed a fair way down, though the fierce glow reached up to the balcony level. The platform was burning good style. I had one squint down – the blast would have singed your eyebrows – saw the hot, glowing centre of the fire and the stark black shapes of oil drums and tyres in it, then let the trap go as a crate of Very flares ignited and the bloody rockets started going off in all directions. They hosed the interior of the tower with sprays of light and scattered blobs of burning chemical everywhere. I heard the stuff whacking against the boards and was enveloped in a cloud of dense choking smoke, black now, not brown. The tower shook again in response to a thunderous rumble and, to my horror, I saw part of the planking around the trap door fold inwards and drop away, leaving a searing red gap.

The wind strode across the wastes, curled within the walls of Ashfra and found the aperture at the root of the watch-tower. And roared. And another chunk of the circular wooden deck on which we stood collapsed.

'*We have to go, boss. Jesus, better a bullet than this.*'

Deacon was standing on one leg, like the wise desert hunters who cooled one foot at a time, like storks. He appeared to be calm, you might almost say amused by the situation. He had put on the dark glasses again. But even the Deke was sweating. He backed against the outer wall where the heat was marginally less intense, forearm pressed against Seback who was gagging with the fumes that poured up through the charred boards. If the flames didn't consume us then the smoke would smother us. Nasir's blokes were still gleefully pitching fuel into the tower. Palm wood and diesel oil in combination created a reeking gas that brought tears to the eyes, wound around the larynx and lungs like barbed wire. The sturdy and enduring tower of Ashfra would never be the same again and, if the rebels kept at it, would be nothing but a blackened shell, come noon.

I dragged the rope ladder away from the fire spots and fed it into the embrasure on the outside wall. There were no rings or bollards to anchor it to, however, and the rope was too thick to make a secure loop around the stonework. It was the Deke who solved the problem. He used two of the three Thompsons as spar-jams. Winding and knotting the rope around them, he fitted the submachine guns across the narrow opening. Bundled, the apparatus looked pretty unsafe. But with pressure on the rope, the guns *might* lock and *might* be strong enough to support one man at a time. The point was bloody moot. Once we started down the exposed outer wall those wogs on the ground would have a wonderful time nicking bits off us with their high-powered rifles.

A second shooting party had taken up position at the top of the stone steps at the end of the broadwalk. They had brought a kind of shield with them, a panel unscrewed from the Sikorsky. There were only about four of them but they kept up a regular pattern of fire which obliged us to keep our heads down. Smoke was thickening by the second and, what with the tears and the sweat, I couldn't see a bloody thing. I had to grope to find the remaining Thompson and the magazines. The tower had been transformed into a vast chimney.

Seback was on all fours, retching up his guts. Through the cloud of smoke I could just make out the Deke. He was loading up the Vaughan with the last of his shells.

'I'll go first, Dingo,' he said. 'Give me what cover you can.'

He knew damned well that the first man out would be at the gravest risk. If, by some miracle, he did get to the ground alive then he would be able to give us a modicum of protection. So far, Nasir hadn't brought a main force out of the fort, only the firing squad to guard against escape. But desert tribesmen, never mind mercenaries, were no mean shakes with a rifle.

'Him next?' I shouted, meaning Seback.

'Absolutely,' Deacon said.

He pushed the rope which lay in the embrasure like a huge, ugly tabby cat and it fell away in a lump. A second later the Thompsons rattled and jerked and held, braced – only just– across the narrow gap. The Deacon took the Vaughan in one hand, holding the shotgun like a pistol, and stepped into the embrasure. He tucked the rope under his right arm and gripped it with his fist and stepped out over the ledge. The Thompsons skidded and I planted my foot against them to make them bite. Seback was clinging to my leg, coughing horribly, hawking and spitting. I groped for his collar and pulled him to his feet.

'You're next, mate.'

He let me guide his hands to the rope. He pawed it, then crawled on to the embrasure, cramping his shoulders inside it.

Behind us the floor had blackened like a frying-pan. Sparks and thin tips of flame licked through the fumaroles.

I heard no shots from below. Fact is, I couldn't hear or see anything. Tension still commanded the rope, though, and the guns were stiff under my heel.

Shots. Muffled by the roar of the fire but audible. Somewhere outside. The rope slackened and twitched. The Thompsons slumped downward as if exhausted.

I punched Seback on the buttocks.

'GO, BLOODY HELL, GO.'

Seback crawled out of sight and the guns snapped hard against the stone again. I couldn't give covering fire. I couldn't see to aim. It didn't matter, anyhow. The Deke was either down or dead.

Dead, I reckoned, since I'd forgotten all about Masud al Hasan and just how bloody-minded he could be, even for an Arab.

*

It had never been Masud's intention to obey the command given him by the English officer. However much he respected Major Deacon it was not in his nature to be dismissed from the action as if he was a puny child. He still had hopes that he might find a means of entering the fortress without having to scale the walls. In addition, he had calculated that the Land Rover, even with its extra tank of petrol, would not carry him far into the upper reaches of the Wadi Yafayn and he did not wish to be humiliated by having to be 'rescued' after the operation was over.

Ashfra drew him inexorably. Even as he walked away into the desert he could feel it sucking at him as the moon sucks at the sea.

Moonlight was the factor that enabled him to succeed. If the night had been dark or the sky layered with cloud he could not have found his way back across the plain and would not have been able to see the bulk of the Land Rover sitting, black against the silver wash. He came off the plain about a quarter of a mile to the west of the vehicle but the contours of the little ridge were etched by dark shadows and he trudged along it, tireless and unrelenting, until he found what he sought.

Once inside the Land Rover, Masud felt confidence well within him. He rested for a short while, drank water and ate a handful of dates. He checked out the weapons and brought a rifle and two handguns into the cabin, then he started the engine and eased the vehicle away from the area of soft sand. He nosed east for several miles. In his mind's eye he had formed a picture of the route he would take across the moonlit waste. It would bring him to the fort through the stunted palms. He navigated with caution, risking the headlamps at first but not later, after he had swung towards Ashfra. It took two hours for the journey. During the final mile Masud was drawn not just by the bulk of the fortress but by the glow that hung over it and by the unmistakable patter of gunfire.

At length Masud brought the Land Rover to a halt, east of the fortess, about five hundred yards from the gate, tucked into a grove of four palms which stood apart from the houses.

He cut the engine, climbed out of the cab and, with gun in hand, slipped forward, skirting the wall in a line some three hundred yards out. Kneeling, he watched events unfold; smoke, shooting, the siege. He understood the position perfectly, smiled at the realisation that nobody knew he was there.

When the gate opened, Masud pressed himself flat to the ground. Six tribesmen – of the Shawekah clan – ran out. The gate closed. They had an objective; to protect the outer wall. Smoke formed a huge, bulbous canopy at the top of the tower. Major Deacon would be on top of the tower; there could be no other explanation. Masud hesitated. He was afraid that something would happen before he could spring back to the Land Rover. He knew how important speed would be, whatever course events took in the hour before dawn.

He crawled further away from the palms, however, pulling a rifle with him. He would have preferred to use his dagger but he had counted the heads – six of them – and did not think he could take out six with a blade. His own safety was of paramount importance. He did not dare risk injury or the major would truly be stranded. He took position, flat against the sand. He was one hundred yards from the gate, sixty from the marksmen who had found cover in a shallow sand-pit off the long gable. He spread his legs, hefted the rifle, sighted, centred the heads one by one then lowered the rifle to the ground once more.

Wind crept across the sands. He heard shouting and gunfire from within the walls. Smoke billowed against the moon. Around the sand-pit the marksmen excitedly changes positions. Shawekah tribesmen were reputedly villainous and full of guile. It would give him pleasure to shoot them.

The marksmen saw the rope before he did. They became even more excited, hopping out of the shelter of the sand-pit to fashion a crescent of guns around the wall. The top of the tower was entirely blotted out by smoke. Flames showed too. The rope, ticked with rungs, hung down the outer wall. It did not reach the ground. Masud al Hasan stroked his beard with the fingertips of his right hand. He was cold but not shivering. He dabbed spittle on to the tip of his little finger and brushed it over his eyebrows. He wiped the fingertips against his breast and, as the marksmen hoisted up their weapons, cradled the rifle properly. The man – Deacon? – came out of the smoke. He had a gun in one hand. His sureness on the rope was marvellous to see. He dropped from rung to rung, appeared unhurried, unconcerned.

Masud al Hasan pulled the trigger. He was no dead shot but the range was short and he had the advantage of surprise. Confusion among the Shawekah marksmen aided him. Three tribesmen reared and tumbled. The others leapt away. Masud chose one. He pressured the trigger and watched the Shawekah warrior spread-eagle against the faint light of the wall. He rose on one knee, swung the muzzle of the rifle and picked off a fifth rebel a split second before the man sprawled into the sand-pit. Still Masud did not reveal himself to the remaining tribesman or to Deacon who, as if he had noticed nothing, continued to descend the rope-ladder at his own sedate pace.

Holding the heavy rifle in both hands, Masud sprinted for the Land Rover.

Prudently he had left the door of the vehicle wide open. He threw the rifle ahead of him and squirmed on to the driving seat, groping for the ignition key. The engine turned over, caught and roared. Masud flung it into gear. He tramped on the big metal pedal. The Land Rover squirted out of the shelter of the palms on to the flat road which bounded the base of the wall. Masud flicked on the headlamps. In the beams he saw the gate of the fort begin to open. Then he was past it and Deacon, like a convict escaping from prison, was outlined on the tail of the rope.

Deacon dropped and pitched to the ground. Masud dabbed on the brakes, jerked clumsily at the steering wheel. He scythed the Land Rover towards the British officer, braked again. Ahead he glimpsed the spurt of a rifle on the lip of the sand-pit. He braked hard, stamping on the pedal. The Land

Rover swung broadside and the passenger door flapped open.

Major Deacon shoved the shotgun into the cab and swarmed after it. He said not a word to Masud al Hasan, merely pointed at the sand-pit ahead and held the Land Rover's passenger door open with his fist. Masud grunted and powered the vehicle on. The remaining tribesman, caught in the headlamp beams, squared to the machine as he might have to a charging buffalo. One headlamp was shot out. Bullets scarred the windshield without breaking it. Masud fisted the wheel. The Land Rover sheered away. For perhaps five seconds the tribesman was in range of Deacon's shotgun. The report of the Vaughan was deep and profound. The tribesman recoiled as if struck by a lance. Lifting from the sand, he toppled backwards, arms outflung. Masud braked the Land Rover with such alacrity that Deacon was flung forward against the windshield.

'Major Deacon, if you will drive, I will fight.'

'Sound idea,' said Deacon.

The men changed places.

Masud extricated the rifle from beneath the seat, worked the bolt, ducked again and found the pistol. Deacon propped the Vaughan in the foot well, jammed against the off-side door. He slung the Land Rover into reverse.

On the rope-ladder was a second man.

Leaning from the open door Masud saw the figure drop as the Land Rover rushed towards him.

'You captured him?' Masud cried. 'It is the American, is it not?'

'Indeed it is.'

'What of Nasir?'

'No,' said Deacon. 'Hold tight.'

Half-way down the rope now was the Australian lieutenant, dropping hand over hand, using his feet hardly at all. Below, on the dirt, Seback crouched on his knees. Though the fall had winded him he was alert for an opportunity to escape. The gate of the fortress had been cranked open and several tribesmen had put their noses round the edge.

Deacon slotted the Land Rover by the base of the wall. Bullets peppered the vehicle. The American crabbed towards the Land Rover as Harper plunged from the rope's end to the ground, whipped the submachine gun from around his shoulders and, straddle-legged, spewed the gate with a short savage burst. Masud too dropped from the cabin and, hugging the panel, gave covering fire. Trapped by indecision, Seback stood upright.

The bullet caught him in the throat. It passed across the windpipe and tore away the larynx. Seback snapped both hands to the wound, pressing fingers into flesh to staunch the flow of air and blood. He uttered a choked, high-pitched cry of despair then slithered backwards against the cab step, back arched and legs twitching. On the breast of his undervest gouts of bloody matter painted a weird heraldic shield.

'Dingo,' the Deke shouted. 'Push him into the seat.'

The Australian dropped the Thompson and caught the American's body and lifted it into the cab. Seback, fully conscious, did not appear to be in pain. His eyes popped with shock, though, and his mouth was wide open as he sought vainly to draw breath through the flood in his gullet and chest. Harper could tell that the wound was mortal, that Seback was as good as dead.

Leaning away from the steering wheel, Deacon anxiously enquired, 'How bad is it?'

Scowling, Dingo shook his head.

Neither man made any attempt to slacken Seback's fingers from his neck. Desperately he squeezed with both hands, seething and rasping, until a thick trickle of bright red blood oozed between his knuckles.

From the side of the Land Rover, Masud said, 'Major, they are coming.'

'Leave him, Dingo,' Deacon said.

'Dump him?'

'God, no! Leave him with me. You and Masud take the back.'

Harper slammed the door of the Land Rover, picked up the

Thompson and turned his attention to the gate. One rebel Land Rover had emerged. It had halted again, however, offering mobile protection to the armed tribesmen. Another vehicle followed, snouting cautiously out of the gate. Smoke, drifting from the tower, partly obscured Harper's view. From the battlements above, however, a rattle of gunfire hastened him on. He grabbed Masud by the shoulder and, as Deacon jerked the Land Rover into motion, Australian and Arab swarmed into the rear.

'Grenades?' Dingo asked.

'I have none,' Masud replied.

'I got three,' said Dingo.

'We will run?' Masud said.

'Somehow,' Dingo said, 'I doubt it.'

Dingo Harper

Laymen and civilians might suppose that what the Deke did next was an act of folly. But when you transfer into Special Air Service or any other crack unit, you take on the responsibility of the traditions of that regiment. In the SAS that means getting the job done, and done well. The job that Major Deacon had been summoned to Oman to do had not been done well. It wasn't the Deke's fault, of course, but that didn't matter. By reversing the Land Rover, the Deke was merely scrawling his signature to the bottom of the page of the battle. Fact is, flight wasn't possible. We couldn't have escaped by scooting off in the Land Rover. Nasir had three identical vehicles. They would surely have outflanked us. The distances were too great, the terrain too flat. There was just no place to run to, no place to hide. What seemed at the time like stupidity was, in effect, a beautiful piece of defence. Deacon's last stand.

The manoeuvre took the wogs completely by surprise. The lead rebel transport had already gunned speed to begin pursuit when the Deke flung our Land Rover into reverse gear and projected it backwards towards the gate. The driver of the rebel vehicle panicked. He ploughed the bloody machine off the track and smack into the wall at the base of the tower. For good measure I threw a grenade overarm. Out of the tail of my eye I saw it explode under the rear axle, tossing out a wheel. The group of rebels who had been packed into the back of the Land Rover were dazed by the crash. We could have made mincemeat of them as they fell willy-nilly from under the canvas flap. But slaughter of that sort isn't part of the sport. Besides, our purpose was to immobilise Nasir's forces as best we could, prevent pursuit and thwart the raid on Zambat. Without transport Nasir had no hope of carrying out an ambush on the oil station.

Our Land Rover was still weaving backwards. The mob of Arabs who had been sheltered behind the lead transport were left exposed. Gaining on them by the second, Masud and I couldn't miss. Bodies fell like ninepins. Retaliatory fire was negligible. Those tribal mercenaries were far too busy trying to get the hell out of the way of the speeding vehicle. I wished I'd had the foresight to snatch Deacon's shotgun from the cab. The riot gun would have been ideal for the work. But I had to make do with a Thompson, which was no bad substitute. Leaning his buttocks against the metal side of the Land Rover, Masud fired the rifle from the hip like an old-style brigand.

The Deke kept his boot on the accelerator. The bloody vehicle was still gathering speed when we ripped past the second rebel transport, halted square to our line, like a bus at a T-junction. From the rear the mercenaries were scrambling to get out and several had sprawled to the dust. Behind that buggy the third and last of Nasir's wheels was drawn up in the gate. I admit I didn't catch sight of the Egyptian. Later, Masud claimed he saw him in the cabin of the trail vehicle, leading from the rear. If that was the case, the bloke must have been blessed. He didn't cop it, alas, and lived to fight another day, in another war. But I wasn't much concerned with Nasir Salim Azzi at the time. I was worried about blotting out the remaining wheels. With a pouch of grenades it would have been easy. All that remained on my belt, though, were two Dopplers, not enough to bring the house down.

Seback's estimate of fifty hand picked fighters was about right. It looked like a frigging army, though, littered in the gate area. If Deacon had been a mite more cautious we wouldn't have got off with it. As it was, the boss had wound the Land Rover up to maximum reverse speed. The brute was fair howling along. Since the instant he'd snapped back the gear lever only seconds had elapsed and incidents of that wild ride did not come separately but simultaneously. Any sort of concerted effort, a deliberate volley of fire from the battery of M1 carbines, and we would have been carved to bits as we rocketed past the gate. None of the blokes in the backs of the rebel transport knew what the hell was going on. They didn't even have the wit to hoist their rifles into a firing position, let alone take aim. They got in each other's way too. The unexpectedness of Major Deacon's backwards drive knocked it off for us. Grenades two and three, the last of my arsenal, went towards the trucks. But it was the hail of bullets from our guns that did the real damage. We roared right past the gate.

I thought that would be it, that the Deke would swing us out across the wasteland into the sands of Zambat. But the Deke was thorough to a fault. He eased down, fair enough, and halted sharply, practically pitching Masud and me over the tailgate.

I heard him shout, 'All set, Dingo?'

He had swung himself from the cab and reared up, one hand on the roof.

He thrust the Vaughan towards me. I took it. I knew what the gesture implied. The Deke was grinning. The bastard loved all this. It was far beyond cynicism. He was as happy as a colt in a spring pasture. Only soldiers would die here, not women or kids or old men. It was like a one-horse cavalry charge in the pearly light of a far-off dawn.

'One more time, boss,' I yelled.

Masud al Hasan shouted in Arabic, laughing like a maniac. We were hyped up higher than kites. Moments like that are your true compensations for the boredom of routine. Real soldiers' pay.

'If you insist, Dingo,' said Deacon. And ducked back into the cab.

I thought he would whisk the Land Rover past the gate and head straight out along the track to the oasis, from which direction would come our aid in the form of a truck-load of Life Guards or SAS 'K' Squadron. Not Major Deacon. He required eye contact. Pushing our luck to the limit, the Deke took us back to the rebels' transport at a regal pace.

One rebel Land Rover had been damaged by our initial broadside. It wouldn't start. A dozen uniformed troops pranced about it. The scene was bizarre, like a French operetta. Umber smoke cloaked everything. The dust of the explosions salted the breeze. The sun, just up, stabbed long shadows across the fortress. And all those Arabs, some in combat gear but most in ragged robes and pantaloons, draped with cartridge belts, froze in the midst of frantic activity as our Land Rover cruised back along the track towards them.

Masud was still laughing, a svelte sound now. He held up one British-made hand grenade which he had discovered in the back of the Land Rover. I leaned on the little agent, pressing him under cover of the panelled side. We poked our gun barrels over the rim. I had the Vaughan and a half-clip in the Thompson.

Masud had a rifle and pistol and one jovial spud. We were bound to take a hell of a pounding.

The concentration of gunfire was terrifying. But it came just that second too late to do for us. Masud got the grenade off. He sank down again and I pulled the trigger of the Vaughan. I was forced so low that I couldn't really see anything except the upper reaches of the wall sailing oh-so-slowly past.

I hadn't been in Arabia long enough to realise that the sons of the desert were incredibly brave in certain circumstances. Pride and anger stung them now. They rushed us, running under and through the fire from their own guns. The Deke had judged it well, though. He tramped on the accelerator as the mob gathered from behind and around the transports. Thirty seconds of bedlam ensued. I'll never forget it. I was scared to death. All the swagger had gone out of me, though Masud al Hasan, born into the tradition, was jabbering gleefully by my side.

Long brown fingers hooked on to the metal. Faces appeared at the edge of the panels. At the back of the cab two young rebels had linked arms like lovers, each with a grip on a winching peg. I realised now why the Deke had passed me the shotgun. The blast was enormous. The pair of rebels dropped away, disintegrating into the dust like apparitions. Leg cocked, robe swaddled around his hips, a Shawekah tribesman was almost upon us. If he had managed to twist the rifle in his grasp and find a downward angle he would have punched a huge hole through Masud's skull. But Masud, too swift for him, swung the rifle and ripped the sight across the invader's eyes and nose. Still the rebel came on. I threw myself back, squatting in the rocking corner, and pumped the Vaughan's trigger. The rebel's head burst like a rotted melon. He vanished, torn away by blast and by the violence of the swerve as Deacon hauled the Land Rover off the track and headed it out across the sands.

Two pairs of hands remained clinging to the panel. I saw Arab features, visages of frontiers I had only read about, ignorant yet magnificent, raised above the edge. One had a bayonet clenched crosswise in his teeth. I had no time to react. The Land Rover was fair leaping about and I was off balance. Masud claimed the last victims. He rammed the rifle butt into one man's gullet, then, with a ferocity I could never match, closed his empty fists around the bayonet and thrust it deep into the poor bastard's mouth. Snapping it down with all his weight, he tore off the jaw. A final sticky scream gave us an epilogue. Gunfire faded to a distant song. Staring behind, I saw the corpses dotted behind us, leading my eye to the fortress and the column of smoke painted against the morning sky.

I would fight with the Deke again, in Borneo and in Aden, but that was my one and only taste of an old-style war, barbarous yet clean.

Eight or nine miles into the sands, the Deke lagged the Land Rover to a halt. He drew himself stiffly from the cabin and called out, 'Any damage?'

'No, boss. Not to us.'

He stood on the step of the cab and stared back across the wilderness. We could still make out the smoke, the daub of Ashfra's walls, but that was all. No pursuit, no trucks or camels or swift Arab stallions. We had stopped Nasir Salim Azzi cold.

I clambered down from the back of the Land Rover.

'How's Seback?'

'He's dead,' said Deacon.

Masud was guzzling water from a canteen. He paused, beard jet-black and glistening, and rolled his eyes, then he put the canteen down and went round to the cab and looked at Seback's blood-spattered corpse.

'At least we didn't do him in,' I said.

Deacon shrugged. He seemed drained now, as if his cells had sensed that it was over and had gone pulpy on him.

'What do we do?' I said. 'Bury him in the desert?'

'Certainly not. Cover him up,' the Deke said, 'and take him back.'

I glanced at the Land Rover. One tyre was almost flat. The panels and sides of the cab looked as if they had been clawed by a gigantic cat. The windshield was crystallised.

'In this?' I said.

'We'll ride as far as we can.'

'Then hoof it, I suppose?'

'We'll be found. They'll be looking for us by now.'

'I hope you're right, boss.'

Deacon didn't answer. He squinted through his tinted spectacles at the sky. There was no sign of the RAF and the horizon, in all directions, was free of the puffs of dust that might indicate a mobile unit hastening to our rescue.

We moved Seback's corpse from the driving cabin, wrapped his head in my jacket and placed him in the back of the Land Rover. Masud al Hasan volunteered to 'guard' the body. Deacon would not let me take the wheel. He did the driving himself. What driving there was to do.

After twenty miles, the Land Rover packed in. We were close to the saddle at the head of the Wadi Yafayn. I shared the cab with the Deke, scalded by the hot draughts of air that fanned through the oblong space where the screen had been. I was almost relieved when the bloody vehicle gave up the ghost. Not to move, not to hurry, not to be dinned by noise and skinned by the artificial wind of travel. To drink, to lie down, to let my muscles slacken; it was a kind of paradise, there in the rock-strewn nothingness of the country between Zambat and Yafayn.

We had water and a little food and the shade of the broken-down Land Rover to lie in. The Deke slept for most of the day, while Masud and I kept watch by turns.

I remembered another little verse by Ezra Pound that seemed somehow appropriate:

Sun up; work
sundown; to rest
dig well and drink of the water
dig field; eat of the grain
Imperial power is? and to us what is it?
The fourth; the dimension of stillness.

George Robert Seback, poor bastard, might understand that now – even if I didn't.

About three in the afternoon three Venom fighters streaked across the western sky and dipped low over Ashfra. They returned in a great boomerang of sound and made a second run across the fortress. We heard no shelling, however. Nasir and his hired tribesmen had sifted into the desert as silently and swiftly as raindrops into parched ground. All that was left of that particular phase of rebellion was a box of letters and the corpse of an unidentified American agent.

A couple of hours later, on the trembling edge of dusk, a 'K' Squadron patrol made contact and took us back to Zambat for debriefing. It was almost over. Was over, except for one small chore that Major Bill Bressol asked the Deke and me to do, three days into February and safe out of Oman.

The town of Jidda lies towards the northern end of a west-facing bay so cluttered with reefs that only the proximity of Mecca could have made the difficult harbour tenable even on the Arabian coast. Out of the tranquil darkness of the outer anchorage a *sambuk* of 12 tons burden nosed cautiously up the boat-channel at half water and, under cool grey cloud, moored at the quarantine quay. The ornate arches of the buildings which fronted the quay were deserted at this very early hour. Professional beggars and destitute pilgrims had not risen from their ragged mats and boatloads of the Faithful had not begun to arrive from the stout, overloaded sea-craft in the shipping lane beyond the reef. At the Government jetty, not far off, nightwatchmen were too sleepy to pay much attention to the *sambuk* and the unloading of its strange cargo.

At the end of the quarantine quay, discreetly parked in an empty vegetable stall, was a cream-coloured vehicle, a Dodge ambulance. It was not the ambulance that served the western legations and consulates but closely resembled it. At the wheel a handsome young Arab in a suit of pale linen waited. At a signal from one of the men on the quay he nosed the ambulance forward. He braked, climbed out and assisted in loading the cargo into the rear of the Dodge. He did not return to the wheel, however. Instead he took his place in the rear with the heavy oblong box which, now that day had come, had developed a faint misty dew on its upper surfaces.

Another man and his companion occupied the front seats. The vehicle rolled slowly from the quay into the circular road which followed the wall of coralline rock and mud brick through the old quarter of the town. Houses of three and four storeys hovered over the roadway, window bays closed with wooden lattices, this being winter and the natives of the coast being sensitive to cold. The ambulance passed through an open square and prowled across the end of the main market beneath the finger of a dainty little mosque. It jounced over the tracks of the decauville railway, which had until recently connected the Mining Syndicate's private jetty to its shore establishments, and passed through the postern which carried it out on to Al Madinah Street.

Ten minutes later the ambulance entered the blue-chip district of banks and consulates where there were trees and shade and the avenues were broad. The ambulance curved round a corner and entered the gate of the American legation. A strip of grass and two tamarisk trees gave the impression of a garden but the frontage of the building was modern, more suited to San Diego than the Red Sea coast. There were no guards at the gate, which lay wide open, this being a nation friendly to Americans, bound by ties of commerce and technology and a history of mutual exploitation. The ambulance halted quietly by the front door.

The handsome Arab dismounted and slid out the box on a hospital gurney, supporting its weight with his forearms. He was joined by the other men. Together the three withdrew the box and gurney and rolled it to the bottom of the four steps that led to the door of the US legation.

There was no sign of life within the building.

'Go on. You do it,' said one of the men to the Arab.

The Arab mounted the steps. He paused, then put his clenched fist to the door, ignoring the Boston bell-pull that hung by the post. Within the high hallways and corridors of the building the echoes of his booming summons could be heard by the men outside. The Arab stepped back and took his place behind the sweating box, between the officers.

A youthful Nebraskan, not too long attached to the legation, was on duty that particular morning. His name was Tom Houghton. He arrived at the door in person, dressed in haste. A legation servant had also appeared from the basement but Houghton waved the Arab away and, with just a trace of apprehension, unlocked the mighty door.

Blinking, though there was no sunlight yet, Houghton stepped barefoot on to the steps and stared in bewilderment at the box and the three men by it. The Arab in the centre of the group was the most handsome and smartest of the three. The other two were soldiers though their casual tunics bore no rank markings and no regimental logos. One was considerably older than the other. He had a starved, scraped appearance and pure white hair. His expression revealed nothing. His eyes were masked by dark glasses. The second soldier was tall and muscular, ash-blond. He wore the sort of arrogant smile that made Tom Houghton cringe.

'Who are you? What do you want?'

'British army,' said the younger officer. 'We brought you a present.'

'Present?' said Houghton, descending the steps. 'What is it?'

'Open it,' said the lean one. 'It isn't sealed.'

There was a handle, the kind that Houghton had seen in funeral parlour windows in shabby towns back home, a cheap object of plated iron. It was affixed to the lid of the oblong box which was fashioned of teak with a veneered top surface. Tom Houghton knew what it was and what it might contain. He glanced up at the open door of the legation. He was hopeful that the servant had roused his superiors and that they would come padding downstairs before he was obliged, out of pride and courtesy, to obey the Britisher.

Tom Houghton closed his mouth firmly and, with both hands, lifted off the coffin lid.

Cold air and a faint whiff of formaldehyde rose from the metal-lined box, from the corpse laid out on a bed of shaved ice which had already begun to melt a little and form droplets on the dead man's brow.

'Yours, I believe,' said Major Deacon and, turning, walked quickly back to the ambulance and with his companions drove out through the gate to be lost within minutes in the waking confusion of the port.